Plan of the Day

Wings Press, Inc.

Dick Shead

Plan of the Day

When Aden finished her set, she left her guitar on stage and sat with Steve at the table they had claimed for the night. She was beaming as the people around her congratulated her on her voice, "That was more fun than I've had in a long time." Her smile faded as Crusher walked up and said, "Hello, Aden."

They both flinched as they turned to look up at him. "Crusher! What are you doing here? How did you find us?"

"I been going town to town and bar to bar looking for my girlfriend. Don't matter how I found you. Get your guitar and let's get out of here."

"What are you talking about? I'm not your girlfriend and after the way you acted last night, I can't believe you think I'd go anywhere with you."

Crusher was used to drunks talking back to him and fighting in bars. As a bouncer it was more or less normal. He grabbed Aden by her right arm and tried to pull her up. "I said let's go!"

Steve stood. "Hey! Get your hands off her. She said she doesn't want anything to do with..."

Crusher backhanded Steve. His poor handshake in San Diego hadn't prepared Steve for the strength of the blow as he lost his balance, falling over backward and tripping on his chair. He sat down hard enough that the chair tipped over. Steve's head hit the floor; he wasn't completely out but all he could see were pinpricks of light in the darkness. Crusher, still holding Aden's arm, yanked her to her feet and seized her by the neck with his left hand as he growled, "Get your guitar, we're leaving."

Plan of the Day

Dick Shead

A Wings ePress, Inc.
Action/Romance Novel

Wings ePress, Inc.

Edited by: Jeanne Smith
Copy Edited by: Melissa Scott
Executive Editor: Jeanne Smith
Cover Artist: Trisha FitzGerald-Jung
Images Pixabay

All rights reserved

Wings ePress Books
www.wingsepress.com

Copyright © 2024 by: Dick Shead
ISBN 979-8-89197-985-7

Published In the United States Of America

Wings ePress, Inc.
3000 N. Rock Road
Newton, KS 67114

Dedication

To my wife, Charlene, my son, Tim and our friend, Lenann, who read the manuscript more times than they wanted. Thanks to Jeanne Smith for
finding the problems we all missed.

<h1 style="text-align:center">One</h1>

Strong sunlight flooded the compartment, streaming through the colorful sheer fabric on the window. He awoke from a sound sleep and rolled out of the sack thinking, *Sunlight? A curtain on the window? A window? Where the hell am I? What time is it? Crap, I won't have time for chow, the chief will have my ass if I'm late for muster.* He shook off the sleep and got his eyes engaged. The surroundings suddenly jumped into focus. He breathed a sigh of relief as he looked around his own room in his parents' house, with his old books on the shelf and his old posters on the walls. He wasn't rolling out of a three-high bunk in a gray metal compartment on a U.S. Navy tin can.

It began to sink in. He, Steve Luce, Fire Controlman 2nd class, was out of Uncle Sam's Canoe Club and back home in Cedar Crest, New Mexico, a small community on the east side of the Sandia Mountains. He had arrived the night before after riding his motorcycle from San Diego, a fourteen-hour ride. No more oh-eight-hundred musters, no more midrats, that great meal served between 2200 and midnight, before catching the midwatch. No more supervising a crew fighting the corrosion on a GBGB (great big gray boat). The *USS Sterett* was now an object from his past, and the first part of his plan was complete.

The plan had formed itself about the time he started high school. Over the next four years he embellished it, but the core idea stayed the same. It had transformed over time and many iterations—the basic idea was that he would continue his education and go to college.

In middle school, Steve had decided he would be a mechanical engineer. He had taken an interest in motorcycles and started riding at age thirteen on a 100cc Honda. His freshman year of high school he had moved up to a used Suzuki 250cc bike. During his junior year, he started working part time at Simonson's motorcycle shop. The shop didn't stock new motorcycles but sold customers' bikes on consignment and worked on most brands. Over a two-year period, he had been both an employee and a customer, making payments on a fairly new Honda 500cc sport bike. Working on the machines had boosted his interest in mechanical engineering.

His plan after graduating had been to work full time that summer, saving most of his wages. In the fall he would enroll at the University of New Mexico using the state scholarship program and continue with the job part time. He would graduate in four years, post-graduate plans to be determined. In his spare time, he would continue working at Simonson's.

New Mexico has a state lottery that pays tuition for local high school graduates to attend any state college. The full tuition opportunity remains in effect as long as the student maintains a 2.5 or greater grade point average. The money from the job would cover his books and living expenses. His parents agreed he could live at home without paying rent as long as he was in school so his expenses could be kept under control. He had a sixteen-month window after graduating high school to enroll. If he missed the window, it was up to him to come up with the tuition. It was all laid out and the plan was coming together... until Steve himself threw a monkey wrench into the works.

As July became August, doubts were creeping into his mind. He no longer wanted to continue school or work as a mechanic. Three things were driving his thinking. One: he was tired of getting his hands greasy and busting his knuckles on stubborn nuts and bolts, and he felt too restless to sit in a classroom for four more years. Two: was mechanical engineering what he really wanted to study? Another thought was starting to occupy his mind, *after graduation what else is out there? What am I missing?*

He was debating whether to go on to school or take a break. He could take a year off without losing the state scholarship. But what would he do in that year? If he didn't go to school, he would have to get a full-time job and find a place to live. His parents were nice about it, but they let it be known that if he wasn't a student he was on his own. If he didn't start college within the time limit, he would lose the scholarship; he knew his savings wouldn't cover the tuition and books for a semester, let alone four years of school. His parents would help but they had expected him to get the scholarship and hadn't set much aside for a major expense. He had heard the horror stories about student loans and didn't like that idea. Researching the G.I. Bill solved his dilemma. He would take advantage of Uncle Sam's promise to pick up the tuition tab after Steve served four years working for his friends and neighbors... he decided to join the military. The parents were upset, but he was eighteen and, after much talking, they began to accept the idea.

The Army and Marines didn't sound like his cup of tea. An Air Force recruiter told him he needed a bachelor's degree before pilot training, so he wasn't going to be a pilot. The Air Force would probably make him a mechanic, something he was trying to get away from. Also, many of the bases were in less than desirable locations.

Whenever he read or saw an article about the Navy, they always seemed to be going somewhere interesting. The chief petty officer at the recruitment center convinced Steve it was a chance to see the world. Coming from a land-locked state and never having even glimpsed an ocean, he decided to see what he was missing and joined the Navy. The chief guaranteed Steve his schooling was covered after completing his enlistment. Steve found out the chief stretched the truth about a lot of things, but the school guarantee was real. And now he had completed his enlistment.

He pulled on a pair of jeans and a Navy T-shirt off the top of his unpacked sea bag. After a trip to the head, he checked himself out in the bathroom mirror. He stood six foot two and had weighed 175 pounds when he enlisted; four and a half years hadn't changed him much, merely burning off the last of his baby fat and leaving the muscle. His brown hair, still reeling from a Navy haircut, was just long enough to part. Looking in the mirror while washing his face, he read the slogan on the shirt, *Navy, blowing shit up since 1775*. He thought about his mother, whom he had never heard use a curse word, and changed to one that just said *Navy*. He also reminded himself to not use 'fuck' as his go-to adjective.

"Good morning," Steve said to his mother as he walked into the large, sunny kitchen.

"Good morning my blue-eyed boy, sit down and I'll serve breakfast. I'll bet you're not used to that after four and a half years in the Navy."

"You're right. It smells great. The galley served good meals but cooking for three-hundred sailors three times a day plus chow for people on the various watches didn't give the cooks time for special treats."

"There's cream for your coffee in the yellow pitcher. Sugar is in the bowl."

"Thanks, but I drink it black now. I've been doing that long enough that milk and sugar makes it taste funny."

His mother looked sad at the news of a change in her little boy but didn't say anything. Instead, she talked about the neighbors and the latest news from Albuquerque, the city on the other side of the Sandia Mountains in the Rio Grande valley. She told Steve he had just missed the spring's windy season. It had exacerbated the fire season, causing several fires in the Manzano Mountains south of the Sandias. Fire, drought, and corrupt politicians were the only natural disasters that ever affected the state.

"So, what are your plans for the day?" she asked.

"Thought I'd ride by Sandy's and then check on my old job. If I can get it back, I can hang out there until first semester at UNM."

His mother looked worried. "Have you heard from Sandy lately?"

"Not in the last six months. I haven't heard from her since I extended my enlistment so I could complete the cruise. But we've been moving around so much I don't think most of my mail caught up with me. I tried to call a couple of times but never got in contact with her."

"Well, don't be surprised if you don't have much luck today."

"Why? What do you know?"

"Nothing for sure. It just seems strange that she suddenly disappeared from your life."

Steve had the feeling his mom knew more than she was saying. The third thing influencing his decision not to go to school had been his girlfriend, Sandy. The two had dated all the way through high school, where they were a popular couple. She was a cheerleader and he played on the basketball team; all of their friends thought they were the perfect pair, as did Steve. It was only at the end of his senior year that it occurred to him that perfection changes. In high school, Sandy had been a knockout blonde, slim and almost as tall as Steve when she wore heels. She could have dated any boy in school, but Steve made her laugh, and they shared the same opinions about many of their classmates and teachers. The physical qualities of their relationship made Steve overlook her lack of curiosity on any subject other than clothes and their circle of friends. She tended to jump to conclusions without any evidence and there were a few subjects he knew how to avoid. Still, he thought he'd found the "only one" the first time out of the gate. He didn't realize how much a person's interests can change in the years between eighteen and twenty-two.

Sandy had been upset with Steve for joining the Navy. She had assumed the two of them would complete college together and then get married when Steve got his business degree. She had laughed and said he was silly when he told her he wanted a technical degree. "You need to be a banker or stockbroker so we can live the life I want to become accustomed to, honey."

He had remembered she was always convinced they would have a lot of money. That seemed really important to her. Her father had divorced her mother when she was very young. He signed the papers guaranteeing to support his daughter, then promptly walked out of the courthouse and disappeared from their lives. This left her mother as the breadwinner of the family. Sandy's mother had worked as a sales clerk and as a checkout person at a Costco's to support the two of them. Sandy had nice clothes, but not as many as she would have liked.

Sandy's focus on money had become a larger and larger obstacle between the two, and their disagreement over Steve's choice of major was one more reason Steve had decided to join the canoe club. He couldn't see himself sitting in an office somewhere working on the books, or whatever. That was Sandy's dream. By the time he enlisted, he knew they were incompatible as a couple. He realized he wanted to break up with her but, since she was his first girlfriend, he didn't know how to do it. Friends on the team gave him advice to just tell her it was over, but he couldn't see himself being that coldhearted. Another reason to join the Navy.

The chief petty officer at the recruiting station was happy to welcome him in and answer the question, *what else is out there?* Especially after he took the ASVAB test and qualified for just about everything. "You could be a fire control technician or aviation electronics technician. Those ratings are a good grounding for an engineering career if and when you get out."

Sandy went to the prom with him but let him know he was on thin ice as far as their future was concerned. Still, she wrote to him all through his enlistment and dated him when he came home on leave. She didn't seem to have any interest in finding a new boyfriend. She also dropped out of college. She said she just didn't find it interesting. Steve deduced from her letters that she was astonished to find that her looks and personality didn't help with her classes as they had in high school. He remembered how much of her homework he had helped her with, often actually writing the papers. She sent news that she was going to become a manager at the grocery store where she worked, but that hadn't happened by the time Steve received his last letter from her. Now, after chasing skirts up and down the coast of North America and WestPac for the better part of four years, Steve had lost most of his naivete and knew what he had to do to break things off with Sandy.

Steve finished his breakfast and got ready to head out. His bedroom, at the back of the house, had two doors, one into the house and one into the garage. He went out to the garage and hit the switch to open the door. The garage contained his parents' SUV, his ten-year- old Honda Civic and his Honda motorcycle. Except for a few days while on leave, he hadn't driven the Civic in the three years he had been stationed on the ship, but he had ridden the bike to San Diego after he found out his ship was home-ported there. The bike was showing some signs of corrosion from being out on the coast, but it still ran well. He had managed to ride it home with his sea bag and all his belongings lashed to the back of the seat and rear fender. A couple of backpacks tied together over the sea bag served as saddlebags for the extra civilian clothing.

Cedar Crest is a village stretching along State Highway 14 running north from Interstate 40. Follow it far enough and you wind up in Santa Fe. All the commercial businesses in Cedar Crest are along the highway with side roads leading to residential areas on either side. The locals call the road "North Fourteen" and the tourist bureaus refer to it as the Turquoise Trail. It has the slope of the Sandia Mountains to the west and a series of hills leading to San Pedro Peak on the east side. The open spaces are covered in juniper bushes and some ponderosa pine. There used to be a "South Fourteen" running south from I-40 but for some reason, the state changed it to State Road 337.

Steve headed out to the highway and south toward Sandy's side road. It wasn't that far away and soon he pulled up at her family's house. Sandy's mother answered the doorbell. "Well, hello, Steve," Sandy's mother said. "Are you just visiting?"

"Hello, Mrs. Curry. No. I'm out of the Navy and back for good. I got back yesterday. Is Sandy here?"

He watched a range of emotions play across her face before she said, "Sandy doesn't live here anymore. And this time of day she will be at work, I think. She's still working at the same grocery store. Sorry you wasted a trip. It was good seeing you." She started closing the door while she was still talking, taking Steve by surprise as he stared at the closed door. There was nothing to do but get back on the bike and ride.

Sandy had worked at a grocery store on the east side of Albuquerque since her senior year of high school. Steve guessed that was the one her mother meant. He headed down the road to I-40 and through Tijeras Canyon into town. The motorcycle shop where Steve had worked was not far from the grocery store, so he wasn't wasting a trip even if he didn't find his girlfriend. He turned north off I-40 onto Juan Tabo Boulevard and traveled the few blocks to the store.

Steve spotted Sandy as he walked in. She was facing him, working at a checkout counter halfway across the store. He started walking toward her, then stopped when she turned to say something to a bag boy, and he saw the bump in her belly. Steve knew you weren't supposed to assume or ask a woman if she was pregnant. Sandy didn't seem to leave any doubt. He continued walking. As he got closer, he noticed the changes in her appearance—her hair seemed limp and thin, brown patches were on her cheeks and under her nose. She looked exhausted.

When she was through with the customer, she looked up and saw him. She looked startled and said, "Hello, Steve. What are you doing here?"

"I'm out of the Navy. Your mother said I might find you here. When's the happy day?"

"You're out? I thought you re-enlisted!"

"No, as I told you in my last letter, I extended my enlistment for six months to ride my ship back home from WestPac." He gestured at her stomach. "Who's the lucky guy?"

"You're out of the Navy? Your letter sounded like you were going to make a career out of it. I thought you were gone for good."

"I told you it was just an extra six months. I don't know why you would have thought I was going to stay in. So, what's going on here?"

A customer pushed her cart to the checkout counter and started unloading groceries onto the conveyer belt. Sandy started scanning items and didn't answer. Steve stood waiting and trying to figure out what he was feeling. When she finished with the customer, she turned back to him. "I'm having a child with Joe King."

"Joe? I was going to call him today. How did that happen?"

"He joined the Air Force just after you joined the Navy. He got a four-month early out at the end of his enlistment. They didn't want to transfer him to a new assignment when he would only be there for such a short time. He's been home almost a year now. He's got a job as a mechanic at one of the Ford dealerships. We started hanging out just as friends but after your letter saying you were staying in the Navy, we got serious."

"I can tell. And, as I told you, the letter only said I was extending for six months."

"Doesn't matter. You can go to hell. We're getting married after the baby is born and we don't need you in our lives. Please leave."

A rent-a-cop came over. "Is there a problem?"

Steve shook his head. "No problem. I made a mistake. I'm leaving. Just out of curiosity, where was Joe stationed?"

"Stationed? When he was in the Air Force? He was stationed at Thule Air Force Base in Greenland. Why?"

"As I said, just curious. Goodbye, Sandy." The guard watched him walk out. He was upset but, after his mother's evasions and Sandy's mother's reaction to him, he was not surprised. "Well, can't shop here anymore." He mentally congratulated himself for having the foresight not to wind up in Greenland for the best part of three years.

Climbing back on his bike, he headed for Simonson's Cycle, still a small shop that flourished as a hangout for local customers who were expected to lend a hand if something required muscle. He took Lomas Boulevard west a couple of miles to the shop's location. Seeing the empty parking lot, he had a bad feeling. Then he saw the sign was missing from the building and fire-scorched, empty windows told the story. *Maybe they moved* he thought, hoped. He pulled out his phone and typed the store name into the browser. An article showed up from the *Albuquerque Journal* telling about a fire and the closing of the store.

"Well, damn! No girl, no job. What the hell am I doing here?" he muttered to himself. His plans for his future were starting to fall apart.

He headed to a coffee shop he remembered and was relieved to find it still there. Steve sat nursing a cup of coffee feeling sorry for himself. His big homecoming was turning into a big bust. He tried calling several friends from high school but they had all moved out and were working and/or married. A few had left town for different schools or jobs. Their parents gave him their new phone numbers but he decided he wasn't in the mood to call anyone after all. He certainly wasn't going to call Joe King.

Back at the house, his mother asked, "Did you find Sandy?"

"Yeah. She's pregnant. Looks like she hooked up with Joe King. Simonson's burned down. I guess he decided to retire."

"So you're not getting back with Sandy? I was afraid something like that had happened. I saw Sandy's mother at the store several times and she made a point of not seeing me. I'm sorry for you. What will you do now?"

"I wasn't going to get back with Sandy anyway. I was going to tell her I think we should see other people. Now I don't have to. What will I do now? Find a job and make some new friends. Most of my old ones that are still here are married. Gonna be a long summer until school starts."

Two weeks later, Steve was thinking maybe he should have shipped over. He knew things would pick up when school started, but this summer was turning out to be the shits. He talked to Simonson at his home. The store fire had started from a faulty electrical fixture and the fire had spread to a gas tank sitting on the workbench; it had been removed from a motorcycle to have a leak repaired. The old, wooden workbench, soaked through with gas and oil, lit off, torching a blaze that quickly engulfed the shop area. Al's customers pushed a couple of motorcycles outside but most machines and the building were a total loss. Al had opened the shop in the sixties and just decided he'd had enough. "I didn't like most of the young people coming into the shop anymore. They have too much money and too many wrong ideas. I guess I'm turning into a curmudgeon. I know I don't need the crap. Anyway, I wish you well."

Joe King called Steve a couple of days later. "Hey buddy. How's it going?"

"Okay. I guess congratulations are in order."

"Yeah, I wanted to talk to you about that. She told me you reenlisted and were not coming home. I was just giving her a shoulder to cry on. I guess it got a little out of hand."

Steve laughed without mirth. "I'll bet she never finished reading my letter. I told her I was extending for six months to ride the ship home from the Persian Gulf. I couldn't start school until this fall, so there was no hurry to get home. So now you're going to be a dad and a husband."

"Well, it kind of looks like a dad at least. To tell you the truth, I don't mind paying for the kid but I'm not sure I'm ready for marriage. I mean we're living together, but I don't know how long that will last. How did you put up with her mouth and her opinions for three years?"

Steve was shocked at Joe's confession. He found he still had some feelings for Sandy. "Just don't fuck her over. I'm not the man in her life anymore, but still, I wouldn't like that."

"I hear you, man. I'll work something out. Want to get together for a beer or something?"

"No. Goodbye, Joe." One more friend gone.

About that time, Steve received a packet of letters from San Diego. They had been following him around the Pacific for the last couple of months. Sure enough, there was one from Sandy informing him she was upset with him re-enlisting and that she was seeing Joe King. She told him not to write—she didn't see any future for Steve in her life.

Steve checked several of the motorcycle shops around town, but none of them needed a mechanic. They all kept his phone number on file. He found a job in a bicycle shop assembling bikes and making adjustments for customers. It didn't pay as much as an auto mechanic and he had to be nice to idiotic bicycle fanatics, but he didn't like working on cars and the hours were flexible. It gave him some spending money but he hadn't made any new friends to spend it with. It did give him a chance to wear his T-shirt with the saying on it "Ew, People." At night he got out the Civic and hit a few bars. He met a few new women but none struck a spark.

The event he was looking forward to in his immediate future involved his shipmate, Larry Kruzick. Larry's enlistment was up in a few days and Steve looked forward to his planned visit on his way east. Kruz was another biker. The two had taken some memorable rides around the Laguna Mountains and into northern Mexico, going as far as Ensenada, about sixty miles south of the border while stationed in 'Dago.

Two

Crusher woke up slowly, aching in every joint from sleeping on his two-bit mattress in his two-bit room in San Ysidro, California. San Ysidro is just north of the Mexican border and a suburb of San Diego. His mouth felt and tasted like the inside of a sewer pipe. He was going to have to brush his teeth one of these days. He pulled on a cleaner T-shirt and pants, then slopped water on his face and over his head to help with the cobwebs. He stood about six foot three when he stood up straight. He was skinny from not eating but he had enough muscles and dirty-fighting experience to work as a bouncer.

Debating between a beer and meth for breakfast, he remembered the girl sleeping on his couch. She was a singer who was trying out for a job at the bar where he worked. She'd just gotten into town, didn't know anyone and no one knew her. She had wandered into the bar the night before, too late to be part of last night's act. The band said they would give her a chance to perform tonight. Crusher had use for an unsuspecting broad, saw

14

an opening, and made friends with her. At an all-night diner, he tried to convince her he could get her a better paying job in Mexico. He had offered her a couch to sleep on, no funny business, promise. She accepted the couch, saying she didn't know San Diego and was almost broke.

His thoughts turned to the offer he had from some small-time dealers to buy cocaine in Mexico and bring it back to the States. All he had to do was carry $40,000 south for the buy and smuggle the product across the border. In the world of drug running, it was a small-potatoes deal but a big gain for him. He'd get $5,000 for his trouble. No one mentioned what would happen if he tried to take the 40K, they didn't need to; he knew what kind of people he was dealing with.

He had devised a plan that would keep him out of harm's way, but he needed the help of a respectable-looking woman. She wouldn't even have to know what she was doing; in fact, it would be better if she didn't know, the acting would be more natural. The one on his couch was going to fit the role perfectly. The problem was he didn't have a lot of luck connecting with women. It went beyond his bad breath and body odor... they just didn't seem to like him. He had approached one woman he knew slightly and had explained the deal to her with a promise to cut her in on the profits. She not only wanted nothing to do with it, she threatened to go to the cops after he explained the whole plan to her. He hoped he'd fixed the problem, that she was too scared to rat him out. Anyway, she couldn't talk much with her jaw wired shut. But now he was wondering if he should have offed her. He didn't plan to tell this new piece anything about the drug deal.

Crusher shook the toe of the woman sleeping on his couch and said, "Wakey, wakey. Time to rise and shine."

The woman stirred, sat up, and looked around. "Good morning. What's the time?"

He leaned in closer but she seemed to be avoiding his breath. "It's about eleven. Let's go find some breakfast." He was disappointed—she was sleeping wearing a T-shirt and some long, lightweight pants. He didn't get to see any skin.

She was still nice to look at, he decided. About five-eight, slim but built. Her shiny, black hair was in her face but he could still see the big blue eyes and kissable lips. The pale, smooth complexion looked like she came from somewhere with a cloudy sky and lots of rain.

"Let me at your bathroom and I'll be ready in five minutes." She grabbed her small duffel bag and headed for the toilet.

They walked to a tiny greasy spoon in the neighborhood and, over breakfast, he explained the gig to her. "I have a friend in Mexicali, has a nightclub. He's always looking for American singers. Most of the clientele are Americans. He would pay you better than scale, you being a good-looking woman. You could do your gig here tonight, and we could drive over to Mexicali tomorrow. It's not that far, just over a hundred miles east. Then half-a-mile south. Barely across the border. If you don't like the setup, we can drive right back. You can work here for small potatoes or you could start getting the big bucks tomorrow. It's your call."

"I don't know if I want to work in Mexico. I hear lots of bad stories about it."

"Those are mostly in the south and east. You'll be perfectly safe in Mexicali. It's practically America."

"Well, I'll think it over. Thanks for letting me crash on your couch last night. I'm gonna go look for a room."

"You're perfectly welcome to keep using the couch. It's not a problem. And if we go to Mexicali, you won't need a room."

"That's kind of you, but while I'm thinking about it, I'll see what the room market in National City is like." She thanked him again, paid for their breakfast, bought a paper, and walked out the door carrying her guitar and the duffle bag.

Crusher thought about the things he hadn't told her. Yes, it was just across the border but it *was* across the border. No U.S.

police to interfere. Once he had her out of the States and into the hands of his friends, he could do anything he wanted with her. As long as she remained ignorant of the smuggling, he would be nice to her. If she found out what was going on, he would enlighten her that there was only one way she could get back to the States—his way. She wouldn't like the alternative. He planned to hide the money in her guitar case for the trip south; it was a loose, cloth case with many pockets. He would have her drive back to the States by herself. She was a "clean cut" American woman, so the chances of her getting searched were slim. She'd be traveling with her guitar and an amplifier he would loan her, which was big enough to hide five bricks of cocaine once he tore out the electronics and speakers. The sixth brick would fit in the guitar case. The bricks were supposed to be wrapped tightly enough so that sniffer dogs could not catch any scent. Anyway, if she was caught, the bitch would be on her own. He went over everything in his mind. If the broad hadn't made up her mind by tonight, he would drug her and just drive her across the border. Once south of Calexico she could scream her head off. She was his.

Three

It was just past noon in Albuquerque. Steve was having lunch at a sandwich shop near the bike store. It was a new place owned by a couple from Iran, offering a much wider selection than the usual fast-food fare. Already he was hooked on the Philly Cheesesteak and Persian Potato Salad. Today he washed it down with the last of his Coke. He stood to leave when his phone rang. The caller ID was Kruzick. He sat back down. A pleasant thought went through his mind of the many times they had hit the beach together in five or six foreign ports as well as liberty in 'Dago, their ship's home port. Kruz's hitch was just about up and Steve was looking forward to his stop in Albuquerque on his way east. Steve hit the answer button. "Hey, mate. I didn't think I'd hear from you till you showed up next week."

"Fuckin' change of plans. I won't be coming to New Mexico and I need a big favor."

"Shit, I was looking forward to your visit. What happened? And what kind of favor?"

"Uh, I may have fucked up. I shipped over."

"You? You been bitchin' about the canoe club since I met you in A school. You didn't like the chow, your bunk, the deployments, not to mention the officers. Why would you ship over?"

"Well, things changed. You haven't heard me bitch as much since I made second-class. And I can take the test for first class next year. I might make chief by the end of the hitch."

"Amazed, I am. You, a lifer. So what's the problem?"

"The bastards transferred me off the *Sterett* onto the *Antietam*."

"So? You knew they would do that. You'll probably transfer every three years or so from now on."

"Yeah, but the *Antietam's* home ported in Yokosuka." He pronounced it the Japanese and Navy way—-Yo-kos-ka. U before K is often silent in Japanese. "I can't take my bike with me."

"That old rat bike. No loss, sell it or give it away and get something else over there."

"It's not that bike; I bought a new motorcycle. 1 don't have time to sell it and I don't trust anyone here to take care of it. I ship out in three days."

"Three days? That's fast, they must want you pretty badly. What'd you buy?"

"A BMW R1250 GS."

"Man, a Beemer? New? That's north of twenty-thousand dollars! How'd you swing that? Oh, that's why you shipped over."

"Yeah, the bonus was nearly twenty-five thousand. And the machine's price was a lot north of 20k. I got good saddlebags and a good pair of Bluetooth helmets. That added three thousand. You know I never liked used machinery. That last bike was junk before I bought it. I thought I'd have a new machine, spend four years in San Diego with the occasional deployment and enjoy life in the fast lane. If I made chief on the new hitch, maybe stay for twenty."

"And then they transferred you."

"Yeah, I knew I'd get transferred but I thought I'd get another ship out of 'Dago. That's where nine-tenths of the hulls are in the Pacific fleet."

"And you drew the short straw. Can't you take it with you?"

"I don't have time to jump through the hoops. Or the money. Japan really screws you if you bring a motorcycle. The paperwork and the testing can run into thousands of dollars. And if I store it in 'Dago, it'll get garage rot and turn into a dusty, rusty pile of shit.

"My brother's based at Naval Station Mayport. He's a storekeeper on the base. He said he'd buy the bike from me. Make monthly payments."

"How long is that gonna take him to pay it off?"

"Well, he can only afford a hundred dollars a month for now. That will run about twenty years. At some point, he'll be able to increase the payments or I'll get back to the States and get the bike back."

"Man! When you jump, you aim high. So what's the favor?"

"I gotta get the machine to Florida. I need you to come get the bike and ride it to Mayport."

"But I just got home." As Steve said that, he thought about his situation at home. The time away wouldn't make any difference in his social life because he didn't have any. He wasn't that crazy about his temporary job. A ride across country was something he never thought of doing and would probably never do again. "Well hell, why not? That's gonna take some coin. Who's paying for this trip?"

"If you'll come out here, like today, I'll cover the expenses of the trip—fuel, food and lodging and your travel to and from Al-bu-chu-ku."

"You got any money left out of the bonus?"

"Not much and you're gonna get that. I don't have anyone else that can do this on short notice. Can you do it?"

Steve thought about his homecoming: no girl, no job, why was he in such a hurry to get back? "Sure, why not? Nothing happening around here. I'll arrange a flight and be there some time tomorrow."

"Fan-fucking-tastic. I really appreciate this. When you get here, give me a call and we'll get together."

"Okay, see you tomorrow."

Steve considered what he had to do. Buying a ticket seemed like the first thing to get out of the way, then getting a hotel room. He should look at a map and figure out a route; he walked back to the bike shop. "I hate to leave you like this but somethings come up and I've got to quit."

"What? You just started working here. You're giving two weeks' notice?"

"No. I'm quitting right now. I've got to be out of town for a week or so."

"Now? This is our busy time of year. Can't you put if off for a while?"

"Sorry to pull this on you, but it's kind of an emergency and I have to be in San Diego tomorrow."

The manager was silent for a moment. "Payday isn't until next week. Drop by after you get back and I'll have your check for you."

"Thank you. I'm sorry about this." He headed home to arrange the trip.

His mother was watching some judge on the TV. She looked up as he came in. "I'm going to be out of town for a few days."

"Out of town? You just got home, where are you going?"

He filled his mother in on the trip, moving a buddy's motorcycle to Florida. When his father came home from work, he went through the whole story again.

"So you're gonna fly to San Diego to pick up a motorcycle and ride it to Florida?" his father asked.

"Right. I don't need to be here until school starts and this will keep me from doing anything stupid about Sandy and Joe King. I'll just take life easy for a few days."

"He's paying you to do this?"

"Yeah. He'll cover the gas, motels and food. Anything else is on me."

"That's a helluva favor."

"He's a shipmate. He'd do the same for me, if I did anything so stupid."

"So you admit that blowing his entire reenlistment bonus is stupid?"

"Oh yeah, but that's Kruz—easy come, easy go."

"Well, be careful. That's a long trip, especially on a motorcycle."

"It's no longer on a bike than in a car, just a slightly different environment."

Four

Nothing ever went according to plan for Crusher. It never occurred to him that the problem might be his unrealistic ideas and lack of planning. This time he felt his idea to smuggle cocaine using a girly girl for a mule was going to work.

He had some meth after the bitch left him at the café and was still feeling the effects when he went to work. The night started out in a frustrating fashion. He was expecting a dealer to drop by and hand him forty grand for the buy. He would hide the money in the bimbo's guitar case while she was up singing. He was hoping the performance would be bad so the band wouldn't want her back. He needed to make sure the slut would be more than happy to go to Mexico.

Then the broad showed up to play with the house band and was a hit with the crowd. It looked like the band was going to ask her to stay. He could tell she wasn't going to want to leave the job at the bar. He was deciding how to kidnap her when one of the dealers showed up and told him they couldn't get the money to him until the next afternoon. So he couldn't leave town tomorrow anyway. He would have another day to convince the bitch to go to Mexico with him. As it happened, she found a room she liked but she couldn't move in for another day. She asked if she could spend one more night on his couch. He was delighted to offer it to her.

Tuesday

Steve packed lightly, not knowing how much volume he'd have in the saddlebags. He had a couple of T-shirts and one long-sleeve shirt, an extra pair of jeans, his underwear, and toiletries. He packed a pair of sneakers and wore his boots and leather jacket. Anything else he might need he would buy on the way.

That morning, his dad dropped him off at the Southwest Airlines gate at the Albuquerque SunPort and he made his way inside. With his boarding pass on his phone and only carry-on baggage there was no reason to stop at the airline counter and he continued up the escalator to the gate level. Now all he had to do was successfully navigate the security line. After talking to the initial screener who checked his ID and boarding pass, he joined the line snaking through the room to the x-ray machines and got ready to take off his boots. He was startled when a woman in front of him turned around. "This is my first trip through Albuquerque. Are the people always this nice?"

Steve assured her they were. "I know what you mean. I've flown to and from San Diego a couple of times and the security folks there seemed to think we were all terrorists."

"It's not just the TSA officers, the people in line are nice too. They're not surly and rude like most lines."

"Thank you for noticing. Where are you off to?"

"I'm on my way back to Baltimore. I've been visiting a school friend. I've had a marvelous time in Albuquerque. Where are you going?"

"The other direction, I'm afraid. San Diego."

"Well, have a nice trip."

"You too. Come back and see us."

The flight was the usual packed airplane. Since he had a last-minute ticket, he was one of the last to board and wound up in the back row. It didn't matter, the service and flight time were the same. It was an early morning flight so both the passengers and flight crew were rested and in a good mood. After they landed at Lindberg Field and taxied to the gate, he relaxed in his seat and watched while the rest of the passengers struggled to get their oversized bags down the narrow aisle. At least nobody got slugged.

Steve rode a bus from the airport to the old Santa Fe depot near Pacific Highway and Broadway, and from there he caught a bus that dropped him off in National City. Steve felt right at home just outside the main gate to the Navy base. It was just a short walk to a motel. He had picked one close to the gate which would make it easier for Kruzick to find him. After getting settled in his room, he called Kruzick's cell phone, expecting to get his voice mail during working hours. Surprisingly, he got him on the first ring. "Kruz, I'm here."

"Fan-fucking-tastic. Where's here?"

"Nasty City, a motel on Fifth near National City Boulevard." He gave Kruz the name and room number. "So what's happening?"

"I've got all my shit packed. It kind of makes me sad to see my whole world fit in one sea bag. I think I can get liberty at sixteen hundred. We'll see you shortly after that."

"Okay, I'll get some lunch and see you when you get here."

Steve had the motel door open for fresh air and was watching some TV show about flipping houses when they arrived. Kruz must have snuck out early; it was not yet four o'clock. He was on the Beemer with another squid, Freddie the Fox, riding a Kawasaki Ninja 650. Freddie was one of the few sailors Steve knew that didn't go by his last name. Kruz knew him better than Steve did. The two of them came into the room, "Hey guys! Freddie, can't you keep Kruz out of trouble?"

"Hey Lucy, didn't think we'd be seeing you again so soon. Or ever. How's civilian life?"

"Haven't had much of a chance to find out. The situation at home kind of sucked. My girlfriend is pregnant and the bike shop I worked in burned down and is out of business. That's why I'm available and willing to make this ride for Kruzick."

"...and you're saving my life and bike, buddy. Come on out and I'll show you what you'll be riding." The three walked out and looked at the jazzed-up crotch rocket. Kruz continued talking about the bike. "It's got like 135 horsepower, weighs about 550 pounds, six-speed gearbox, lots of electronics and adjustable ride."

The object in question gave off a very Teutonic air of competency. One's eyes were drawn to the large disk brake components on both sides of the front wheel. The mostly-black machine had a front fender hugging the wheel and a fiberglass fairing jutting out above the wheel with a headlight, DRLs and turn signals mounted on the fairing. A windshield rose above the top of the fairing and shielded a high-quality multi-function display. Chrome tubular-steel formed a frame that wrapped around the front of the engine and acted as a crash guard for the cylinders, one jutting out on each side of the bike. Steve recognized this as the enduro package. No wonder the bike cost so much. Kruz had almost every option BMW offered. The large gas tank covered the length of the engine; the seat started just behind the tank and extended over the rear wheel. Kruz had aluminum saddlebags mounted on each side of the rear wheel and one behind the seat. Steve saw that he could have brought a lot more clothes. The bike was truly built for cruising.

Kruz swung the seat to the side, exposing the tray underneath. "Here's the user manual and the tool kit. You can figure out the rest of the stuff as you need it." He closed the seat. "The biggest learning curve is all the switches." He showed Steve the ten switches on the left handle grip and the five switches on the right.

"You don't have to put the key in the switch. It's got a remote key start. One more thing, you need to get the BMW motorrad app. What kind of phone do you have?"

"An Apple, why?"

"The app gets you connected to the map display. You can get it for free from the Apple store. You also need the app for the GPS location device. I bought a third-party locator; it doesn't tie in to the Beemer computer. It shows you its location on your phone."

"I'm starting to see why the price you paid was so high. Is there anything you don't have?"

"Yeah, I didn't get the built-in anti-theft device. I figure with the GPS tracker I didn't need the motion sensor."

Steve made the downloads and sometime later was pumped full with more information about the bike than he could remember. He had the basics, though. The liquid-crystal display had four display modes and page after page of explanation in the user manual. Steve planned to start out in speedometer mode. As he got comfortable with the machine, he could start using other features. Kruz explained how the remote key function worked to start and stop the engine. When he started the engine, it had a pleasant, low-pitched hum. It wouldn't disturb any neighbors.

Freddy spoke up. "We've got to be going. It's nearly sixteen-thirty."

Kruz added, "Damn, I wish we could stay longer but we both got the duty tonight. Chief Weyland let me skip out so I could get the bike to you but we gotta get back. Here's the title and a notarized letter saying you have permission to use and sell the bike." He handed Steve the items telling him how to get in contact with his brother, Frank, along with a package that held a large wad of cash. "Wish we could stay longer. But I'll get to Al-ba-kerk one of these days."

"Yeah, when you retire in twenty years."

"Fuck you, Lucy. And thanks for the help. Keep the rubber side down."

The two piled onto Freddy's Ninja and headed back for the base. Steve decided to go for a ride and get used to the new machine. He pulled on the crash helmet, a full helmet with earphones added in and noticed another in one of the saddlebags. Following the start procedure, he headed out for Point Loma. He would get some city practice before going out on the freeway. The bike was heavier than his Honda but handled well. He soon enjoyed the smooth-running engine and easy shifting as he eased his way through traffic. He was quickly at one of his favorite spots, the Cabrillo National Monument, and pulled into a parking lot to stop and watch the Pacific Ocean for a while, one attraction New Mexico lacked.

The sun was just above the ridge forming Point Loma when he got back to the motel. He had gassed up the machine and felt he was ready to head out first thing the next morning. He passed an hour reading the user's manual and decided to get something to eat. A walk down the block took him to a small café where he had seafood and fries; he wouldn't get much fresh fish back home. Out on the sidewalk, he noticed the night people were starting to come out. Walking back to the motel, he passed a hole-in-the-wall bar with live music blaring through the door. The sign said, The Happy Hideaway. He didn't remember seeing this place when he was stationed here. *One beer won't hurt me* he decided and went in.

Steve walked in past a bouncer sitting on a stool near the door. He could smell the guy's breath from several feet away. The layout was typical—dim lighting showing a bar running down one side of the room with tables on the other. A small stage was near the back on the table side with a spotlight on the three-piece band. The place was less than half full, most of the crowd in boots and cowboy hats. They seemed out of place this close to the naval station but, in a T-shirt that read, *I had my patience tested - I'm negative*, and sneakers, he was the one that didn't fit in. A small dance floor was empty in front of the stage which held the band playing guitar, bass, and fiddle. A true, old-time country band. He took a seat at the bar and ordered "whatever's on tap." Holding the mug, he spun around on the stool to watch the band as he sipped his beer. The band wasn't bad and the crowd started to build after a couple of songs. He had decided his limit was one beer and was almost through with it when a woman about his age joined the band on stage. She was wearing faded, skinny jeans with a few tears in the legs showing a bit of skin. She had them tucked into stiletto-heeled cowboy boots. Instead of closing the snaps on her long-sleeved cowboy shirt, she had tied up the shirttails to leave her midriff bare. A crumpled, straw cowboy hat sitting on the back of her black hair finished the look. Steve found her striking. Her blue eyes took in the crowd as she plugged her big, flat-top guitar into the amplifier and placed the strap around her shoulders. Steve settled back on his stool. He decided to listen to her set and held on to his almost empty beer mug.

The bouncer pushed past and disappeared in the back toward the rest rooms and whatever else was back there. He was soon back, glanced at Steve and sat on the next stool, giving Steve another whiff of his bad breath. He had an angry look on his face as he watched the singer. He looked like he had missed quite a few meals. He had an average-looking face with a slight case of acne. His mouth was slightly open and Steve noticed the brown teeth. His breath hadn't improved any. Steve nodded to the guy and turned his attention back to the girl. They were applauding after her first song when the bouncer nudged Steve again and said, "So, how do you know Aden?"

Steve turned to face him. "Who's Aden?"

"The singer. You did come in to see her, didn't you? You're the only guy in here by yourself so I assume you're a friend of Aden's."

Steve instantly thought of the chief's favorite saying, "YCAAGDT," as in *You Can't Assume A God-Damn Thing*, but just said, "No, I just happened to be here." He didn't elaborate; it was none of the bastard's business.

"That's my girlfriend. Good, isn't she?"

He didn't know the situation, but Steve was astonished the bouncer thought the singer was his girlfriend. She hadn't shown any warmness to him as he passed by her on his way to the back. He suspected most of the men in the room, more interested in her looks than her singing, had a better shot with her than the bouncer. "Not bad. She sing here all the time?"

"No, she started last night. I got her the job. You come here often? I don't remember seeing you before."

"No, I'm just here tonight. I'm leaving tomorrow."

"Oh, where you headed?"

He thought about his trip. None of this guy's business but not a secret. "I'm off for Mayport, Florida on a motorcycle in the morning."

"Mayport? Never heard of it."

"It's near Jacksonville. Another Navy town."

"Damn, that's a long way on a motorcycle. You do that kind of thing often?"

"This is the first time for me. I'm delivering the bike to a sailor there and looking forward to the ride."

The bouncer offered his hand. "I'm called Crusher."

Steve shook the hand. The grip was limp and sweaty, certainly not a crusher grip. "I'm Steve. Nice to meet you." He furtively wiped his hand on his pant leg.

They both clapped as the singer finished her set. The band, including the woman, strode off the stage as he finished his beer. As he stood up to leave, the woman walked up to Crusher. Up close, she was even better looking. She had snapped up her western shirt instead of the bare midriff but it didn't lessen her attractiveness. "Good set, Aden," Crusher said as he motioned to Steve. "We both enjoyed it."

The woman briefly looked at Steve and turned back to the bouncer. She clearly had something on her mind. "I want to talk to you." She looked at the crowd. "Outside. Now!" She turned and headed for the door. Crusher looked at Steve and shrugged. He got up and followed her out. The way the woman talked, Steve thought he should give them some space so he sat back down as a song on the jukebox played and he watched the dancers fill the small dance floor. When the song ended, he headed out the door.

As he opened the door, Crusher and the woman were standing a few feet away. It was easy to hear the conversation. The woman wasn't yelling but she was mad. "What gave you the right to tell the manager I didn't want the job anymore? You've made some pretty big decisions for my life. I don't like it."

Then Crusher was yelling. "You dumb bitch. You'll do what I tell you. Nobody cares what you like." He was squeezing her upper arm as he drew back his other hand to slap her. Crusher hesitated as he looked at the door when he heard it open. Steve took in the scene, Crusher standing with his arm back, Aden, looking shocked, raising her arm to block the blow. The street was empty, just the three of them as far as Steve could see as he looked around.

Steve started to grab Crusher's hand but instead said, "Hey! Your boss is looking for you."

The bouncer let go of the girl. "What? What's he want?"

"Your boss is looking for you. Somebody's got a beef about the drinks. He's making a nuisance of himself."

The bouncer stared at him and then turned back to the woman. "Shit! We'll finish this later." He ran back inside.

Steve turned to the woman. "Are you okay? How can I help you?

Aden gave him a long look as she was buttoning up several snaps that had come undone. "He was going to hit me, wasn't he?" She said it as if she couldn't believe it.

"Sure looked like it to me."

"Who are you? Are you a friend of Crusher's?"

"I'm Steve Luce. No, I just met him inside while you were singing."

"I'm Aden Carlow. That bastard, I barely know him and he thinks he owns me. I have to get away from him."

"Aden? That's an unusual name. Any story behind it?"

"I don't think this is the time. He was going to strike me. I have to get out of here!"

"Sorry, none of my business. I have a motel room next door. We can go there and figure out what to do next. At least it will get you out of sight."

She hesitated. "All right. I don't want to be here if he comes back out."

As they quickly walked to the motel, Steve asked, "Looks like you really pissed him off. What happened?"

"I just met him a couple of nights ago. Crusher was really nice at first. He said he'd get me a gig at this bar. The band leader told me last night that wasn't true. Crusher had nothing to do with me getting the job. When I got here tonight, the manager told me Crusher arranged a gig for me in Mexico and told him I didn't want to work here anymore. Crusher thinks the two of us are leaving tomorrow for Mexico. I told him I wasn't about to go to Mexico with him and he blew his top. One minute he was super nice and the next he was going to beat me into submission. I don't understand it... he just became a different person."

"Does he use meth?"

"Meth? I don't know. Surely not. That stuff will kill you."

"I know. He's got several of the physical symptoms and he seems to be getting into the paranoia or irritability stage."

"Damn, I'll take your word for it. I haven't been around anyone using that stuff. Obviously, I don't want to be around him anymore. I only stayed friendly because he seemed harmless. I know, that seems incongruous when talking about a bouncer. He offered me a place to sleep." She narrowed her gaze at Steve. "And that's all I did there. Sleep."

He held his hands up in surrender. "The question never crossed my mind. He told me you're his girlfriend and I found that hard to believe." They stopped before a door. "We're here, come on in."

Inside the room, they closed the door and made sure the window shades were all the way down. Aden took in the motorcycle parked in front of the door, the single bed, chair and TV, everything in poor condition. She said, "I'm going to make a pit stop and decide what to do next." She disappeared into the bathroom and soon Steve heard the commode flush. He flipped on the TV to cover up the noise and was standing watching it when she came back.

"He called me his girlfriend? That asshole. So. Long story short, my father came from Scotland. He is a piper and his favorite bagpipe song is *The Barren Rocks of Aden*. My parents named me after the song. Incidentally, do you know why pipers walk while they play?"

"No, why?"

"To get away from the noise."

Steve laughed. "That's kind of weird. Pretty name, though. So, what now?"

She thought for a moment. "Oh shit, I've got to go back and get my belongings and my guitar. They're in the back room at the bar."

"Could I do it?"

"I don't think they would give them to you. Maybe you could go with me? We could go around to the back door while Crusher is watching the front. My stuff is just inside the back door. We should be able to get in and out without him seeing us."

"Okay." He checked his watch. "We might as well go now. The crowd is probably as big as it's going to get. He should be busy out front."

They made their way outside, both of them checking that Crusher wasn't outside looking for them, and walked away from the bar to the end of the block. They hurried, as much as Aden could in her stiletto-heeled boots, down the side street and into the alley running through the middle of the block. It was dark in the alley and their footsteps seemed to echo off the solid rows of buildings on either side. Fortunately, the bar had its name on the door or they would have missed it. It was locked, so Aden knocked softly on the metal door. After several tries, a waitress opened the door an inch and asked, "Who's there?"

"It's Aden. I just need to pick up my guitar and stuff."

The door swung open. The waitress was dressed in boots, shorts, and a shirt similar to Aden's. She was perhaps a little too old for the outfit. "We wondered where you went. We had several requests for you to sing another set. What happened?"

The three stood in a hallway. On one side was a storeroom filled with liquor cases and beer kegs. Across from it were the rest rooms. The light was dim, but in the storeroom, Steve could see several guitar cases and a small duffle bag in an empty corner. Aden said, "Crusher came on a little too strong. I've got to get away from him. Thank the manager for me and the band for letting me play tonight. I'll just grab my stuff and we'll go out the back."

"What? Don't you want to get paid? I think you got a lot of bills in the tip jar."

Aden stood thinking. "Do you think you could get the money for me without Crusher finding out? I don't want to see him."

A small smile formed on the waitress' face and then she looked sympathetic. "I hear ya, honey. I'll see what I can do." She headed for the front of the bar.

Aden slipped off her boots and put on a pair of sneakers. "Now at least I can walk and run if I have to." She stuffed the boots and straw hat in the duffle bag. Her guitar went into a cloth guitar case with shoulder straps on it so she could wear it on her back. The two of them waited for the waitress.

They heard someone yelling as the waitress hurried through the door. "You better get the hell out of here. Crusher saw the boss write you this check and is looking for you." She shoved a handful of bills and a check at Aden as Crusher came through the door.

He pushed the waitress sideways and she hit the wall hard. "Ow!"

Crusher ignored her and advanced toward Aden. "You bitch! I knew there was something going on between the two of you. You're not dumping me for him!" He was wide-eyed and spittle flew from his mouth as he pulled out a butterfly knife and flipped it open with one hand. The waitress screamed and Aden backed up. Crusher turned his attention to Steve. "You lied to me! The boss didn't want me." He looked at Aden. "And you seem to know each other!"

He pointed the knife like a sword and lunged into an attack. Steve grabbed the first thing at hand, a cardboard case holding whiskey bottles, and swung it between himself and the knife. He felt the blade go into the cardboard and twisted as he pushed the case into Crusher's face. Crusher stumbled and Steve tripped him, leaving the bouncer flat on his back on the floor. He smashed the case down on Crusher's head, breaking at least one bottle. Crusher dropped the knife from his hand so Steve kicked it into the corner. The waitress ran out of the room headed for the front. "I'm getting the manager!"

Aden had her guitar on her back, the money in her pocket and the clothes bag in her hands. Steve yelled after the waitress, "Sorry about the whiskey, thanks for the help!" Grabbing Aden's arm, he pushed her into the hallway and toward the outside door. He got the door open and pulled Aden through. He looked down the hall as Crusher came out of the storeroom and ran toward him. As Crusher reached for him, he slammed the door shut and felt the shock as Crusher hit it. Steve heard Crusher moan and the sound of a body falling. The door hadn't locked and curiosity made him open the door and peek inside. Crusher was not moving, lying on his back with a bloody nose. Steve shut the door quietly, took the duffle bag from Aden, grabbed her hand and started running down the alley. He looked back just to double check that Crusher hadn't followed them out. They reached the street and had a final look back to be sure the alley was empty. "That went well. Let's get back to the room and figure out what's next."

Five

Crusher opened his eyes and found himself staring up at the dim ceiling with pinpoints of light dancing in his vision. The manager was bending over him lightly slapping his face. The waitress was there as well. He realized his nose was bleeding and he had a lump on his forehead. Staggering to his feet, he looked at the back door and saw a bloody splotch where his nose had hit it. He opened the door and looked out back—no one in sight. He went back into the storeroom and checked the guitar cases. The one he was looking for was missing.

The manager looked at the broken case of whiskey and asked, "What happened?"

"I caught a guy with that singer trying to grab a case of whiskey and make it out the back door. He hit me with the case and the two ran off. When I started to follow them, they slammed the door in my face."

The manager looked at the waitress who slowly shook her head. The manager winked at her. Until then, Crusher had been a good bouncer. It looked like it was time to find a replacement. "Can you work?"

"Hell yes. I'll be right out front." The manager was reviewing replacements for Crusher in his mind as he and the waitress went back to the front and Crusher headed for the restroom. Crusher, whose real name was Norman Drumpf, clearly was a meth addict. He had experimented with different drugs since high school but had been using meth steadily for about six months. He had a dealer he didn't much like and he didn't like paying the prices the dealer demanded. When he had complained, it paid off. His dealer made him an offer. If he would carry some cash to Mexico and bring back a cocaine shipment, he could get paid for the trip and pay wholesale prices for his meth. He agreed and the dealer hooked him up with the supplier.

So this night Crusher's plan had started. The dealer had met the bouncer by the front door and passed over a brown-paper package containing $40,000. While Aden was on stage, Crusher had walked into the storeroom and hidden the money in Aden's guitar case. Four hundred $100 bills forms a stack one point seventy-two inches high—call it an inch and three quarters. Not that big. Crusher had placed the bills in a compartment holding a spare guitar strap and some sets of strings. It was wide enough to split the bills into two piles side by side so it made even less of an accumulation in the bottom of the compartment. He had placed her spare guitar strap, packages of strings, a container of picks and the string winder on top of the strap so there was no reason Aden would be digging down in there.

After she stayed a second night on his couch, Crusher had assumed he had Aden in the palm of his hand. She would grab at the higher pay of a job in Mexico and would fall in with his plans to go to Mexicali with him. It was right on the border just a few hours east of San Diego. He had promised a high-paying gig. It never occurred to him she would turn him down. Now he had to find her. He had no idea where she would go if she stayed in San Diego.

It looked like she hooked up with that asshole from the bar. He was certainly helping her tonight. She would probably spend the night with him. If the asshole—he couldn't remember his name—was to be believed, he was heading east first thing in the morning. Maybe she would go with him? Crusher had to hope they were together and he could catch them on the highway. He tried to remember where the bastard said he was going. Florida? Mayport! He was riding to Mayport, Florida. Crusher walked into the rest room and cleaned the blood off his face. The lump on his forehead was tender but didn't hurt much. As he cleaned up, he made his plan: pick up his paycheck tonight, grab some clothes and his Saturday-night-special pistol, gas up the car and head for El Cajon. At that distance from 'Dago, the city traffic would have dropped out and he could watch the traffic on Interstate 8 as it headed east. If he caught them before they passed Calexico, actually anywhere along I-8, he could grab Aden and continue with his plan. He had another thought—if this didn't work out and he didn't get back the money for the drugs, at least he would have a head start on the killers that would soon be after him.

Six

As a precaution, Steve wheeled the motorcycle into the motel room, in case Crusher came looking for them. He knew Steve was riding a motorcycle. The two of them closed and locked the door, put on the chain guard and made sure the shades were all the way down. With the bike in the room, it didn't leave a lot of space for people. Steve sat on the bed while Aden took the chair. She was the first to speak. "Well, this night didn't go like I thought it would. I expected to do another set and get invited back to join the band."

"How long have you been singing?"

"Professionally? Actually, this was my second night. Last night was my first. I've always enjoyed singing but have never tried it as a way of making a living. I just came down from Seattle and have been looking for work."

"You haven't sung anywhere before?"

"Not professionally... I've sung in some amateur gigs."

"And you're from Seattle?"

"Yes, why?"

"I was just wondering why you came all the way to San Diego to start your career."

"You noticed that, huh? There're several reasons. It was a good time to leave Seattle. The music scene there is mostly rock and alternative rock; grunge is dying down but is still strong. I'm more of a country and ballad singer."

"All good reasons to leave Seattle, but you passed lots of towns you could have stopped in."

"Yeah." She sighed. "Okay. I am also getting away from my folks. They're good people but they almost shit a brick when I said I wanted to quit my job and try singing for a living. After the things we said to each other I wanted to get as far away from them as possible. This seemed like the place to start."

"Well, I can relate to that. My folks were unhappy when I joined the Navy. They thought I was wasting time and they were afraid for my safety. I'll bet your parents were just having the same thoughts."

"If they were, they could have expressed it better."

"Well, not my business. What will you do now?"

"I'm not sure. I met Crusher two nights ago when I went into the bar looking for a singing job. The band leader told me to come back the next night but Crusher said he could find me a better job across the border. He wanted me to go to Mexicali tomorrow and I almost did it. I finally decided I don't know him that well; you notice he lacks certain social skills. Then he started making decisions for me without my knowledge. That's what I was telling him when you saved the day. Boy, that got out of hand in a hurry. Am I glad to get away from him.

"So, I need to start looking for another job, but I have the feeling San Diego isn't the place for me right now. I'm not comfortable in the same town as Crusher."

She looked at the motorcycle. "So what do you do when you're not rescuing damsels?"

"I'm just out of the Navy, killing time until college starts in the fall. I'm on my way to Florida in the morning."

"You're really riding that to Florida? Why?"

"Oh, a buddy is paying me to deliver the bike to his brother in Mayport, Florida." The idea appeared in Steve's mind without him thinking about it. "If you don't mind riding a motorcycle, you're welcome to come along with me. I think you're right about 'Dago. It might be wise to try another town. I'll be passing through Tucson, Houston, New Orleans on the way. Plenty of places to find a job. When you've had enough, just hop off."

"No. I couldn't. I've never ridden on a motorcycle and, quite frankly, I know less about you than I do Crusher."

"Well, I hope I'm nothing like Crusher. But I understand your answer. I don't know why I suggested it. Forget I said anything."

She seemed to be thinking it over. "So tell me something about yourself."

"I'm from a little town in New Mexico called Cedar Crest... it's near Albuquerque. I joined the Navy after graduating high school. I had planned on going to college but realized I didn't know what I wanted to study. I spent the last three years on a ship touring the west pacific, the I/O and all the way to the Red Sea. I could tell you lots of sea stories but you wouldn't believe them. As you shouldn't."

"Do you have a girlfriend?"

"Not anymore." He laughed cynically. "When I got home, I wanted to tell my high school sweetheart that we should date other people, but before I could say anything she informed me she is marrying my high school best friend as soon as their baby is born." He frowned. "Funny, I was going to break up with her but it still pissed me off."

Aden laughed. "Sorry. Hard to lose a love. "

Steve continued. "Unless he dumps her. When I talked to him, he was having second thoughts. I knew she wasn't the sharpest knife in the kitchen, but it never bothered me until she threw me over for someone even more bubbleheaded than she is. Oh well, not my problem anymore."

"What's the I/O?"

"Oh, the Indian Ocean. We transited it on the way to the Mideast."

"Huh? I never heard the term. I don't have anything to wear on a motorcycle. How would we carry anything?"

Steve pointed at the saddlebags. "It will be breezy—actually windy. The pants you're wearing are fine for a performance, but you'll need something in better shape for the ride. You'll also need a jacket, preferably leather. It's kind of a safety issue and the stiffness keeps your clothing from beating you up as the wind hits it. I have an extra helmet, with the full enclosure and headphones so we can talk to each other; it's almost like riding in a car. There's plenty of room in the saddlebags. I didn't bring much in the way of clothes myself. I guess you would have to carry your guitar on your back."

"I have other, better jeans. Maybe I could find a singing job along the way. How long is the trip?"

"You might find a job. We can surely make the time for you to look for work. I figure four or five days for the trip. There's no hurry." He had planned on making it in a little over two days but knowing Aden was a novice rider and would be looking for a place to get off and play, he would break the trip into shorter segments. He realized he was hoping she would ride along.

"What do you get out of this?" She looked around the room. "And what are the sleeping arrangements?"

"I get the pleasure of your company. Nothing else. We can get separate motel rooms. We're traveling on the cheap, though. Not gonna be high-class hotels."

"I'm used to that."

He needed something to show her it could work. "If you cash your check in the morning, we can swing by a motorcycle shop for a jacket. Then we'll head out."

"Well, if you don't mind the time, maybe try a flea market first or a secondhand clothing store. I'm really trying to travel on the cheap."

"Okay, do you need to go anywhere now? Apartment? Friend's place?"

"No." She blushed. "I was staying with Crusher. I didn't leave anything important at his place. I don't know anyone else in San Diego."

"No problem. You can stay here tonight. You take the bed and…" He looked around the room. The choice was the chair or the floor next to the bed.

She sighed. "If you stay on your side, we can share the bed."

Steve was taken aback but he said, "Works for me. I'll even give you first choice on sides."

Aden picked the left side. She disappeared into the bathroom with her clothes bag and came out after a while wearing a long T-shirt and pajama pants. Steve turned out the lights before using the facilities and brushing his teeth. He made his way across the dark room, took off his jeans and slipped into the bed. A "Goodnight. This is a test." came floating from the other side along with a chuckle. He answered as he rolled onto his left side and tried to ignore the person behind him.

Wednesday

Crusher rolled out of bed at 5 am. He had worked until 2:30 in the morning and spent half an hour driving around the neighborhood looking for Aden and Steve. He thought he might spot the motorcycle parked at a nearby motel but no luck. That made it a short night for him, but he had no idea what time Aden and the asshole would hit the road and he damn sure didn't want to miss them.

He felt like shit but a little pick-me-up did wonders and he was on the road by six. He got off the freeway at Los Coches Road on the east side of El Cajon and loaded up with coffee and a McSomething from a McDonalds. A park and ride was located just past Micky D's. Crusher pulled into a space in the back facing I-8. This was far enough away from San Diego that the city traffic had thinned out some. He was surprised at the number of trucks. Amid the cars and trucks passing by, a motorcycle would surely catch his eye. He unwrapped his food, sipped his coffee, and settled in to wait.

Seven

Steve and Aden got up at seven when Kruz called him. "Hey Lucy, you on the road yet?"

Steve decided not to mention he would have a passenger. "Not yet. Thanks for the wake-up call. I'm gonna have breakfast and then get going. I'll probably stop in Tucson tonight."

"Sounds like a plan. Thanks again for doing this. I'm headed over to North Island this morning. Catching a Papa-eight flying to Hickam Air Force Base and Yokosuka. Let me know how everything goes."

"Will do, shipmate. Take it easy and don't piss off the Japanese—we need good allies."

"Fuck you, Lucy. Take it easy on the ride. I told Frank you're on your way and he says he's in no hurry, so no reason for you to be."

They disconnected as Aden came out of the bathroom. She was wearing jeans without holes, a lightweight shirt with long sleeves and sneakers. They didn't talk much as each thought over what they had said the night before. After Steve cleaned up, they walked down the street to the café where he'd had dinner the night before. They were both watching the street and the neighborhood for Crusher.

"So. You still interested in the ride?"

"Yeah, I guess so. I've never ridden on a motorcycle. But as you said, I can get off anywhere." She grinned. "Even between here and the city limits."

"Nothing to it. Just hold on to me and stay sitting in line with the machine. When it leans, you lean. You'll figure it out fast."

After breakfast they headed back to the motel room and stowed their gear in the two side saddlebags. Together they figured out how the Bluetooth feature in the helmets worked. They would be able to talk to each other while riding. Steve wasn't surprised to learn that Aden had a very sharp mind with a good grasp of the technology.

Aden used the browser on her smartphone to locate a bank and a used clothing store in the area. The store opened before the bank, so they rode over there first. Aden carried her guitar on her back, the two shoulder straps holding it in place. The rear saddlebag was far enough back that Aden had room for her guitar to fit in front of it. "How does it feel?" Steve asked.

"It's okay. I'm used to carrying it this way. Actually, the bottom is sitting on the seat which takes the pressure off my shoulders."

"If it gets to be too much, when we get on the freeway maybe I can carry it between us."

"No problem for now."

In the used clothing store, Aden found a lightweight, good-fitting leather jacket for about half the original price. Steve paid for it and they headed for the bank. By the time Aden had cashed her check and paid Steve back, it was almost ten o'clock. Time to hit the road. Steve thought about topping off the gas again but it seemed unnecessary. They headed out for the 805 and MLK Jr.

freeways. Those would take them to I-8 as it swung east for El Centro and points beyond. Traffic was the usual heavy flow but moving smoothly. At Spring Valley, he switched to the 125 freeway and rode it the few miles around La Mesa to I-8. When he turned onto I-8 it was about eleven o'clock. As they passed by El Cajon about five minutes later, Crusher was snoring softly.

Eight

Crusher gave a snort and sluggishly staggered back to wakefulness. He shook his head and sat up in the seat. A glance at his watch showed nearly 12:30. He looked out at the traffic and saw nothing but cars and trucks. Shit, so many questions. Had they gone by? Was the asshole even really riding a motorcycle across country? Was the bitch with him? Was he way off in his thinking? His phone rang and he saw the caller was the cocaine supplier. He swore and answered it. "Yeah?"

"You on your way to Mexicali, bro?"

"Uh... Yeah, we should be there in a couple of hours."

"I'm counting on you to bring the stuff back. You know what happens if anything goes wrong."

"Don't worry. I'll be back tomorrow with your product."

"I guess you know this is a test. You pass, you got a good spot in the business. You fail and you won't have to worry about your future."

"I won't fail. I'll see you tomorrow." The phone went dead. "Shit." He looked at his watch again. 12:45. They must have passed him by now. He had no choice but to go after them. If he was wrong, at least it would take him away from San Diego.

Nine

Crusher was wrong about where the urban area ended. Aden and Steve passed through housing developments and a couple of casinos along the highway until they were east of Alpine in the Cuyamaca Mountains. By the time Crusher woke up, they were east of El Centro where Steve had stopped for gas. Aden said the wind was pushing on the neck of the guitar case, so Steve suggested carrying the case upside down. "The straps are wider than your shoulders, but you can tie them together across your chest. The neck can sit off the side of the seat." She tried turning the case over and it seemed like it would work.

So far, the bike had performed perfectly with a really enjoyable ride through the hills and valleys of the mountains. He was amazed at how light the machine felt when they were moving. The stop in El Centro had been to stretch their legs and see what kind of gas mileage they were getting. Steve ran the numbers using the calculator on his phone and found they were doing a little better than forty miles per gallon, which agreed with the bike's own calculation shown on the speedometer.

"Whew, it's hot!" Aden said.

"Yeah, this is the low point of the trip. We're fifty feet below sea level. Sure holds the heat in."

"Well, this is a first for me. I don't think I've ever been below sea level. But this jacket is too much." She took off her jacket and stored it in the back saddlebag. The temperature was hovering around a hundred degrees in the dry, desert air. Steve didn't say anything, just climbed back on the bike and waited for Aden to fit herself on the passenger seat. The neck of the guitar case hung just off to the side of the seat. He found he enjoyed having her on the bike holding on to him.

The land around El Centro was all cultivated fields. The highway passed through them for twenty miles before they ran out onto the desert proper where the dry, flat sand reflected the heat back at the riders. Steve thought about all the water diverted from the Colorado River to what he had heard was 500,000 acres of land cultivated from the desert around El Centro. They continued for about 45 minutes until coming to a rest area. He pulled in and parked on the sand under a tree for shade.

"I need more water," Steve said as he got a bottle out of the saddlebag. "How you doing?" he asked.

"Okay. I'm glad to stretch my legs. It is easier to carry the guitar this way. Oh damn!" she cried as she took off the guitar case and leaned it against a saddlebag. She noticed the seam on the shoulder of her shirt was undone all the way across the top of her shoulder. "I see why you suggested a leather coat." She grabbed another shirt out of the saddlebag and headed for the restroom.

Steve looked at the big RV with Ohio plates parked under a nearby tree. A man came out of the RV and walked over to look at the Beemer. He nodded to Steve. "How's it going?"

"Okay, yourself?"

"Not bad. Good looking bike. A far cry from what I used to ride."

"Oh, what did you have?"

"An ought-two Honda 450. Good dirt bike. Never did any street riding."

"That is a good bike. I used to work at a cycle shop, and I've seen several used ones sold on commission. Still popular."

"I kind of miss it. I sold it after I got married. My wife didn't want the kids to get the bug for a motorcycle."

Aden was back wearing a different shirt. "This stupid motorcycle is trying to tear my clothes off." She smiled at the man. "Hi, I'm Aden."

"I'm Paul. What's the problem?"

"I rode here from El Centro without my jacket and the wind tore my shirt sleeve loose."

"My wife has a sewing machine in the RV. I'll bet she could sew your sleeve back on. Come over and have some iced tea."

Aden said, "That's the best offer I've had today. Thank you." She looked at Steve. "Do we have time?"

"Sure, we've got a little spare time. Iced tea sounds good. I'm Steve, by the way." They shook hands.

Aden picked up her guitar case and the three walked back to the RV where Aden and Steve were introduced to Peg, Paul's wife. Asher and Cole, Paul's kids, were curious about the guitar, so Aden pulled it out and sang a couple of songs. Asher, the older, wanted to try to play it. Aden showed him how to hold it and play a D chord and an A7 chord. She helped him pick out the notes to a song. "You're going to be mad at me," she told Paul. "You're going to have to buy Asher a guitar."

Meanwhile, Peg set up the small sewing machine and repaired the shirt. "I like to sew. I make a lot of our clothes so I like to have the machine near."

"You did a great job. It's better than new."

"Where are you two heading?"

Steve and Aden looked at each other. Steve answered, "I'm delivering the motorcycle to Mayport, Florida."

"It's not yours?"

"No, it's a long story, but a friend in San Diego sold it to his brother in Mayport but couldn't take it there himself. He asked me to make the trip. Where are you guys going?"

"The other way. We'll stop at Sea World, maybe go whale watching and then head north to Disneyland. Maybe hit some of the other parks around L.A. After that we'll head back to Cincinnati."

"Well, enjoy your vacation." They finished their iced tea and Steve said it was time to go.

"Thank you, again, for the repair job. And the tea."

"No problem, have a safe trip." The whole family went out to watch as Aden put on her leather jacket and the two rode off.

Back on the road, Aden said, "They were nice people. I hope we meet more like that."

"Yeah, I guess most folks are."

"Not so much the ones I've met lately."

Ten

As they neared Yuma, the land turned from desert to cultivated fields again. They crossed the Colorado River and California was suddenly in their rearview mirror. It was about one o'clock when they rode into town. As they gassed up, Steve asked Aden, "How are you holding up? Okay to go on?"

"I'm fine. Adjusting the windshield helped a lot. It's good to stop, though, to straighten out my legs."

"We'll head for Tucson and then decide what we want to do next."

So far, the ride had been pleasant enough, except for the heat. The bike was performing well and Steve was getting acquainted with its features. They were enjoying the Bluetooth feature in the helmets allowing them to talk to each other and listen to music. The road to Tucson was back into the desert and uneventful. After stopping at Gila Bend for gas, the only notable thing that happened was switching to I-10 at Arizola. They made it to Tucson by about four-thirty.

Steve spotted a Costco and exited I-10 on South Kino Parkway. They made their way around to the gas station. After climbing off the bike Aden asked, "This looks like a nice town. What's here?"

"Oh, the Air Force has a base here. And there's the University of Arizona. Other than that, I think it's mainly an agricultural center."

"University, huh? Air Force, huh? Maybe they'd like some music. I think I'll drop off here."

That was disappointing. "The ride getting to you?"

"Oh, the seat is comfortable enough, but I'm stuck in one position for so long. And it's hot."

"Yeah, can't do much about that. If you get off here, you'll stay hot."

"Good point. Let's see what's here anyway."

Steve had planned to keep going another hour or two, but he found he was enjoying the company. "Well, I'm willing to stop for the night. Let's see what we can find for you." He filled the gas tank and let Aden pick a place for lunch of the several fast-food joints around them. She picked Rudy's Bar B Q.

Aden asked the counter server, "Do you know any bars that would have live music?"

"Yeah, there's some down around South Alvernon Way and 29th Street." She looked at Aden's guitar bag. "You looking for a job?"

"Thought I'd check out the market."

"That area is probably your best bet."

"Thanks." They took the drinks and food to a table and sat. "So, this is probably the end of the ride. I've enjoyed it. Thanks for bringing me along."

"No problem. You think you can find a job here?"

"If I can find a bar where the Air Force hangs out, I can probably get in with a band, find some work. I've noticed, in my two days as a professional singer, I do well with the military."

"I'll take you down to South Alvernon Way and we can look around. If nothing turns up, the next stop is Las Cruces and New Mexico State University."

"You don't mind me hanging on to you?"

"No, I'm enjoying the company. You're welcome to stay as long as you want."

They finished their drinks and headed out following the directions the server had given them. South Alvernon Way led into the commercial district and looked promising for what Aden was looking for. They passed several bars Aden didn't like the looks of. It wasn't until they were nearly to the Air Force boundary that they came to a large tavern with its own paved parking lot and a sign that advertised "Eric and the Desert Tramps."

"Let's check this one out," Aden said. Steve wheeled into the parking lot which was fairly empty at that time of day. They locked up the helmets and jackets in the saddlebags and walked in. The layout was larger than the Happy Hideaway... a bar stretched across the front of the room with tables and chairs more to the back. A stage and small dance floor were against a side wall. It was a large building and had a kitchen serving meals, attracting a dinner crowd as well as drinkers. It seemed to be better quality than most and looked to be in better condition.

At the bar, Aden asked for the manager. A middle-aged man with a bit of a paunch came out of an office behind the bar. "Help you?"

"Hi, I saw the sign for live music. Can you use a singer?"

"The band comes in at eight. You would have to talk to them. I have no idea if they want a female singer." He looked her up and down. "I'm in favor of the idea, but I let Eric handle the music. Eric Bender, he's the band leader. Incidentally, I'm Roger."

"Hi. I'm Aden and this is Steve. What time does he get here?"

"About seven. He sets everything up and makes sure the electronics are working."

Steve looked at his watch. "It's five-thirty now. Let's find some food and a motel. We'll be back here at seven."

"Our kitchen just opened. Pretty good fare."

"Let's see your menu."

Roger handed them menus and Steve looked at the prices. "You serve a richer clientele than I'm used to." He turned to Aden. "Let's find a colonel bucket."

"That works for me."

"There's a couple of motels up the street to the north. Several cafés near them. You could try there."

"Thanks, we'll do that." He looked at Aden. "Shall we?"

"Yeah, that will give me a chance to clean up and change clothes."

"Okay, we'll be back. Thanks."

"*Por nada.* I hope you get the job. Tell Eric I recommend you."

"You've never heard me play!"

"I don't need to. I can tell." He reached out to rub her shoulder but stopped when she jumped and moved away. He smirked, saying, "You have a melodic voice."

Outside Aden said, "Well, that was kind of creepy. I don't know if he's a pervert or just lacks social skills."

"I hear you. Let's hope the band is better."

They headed back the way they had come and found a Denny's near a motel that looked in Steve's price range. The motel had a portico, a roof stretching over the driveway, and an outside wall supporting the roof. Vehicles stopping in front of the office were out of sight from the street. Steve parked the bike under the portico and went in to get the rooms. He didn't know then that the portico was going to save him a lot of trouble later that night.

The motel clerk seemed astonished when Steve asked for two rooms, but he was happy to rent them out, two adjacent rooms on the second floor. Aden paid for her own room, and they climbed the stairs to check them out. Steve had a shower and changed underwear and his shirt to one that read, *It's okay if you disagree with me, I can't force you to be right*, before knocking on Aden's door—just next to his. She was wearing the same jeans as earlier but had changed her T-shirt. They walked to the Denny's and ordered dinner.

"Do you know what you are going to sing?"

"Roughly. I'll decide after I meet Eric. I'll see what he tells me about the crowd, and what he and the band know."

"If you don't mind, we'll walk back to the bar. I want a beer, and I don't ride when I've been drinking."

"Not even if you just have one or two?"

"No. I bought my motorcycle from the widow of a guy that had a couple of beers at a poker party and rode home. He misjudged a turn, hit the curb, flipped the bike and ran his head into a pole holding a street sign. He wasn't wearing a helmet. His wife had bought one for him and was going to give it to him on his birthday the following week. Not a scratch on the machine. Anyway, as the pilots say, eight hours bottle to throttle."

Back at the motel, Aden changed to her torn jeans and the shirt she was wearing when they met. That seemed to be her uniform. They were walking to the bar, so she wore her sneakers and carried her high-heeled boots in a bag.

"How did you, ahh, come up with your attire?"

"The band leader at the Happy Hideaway in San Diego suggested it when he interviewed me. He said it's similar to what the waitresses were wearing without looking like a waitress and would get the patrons' attention even before I started singing. I had the boots and hat, I just had to find some torn jeans and the confidence to wear the shirt in this fashion. It seems to work."

"Can't argue with that." She slipped the leather jacket on over her shirt for the walk down the street and carried her old straw hat. "I'm a gentleman. I'll carry the guitar."

"Thank you."

They got to the bar a little before seven; Eric wasn't there yet. Roger showed them to the back room where the supplies were, and the band left their cases. Aden took off her jacket and put on her boots and hat. Steve was impressed how her presence changed.

They were still sitting in the back room when Eric walked in. "Wow! Who are you? Roger said there was someone back here I should hire." He held out his hand to the two. "I'm Eric Bender."

Steve shook his hand. "Steve Luce. I'm just getting Aden settled." They both looked at Aden.

"Hi, I'm Aden Carlow. I'm looking for work. Could you use a female singer in your band?"

"Well, first impressions are good. How's your singing?"

"I could play something for you. Any requests?"

"You know, I like that one about the two gal pals. One leaves town and the other gets married and beat up. I've been wanting to do that one, but it really takes a female to sing it. Do you know it?"

"Yeah, it's one of my favorites." She stood and worked the guitar strap around her shoulders. After checking the guitar's tuning and with no hesitation, she launched into the song. At the end, Eric clapped and said, "I think we can work something out. What do you expect to be paid?"

"How many songs do you want and how much time am I going to be on stage?"

"All good questions. For tonight, how about I call you to the stage for three songs each hour from eight to one? More if we get requests. If this works out, we'll work up some song arrangements for you and the band, but for tonight let's keep it simple. I'll tell you in confidence the four of us get two-hundred and fifty for the night. I don't know what the others will think about splitting five ways. You can have the tips while you're singing. I'll see if I can get Roger, the manager, to kick in another forty or fifty and if he won't, it's up to the others whether or not you stay."

Steve ran the numbers in his head and decided the band was playing as a hobby but Aden said, "That's about what I'm used to. Let's give it a try. How's the crowd?"

"They're mostly airmen from Davis-Monthan Air Force Base. Some will bring their girlfriends and wives." He looked at Steve and back at Aden. "There will be lots of single men and while I'm sure you're safe from a bar fight I wouldn't be surprised if you get some unwanted attention."

Aden giggled and told Steve, "Maybe you'll get to defend my honor."

"I hope not. I get embarrassed when I run in front of women." They both laughed.

Eric went off to talk to Roger while the other three band members straggled in. Dan played drums, Jack played bass, and Jimmy played fiddle and mandolin. Jimmy put the band squarely in the Country/Western category. Aden was discussing songs with the three when Eric returned. "Roger says he'll pay you forty dollars for tonight. We'll see what happens after that."

"That works for me. We've found some songs I know that you do. How do you want to work it?"

"Why don't you and Steve sit in the audience and I'll call you up to the stage for your songs? We'll have your guitar on the stage."

"Sure." She looked at Steve. "Let's go claim a table."

When the show started, Aden and Steve saw that Eric and the Desert Tramps had a big following in Tucson. The bar was full and the band got a big hand before they started playing. Eric led the band through several of their usual songs and then said, "We have a special treat tonight. Give it up for Aden Carlow!"

Aden took the stage while the crowd was applauding. There were several wolf whistles. She gave the crowd a big smile while working the guitar strap over her head, "Is this an Air Force crowd?" There was loud applause. "Well, I'm sure you're all good guys and none of you act like this dude." She immediately broke into a cover of "Goodbye Earl." At the end, the women applauded like crazy, the men clapped and looked nervous. When the applause died down, she followed it with "Wildwood Flower." The crowd seemed to like the old Carter Family song; many got up to dance. She got a big hand at the end and Steve saw people putting money in the tip jar. After one more song, she sat down again for the rest of the set. Couples walking by told her how much they enjoyed her singing. The rest of the night continued like that. On the second and third sets she had some requests and did an extra song each set. The solo males in the crowd saw Aden sitting with Steve and didn't bother her, but Steve could see the crowd liked her and resigned himself to continuing the trip by himself.

Eleven

Crusher, with unbelievably good luck and crazy driving, had caught up with the motorcycle just before they got into Tucson. Fortunately for Crusher, they were still on the highway... he could never have found them on the city streets. Not making the stops Steve had made saved him lots of time and for once his assumption had been right. Not expecting Crusher to follow them, they had no inkling how closely he was watching. He followed them into Tucson and watched them stop for gas and go into a Rudy's. He lost them on their way to the bar when the traffic in front of him stopped at a red light, but he continued in the same direction they were going. Many blocks and several stoplights down the street, he spotted the motorcycle parked at a bar, the Airport Tavern. He saw the sign advertising the band and assumed he was right that Aden was looking for a singing job. He parked on the street and waited for them to come out. Hunger and the urge to piss made him change his mind. He saw a burger joint up the street and decided to make a pit stop. With a full stomach and empty bladder, he came out to find the motorcycle gone. He drove up and down the street a couple of times but didn't see them or it. Steve was parked behind the portico at the time. The meth head drove back to the Airport Tavern and parked in a secluded corner of the parking lot before walking in.

The bartender gave him a dirty look. Crusher was much rougher than their usual customer and didn't fit into the scene. He finally asked, "What'll it be?"

"Gimme whatever's on tap." Crusher put some money on the bar and took a big swig. "Hey, I was looking for a friend that might have stopped in earlier. Her name is Aden."

The bartender didn't show his disbelief, but this guy didn't look like someone the singer and her boyfriend would hang out with. He finally decided it was none of his business. "Yeah, they were in. She was looking for a singing job. They'll be back about seven."

"Thanks, don't tell her you saw me. I want it to be a surprise."

"Uh... yeah, sure."

Crusher went back to his car. It sounded like Aden got a job at this establishment. He would wait for them to show up later. He sank down until he could just see the front door over the dashboard. About seven, he watched the two of them walk in. He decided to wait where he was until closing time but the tendency to doze off caught up with him. He almost blew it again.

A horn honking and a car door slamming brought Crusher back to consciousness. His eyes opened from a sound sleep in which he was dreaming he was in Mexico—and now nothing looked familiar. Where was he and why was he here? Memories came flooding back as he recognized the tavern with the parking lot now full. His watch showed him it was nearly one in the morning. Did they get away from him again while he was sleeping? "Shit!" Was the only word that came to mind. It was time to see if he had screwed the pooch. He rushed inside and immediately spotted Aden on stage as she finished the last song of her set. Her performance had been well received all night and she looked pleased. Crusher saw the asshole sitting at a table near the dance floor. He was watching Aden and stood up to applaud as she stepped off the stage to join him. Crusher took a seat at the back of the room and ordered a beer. He chug-a-lugged it while he waited for her to sit down.

When Aden finished her set, she left her guitar on stage and sat with Steve at the table they had claimed for the night. She was beaming as the people around her congratulated her on her voice. "That was more fun than I've had in a long time." Her smile faded as Crusher walked up and said, "Hello, Aden."

They both flinched as they turned to look up at him. "Crusher! What are you doing here? How did you find us?"

"I been going town to town and bar to bar looking for my girlfriend. Don't matter how I found you. Get your guitar and let's get out of here."

"What are you talking about? I'm not your girlfriend and after the way you acted last night, I can't believe you think I'd go anywhere with you."

Crusher was used to drunks talking back to him and fighting in bars. As a bouncer it was more or less normal. He grabbed Aden by her right arm and tried to pull her up. "I said, let's go!"

Steve stood. "Hey! Get your hands off her. She said she doesn't want anything to do with..."

Crusher backhanded Steve. His poor handshake in San Diego hadn't prepared Steve for the strength of the blow as he lost his balance, falling over backwards and tripping on his chair. He sat down hard enough that the chair tipped over backwards. Steve's head hit the floor; he wasn't completely out but all he could see were pinpricks of light in the darkness. Crusher, still holding Aden's arm, yanked her to her feet and seized her by the neck with his left hand as he growled, "Get your guitar, we're leaving."

"Help!" She had her hands on Crusher's arms but wasn't strong enough to break his grip. "Let go of me, you bastard!

Someone help me!" Crusher's hold on her neck was cutting off her air but she managed to squeak out her plea.

The crowd had thinned out from earlier in the evening, but most of the people remaining were young, fit, and sported military haircuts. They got to their feet as Steve was hit and Aden was pulled out of the chair. A woman standing behind Crusher extracted an extendable baton from her purse. In less time than it takes to say "bang," she had it open and had moved to where she could swing the baton across Crusher's left hand, breaking several of the bones in the back of it. Crusher produced a howl heard outside the bar as tears came to his eyes. He grabbed the broken hand with his right one, letting go of Aden. Abruptly he spun around facing his attacker and swung back his left arm to punch her. A small Marine lance corporal in uniform who happened to be taking a class at Davis Monthan and had stopped briefly in the bar, promptly blocked Crusher's arm with his left arm as he jabbed the extended fingers of his right hand into Crusher's abdomen. They sank in almost out of sight. It would have raised a howl of pain if Crusher had any breath left to howl. When Steve was told about it later, he remembered his chief's description of a Marine, or, as the chief called them, 'Hired guns'—"average Marine is five foot two with a chip on his shoulder."

Crusher was still bent over when the woman spun him to the side so she could strike the front of his knee with the baton, which put him on the floor as his leg collapsed, possibly breaking the kneecap. By this time, Roger was on the scene. "What happened?" he asked the woman with the baton.

"This son of a bitch knocked that fellow out and tried to march off with your singer! I disabused him of the idea." She pointed to the lance corporal. "The Marine here came to my rescue from the bully. I'll leave it to you to call the police. I'm going to skedaddle before the bastard gets his breath back and decides to have me charged with something." She looked at the Marine. "Want to join me in my escape?"

"I'll follow you anywhere, babe. Anyone that handles a club like that gets my vote."

The couple looked at Aden. "We enjoyed your songs. Hope you come back." With that, the baton swinger collapsed the baton and put it back in her purse. She and the Marine walked out to the applause of the crowd.

Roger looked at the remaining patrons. "That's all, folks. I'm going to call the police right now, so this seems like a good point to say we're closing a little early tonight. Hope to see you back here another evening."

Aden was kneeling next to Steve and gently slapping him on the cheek. He opened his eyes widely and sat up. "I'm okay. I just saw stars for a while. What happened?"

"A woman in the crowd broke Crusher's hand and his knee. A Marine hit him in the stomach so hard he still is trying to get his breath back."

The patrons shuffled out, leaving Aden, Steve, Crusher and Roger in the lounge. The band headed for the back room. Roger asked Aden, "Do you want to get involved with the police?"

Aden looked at Crusher. "Not if we don't have to." She kicked Crusher on his leg, which had him grabbing at his knee to protect it. "I told him last night to stay away from me when he tried the same tactics. He's followed us all the way from San Diego." She indicated Steve, who was trying to stand. "I think the best plan is for us to get out of here. Then I would appreciate it if you turned him over to the police. I don't know why the weirdo's following us, but we need to get away from him. Sorry to drive your business away."

Roger waved it off. "Not a problem... the crowd dies down quickly after the band quits. I'll set on this guy for an hour or so until I'm ready to head home. Then I'm calling the police. That should give you time to get out of sight. I'll tell them I don't know where you live, which is the truth. After the police finish with him, I think your ex-boyfriend is going to spend some time in the emergency room. I think that woman broke several bones in his hand, maybe his knee."

"Couldn't happen to a nicer guy. Tell him and the cops we're headed for L.A. If I see him again, I'll call the police." She helped Steve to his feet. "How are you?"

"Okay, I think. I wasn't really out, just seeing stars."

Aden grabbed her guitar and headed for the back room to change her shoes and get her jacket. Eric and the boys were still there. "Well, we and the crowd liked your singing. Are you going to stay around?"

"Ah... no. I think I need to get farther away from that asshole that attacked me tonight. As long as he knows where I am, I think I'm in trouble. We're leaving town. Too bad. I like your style and it was really enjoyable playing here."

"A shame it didn't work out. We thought you fit in really well. If you ever get through here again, stop in."

"Thanks. It was fun. I'm sorry I can't stay."

As they were leaving, Roger handed her a hundred dollars in cash. "This is from the tip jar plus what I owe you. The jar wasn't nearly this full until after the fight. Sorry you don't want to stay. I think you could have been a real draw for this place."

"Thanks, you're a nice man to work for. I really enjoyed your place."

"Thank you."

Aden and Steve walked out and turned for the motel.

Twelve

As they walked along the empty street, Aden noticed the evening had cooled down. "Boy, after the bar it's almost chilly."

"Yeah, that's the desert, low humidity allows the heat to escape." Steve pulled out his phone and checked the temperature. "I read somewhere this is the optimum temperature for naked humans, seventy degrees."

"You bring some strange factoids into conversations." Aden chuckled, reaching up to feel the back of Steve's head. "You have a bump back here. How does it feel?"

"I don't think anything is broken. I just need to get off my feet for a bit. I guess by morning I'll know if I have a concussion."

"I just wondered if it's affecting your choice of conversation topics." Her expression changed. "Do you think he knows where we're staying?" She didn't have to spell out who 'he' was.

"No. He said he was going bar to bar to find you but I suspect he caught us on the freeway and followed us into town. We're lucky he didn't follow us to the motel. If he knew where we were staying, he could have hit us earlier in our rooms. That would have been safer than trying to jerk you out of a club in front of all those people. After the police pick him up and take him to an emergency room, he will spend the rest of the night in jail. I think if we get an early start in the morning, we'll be okay. Are you going on with me?"

"Yeah, it looks like I'll be traveling with you again, if that's all right. I wasn't trying to dump you because I don't like your company. I just thought you might want to continue without the extra weight and I know I'm slowing you up."

"Don't worry about it. You're a lightweight and there's no hurry."

They got to the motel and Steve started to say goodnight but instead said, "I think I'll push the bike down to the portico and leave it behind the wall. Just in case he comes looking for us when he gets out of jail and we haven't left yet. I don't think Crusher will drive in where he could see the bike behind the portico wall." He moved the motorcycle down to the office area and put it against the wall so cars could still drive in. It wasn't much of a defensive move, but it was all he could think of. Anyway, he planned to be gone by the time Crusher got out of jail. When he got back to his room Aden was still standing outside, facing her door. She had her key in her hand but hadn't made a move to put it in the lock. Steve said, "If you think it's safer, you're welcome to bunk with me again."

Aden stood still another couple of seconds. "If you don't mind, I think I'll do that. I don't seem to be able to open this door."

He opened his door and followed her into the room. "Do you need anything from next door?"

"No, all my possessions are in this bag." She held up the tote bag. "Not much to show for twenty-four years of life."

"Wow, Crusher has you in a downer mood. Let's hope we've seen the last of him. Do you want the left side again?"

"Sure, thank you. What is your plan for tomorrow... actually, today?"

"Las Cruces. It's not that far, about four hours, but I have a feeling we're going to get a late start and I think Las Cruces is a reasonable distance. Beyond 'Cruces the next big town is a long way off. If you want to look for another gig tonight, we can check out the area around the university."

Aden thought about it. She probably had enough money for a ticket to California, or back home to Washington, for that matter. Did she want to continue with this weird trip? "Oh, that sounds like the right idea. I'll see how I feel tonight. Is Las Cruces still in Arizona?"

"No, it's in the middle of New Mexico, east-west wise. It's just a little north of El Paso, Texas. I'll head on through El Paso and across Texas tomorrow. If you want to continue with me, I'll be going through San Antonio and Houston, which should be good pickings."

"Well, I'll see what turns up."

"Works for me. Let's get some sleep." They did their ablutions and fell into bed. Steve distracted himself from thinking of Aden's warm body by thinking about Crusher.

"Steve? Are you awake?"

"Yeah, I keep thinking about Crusher and why he's following you."

"I hate to admit it, but he's got me scared. I keep thinking about what could have happened. He was choking me! I'll bet I have bruises on my neck in the morning."

"I'm sorry you're going through this. What can I do to help?"

"Would you mind spooning me? Don't get the wrong idea—I don't want it to go any further but I think I could sleep if you were hugging me."

"Okay, let's give it a try." He rolled over and moved up against Aden's back, his legs up against hers. He reached across for her hand and found it trembling. She really was frightened.

"That feels good. Thank you."

"I'm afraid it's gonna feel too good to me. If you know what I mean."

"Don't worry about it. Just go to sleep. Goodnight."

Steve heard someone knocking on the door of the room Aden hadn't used. He woke to find he was sleeping on his back and Aden was lying against him, her head on his shoulder and her arm over his chest. She woke up when he gently removed her arm, stood and grabbed his pants. He cracked open the door to find the manager about to knock on his door. "Just wanted to see if you're checking out. If so, you need to do it in the next hour, or I'll have to charge you for another day."

"Yes. We'll be leaving today." He looked at his watch, twelve-thirty. The morning was gone. "We had a later night than we expected. We'll be out by one."

"That's fine." He saw Aden in the bed. "Sorry you had to pay for two rooms."

"Yeah… that's not a problem. I'll bring the keys to the office in a little bit." He closed the door. Aden was peeking at him with the covers drawn up to her chin. "Hey Aden, time to get going."

She looked around, saw where she was and gave a grin. Sitting up she asked, "Well look at us. Did I move over or did you?"

"I think we both did."

"I think I was dreaming about you. I hope you live up to the dream." She stood and checked out the bump on his head. "It's still there but not as big. Well, I guess we got caught up on our sleep. How do you feel?"

"I have a headache. It could be lack of coffee. How do you feel?"

She touched her neck and looked in the mirror in the bathroom. "I do have bruises on my neck! It hurts a little. That bastard! He's ruining my life."

"With any luck, we've seen the last of him. Let's get some breakfast and get out of here."

They were on the road by one-thirty. The freeway was the usual train of semis making their cross-country run. When they were settled on the road, Steve said, "Talk to me. Keep me amused."

"Okay, why in hell would Crusher follow us all the way to Tucson? I only met him two days before I met you. He's either completely crazy and stalking me or there is some other reason he's following us."

"Good question. He's clearly not playing with a full deck. I'm sure he's using meth. Maybe that's made him lose a few cards. If that's the last of him, I'd put it down to drugs."

"You two talked in San Diego, does he know where you're going?"

"Yes, unfortunately. I told him Mayport, Florida. I don't know if he remembers talking about it. Surely, he won't search for us all the way there."

"As you said, if we don't see him again, it's probably the meth. If he keeps after us, then there is something we don't know." She was silent for a while and then asked, "You know, after moving to San Diego from Washington, I thought the countryside looked pretty brown. Now that I study it, I see there are subtle variations in the coloring. There's still a lot of brown, but it's starting to grow on me."

"Welcome to the desert. You'll find green looks out of place after a while."

The road stretched out before them, the heat of the day building up and making heat waves and mirages on the road. There were few cars or SUVs compared to the constant stream of semi-trucks moving in both directions. They zoomed past Mescal and the traffic thinned out to just the interstate travelers. Inside his helmet the sounds were muffled. He thought about playing some music over the helmet sound system when Aden's head fell forward and rested on his shoulder. He realized she was sleeping. She still maintained her grip around his waist so it didn't seem like she would fall off. He decided against the music and let her sleep. They rode on in silence.

Steve really thought about stopping at Benson for a cup of coffee and a glass of milk, but Aden was still sleeping. He checked the time, 2:15 pm. From Tucson I-10 made a series of S curves, each S fifty or sixty miles long before the cycle repeated. The country was more of the dry, brown soil with stunted bushes scattered across the landscape. Steve had the cruise control engaged and fell into the traveler's trance as they continued down the road. Around Deming, New Mexico, eighty-five miles inside the New Mexico state line, he thought to himself *what happened to Lordsburg?* It was forty-five miles behind him. He had totally spaced out and they were now only about forty-five minutes out of Las Cruces.

Half an hour later, a Love's Truck Stop popped up out of the desert on the edge of Las Cruces. Steve pulled off the interstate and rode to the gas pumps. The change in motion woke up Aden. "Is this Las Cruces?"

"Yeah, the west side of it. I'll fill up here and we'll look for some place to stay and maybe find a job for you. First, let's get a late lunch."

"I can't believe I fell asleep."

"You didn't seem to be in danger of falling off, so I let you sleep. Feeling rested?"

"Yeah, I'm feeling much better. I couldn't sleep at Crusher's house. I don't know if I was worried about Crusher or the critters that might crawl out of the woodwork. I guess the last couple of nights haven't been that restful."

After filling the tank, he parked the bike and they went into the café, both heading for the restrooms.

When Aden came out, she was pissed. "Look at my neck! It's purple from the bruises. It will take a couple of days to go away."

"You're right. Crusher is stronger than he looks. Does it hurt?"

"Not so much, but I guess I need a scarf. I can't cover this up with makeup."

"That will work. I'm sure we can find something here in 'Cruces." They went in to eat.

Steve, delighted to be back in New Mexico, ordered a chicken enchilada. The waitress said, "Red, green or Christmas?"

Aden looked confused when Steve said, "Green."

Aden asked for yogurt and fruit and got a funny look from the waitress. She looked around at the pot-bellied drivers and said, "Don't get many folks in here going for healthy food." She gave Steve a look. "Sure you don't want to change your order?"

Steve deadpanned. "No thanks, I'll start eating healthy tomorrow."

The waitress gave a long, drawn-out, "Right," and left.

"What do you think of the trip so far?" Steve asked.

"I'm trying to think of what else can go wrong. I'd ask if all your rides are like this but most of the problems have been my fault. What does 'red, green or Christmas' mean with your order?"

"Do I want red, green or Christmas on my enchilada."

"Huh?"

"The kind of chile they make the sauce out of—red chile, green chile or both."

"That's a thing? It sounds like a chant."

"It is. I think we're the only state that has an official state question. I guess you have to be in the club to understand. It's our major crop. You'll even see it on our license plates. Chile capital of the world."

"I learn new things all the time I'm around you. Anyway, Crusher seems to have scrambled my brain. I'm still wondering why he's chasing me. Am I wrong to think there's something seriously out of whack with him?"

"Naw, definitely not. It's Crusher's blunders around you that have me wondering. I think his drug use has definitely scrambled his brain, but he seems to have some plan involving you. From what you've told me, he seems to want to get you into Mexico. My God, coming into the bar like that and thinking he was going to drag you out..."

"You might be right." Aden laughed. "He really didn't expect that woman with the baton. And that Marine helped save the day. Let's change the subject. How did you like the Navy and where have you been?"

"It's fine. If you like to travel, it's the service to join. Although what you see might not be what you want to see. I've been to Yokosuka, Japan; Busan, South Korea; Auckland, New Zealand; Diego Garcia, and the Red Sea. Diego Garcia was something different, just because so few folks have been there."

"I don't think I've heard of it. Where is it?"

"These days it's strictly a military base. It belongs to Great Britain and is an atoll in the middle of the Indian Ocean. We refueled there on our way to the Arabian Sea."

"The Arabian Sea. That sounds exotic and romantic, all those Sinbad and the princess stories, but I'll guess it wasn't."

"Right, we were patrolling off the coast of Oman and into the Persian Gulf. It's hot, windy, and dangerous. Not only are there pirates, but you also never know when some fanatic is gonna shoot a missile at you."

"Did someone shoot anything at you?"

"Not us. But lots of ships have taken a missile or shot down missiles. We were mostly escorting convoys and chasing Iraqi boats that were trying to intercept tankers and merchant ships.

"The Navy and I kinda think alike. We started every day with a plan of the day. That's the way I work. I like to have my whole day planned when I get up. The plan may change during the day, but it gives me a starting point. But enough of this. It's over, and Uncle Sam is picking up the tab for college starting in the fall, courtesy of the G.I. Bill. I'm glad I enlisted. I could have enrolled with a New Mexico scholarship directly out of high school, but I had come to the conclusion that I didn't know what I wanted to study and I was tired of sitting in classrooms. I decided four years in Uncle Sam's canoe club would show me a future. It worked in more ways than I expected. First of all, I found out my girlfriend wasn't the person I thought she was, and I was not going to, and didn't want to, spend the rest of my life with her. She wanted me to get a business degree, but I had no interest in working as an accountant or banker. I was thinking of getting a mechanical engineering degree but now I know I want to go into electrical engineering, although it seems to be merging with computer science. I might consider shipping over, that's what we call reenlisting in the Navy, after I get a degree. Go back as an officer. How about you? If I'm not being too personal, how did you cover tuition?"

"My folks started a college savings account when I was born. I guess they could see how expenses were rising. Theoretically, the state of Washington has a grant program that covers all tuition for low and middle-income families, but I don't think anyone has ever successfully navigated the process. I have a small student loan. So far, I haven't had any problem paying it back. This singing career might change that. So, I'm hearing you had a girlfriend but she's no longer in the picture?"

"Not anymore. She is marrying my former best friend. As soon as the baby is born."

Aden laughed. "I think I've heard that story before. So he was home for four years with your girlfriend while you sailed around the Pacific? They say absence makes the heart grow fonder, usually of someone else."

"Actually, not even that. He joined the Air Force about the same time I joined the Navy. He got out and went back home four months before I was due to get out of the Navy. Then I extended my enlistment for six months to ride my ship back home from WestPac. She decided I was going to stay in forever."

The food arrived and Aden looked at Steve's enchilada. "That looks interesting. May I taste it?"

"Sure, help yourself."

She cut a piece free, leaving the beans and rice. After starting to chew, she opened her eyes wide and reached for her water. After downing half a glass she said, "You bastard! You could have warned me."

"About what?"

"About the piece of volcano I stuck in my mouth."

"Well, you knew it was made with chilies, what did you expect?"

"I expected something like bell pepper."

"It's a little spicier than that."

"I want to see you eat it."

Steve took a bite and realized it was a hot version of green chile. After four years away from New Mexican cooking, he wasn't used to it. Obviously, he couldn't admit it was hotter than he expected to someone from out of state. "It does have some authority." He took another bite. "Nice flavor, though." He was fighting mightily against hiccups but was out of luck—he hiccupped several times, causing Aden to notice.

Aden looked at him and shook her head. "Hot enough to give you hiccups? You have clearly burned out your taste buds as well as losing your mind to eat it in the first place." She looked serious. "So how do you know who the right girl is for you?"

"Good question. Right now, I'd say it's someone with all your qualities." Steve decided he better change the subject. "So... what do you do when you're not singing?"

"Uh, after college I worked at a company in Seattle, a nine-to-five job. But I've always enjoyed singing. Friends have told me I should go professional, so I decided it's now or never."

"San Diego was your first professional performance. Why there? I understand leaving Washington, but 'Dago just seems out of the way."

"You're not gonna let that go, are you? That reminds me, I need to call my mom and apologize to her. Some of the things I said to her are unforgivable. She really upset me, and I won't tell you what we said to each other. Anyway, after storming out of the house, I blew a small bundle to get on the next flight out of Seattle and it turned out to be a flight to San Diego. That's how I wound up there. I haven't been anywhere, and I've always wanted to travel. You actually are helping with that idea. This trip is more exciting than you can appreciate. I want to see the other forty-nine states before going back to Washington. It looks like I'm going to see Florida a bit sooner than I expected. Not to mention a passing glance at Arizona, New Mexico, Texas and the southern states.

"And yes, I'm just getting started. You've been to two-thirds of my gigs. Folks seem to like me so far. I haven't decided if they think I'm a good entertainer, a good singer or they like my outfit."

"I think I understand the outfit. What's the difference between a good singer and a good entertainer?" Steve was trying, without attracting attention, to blow his nose. The chile had cleared out his sinuses.

"You saw my performance in San Diego. What prompted you to stick around—the thought that I might be a good musician, the banter when I walked on stage or because you liked the skin-tight jeans and open shirt?"

"I get your point. Can't it be all of the above? I must admit last night, was it last night? No, the night before. I was getting ready to leave the bar when you came on to perform. I sat back down when I saw you. I stuck around because I liked your songs. You didn't have much banter."

"Thank you. I'll take praise where I can get it. But an entertainer has to be able to hold an audience's attention between songs. I'm working on my patter. Anyway, my career, so far, is pretty short. This bit with Crusher isn't helping any."

Thirteen

Steve would have been upset to know Crusher was not that far behind them. After Roger called the police, a cop had come by and arrested Crusher. The cop patted him down, but Crusher had left his knife and pistol in his car. He was taken to an ER where he had a long wait. They took care of the heart attacks, overdoses, and bleeders first. Finally, a physician's assistant x-rayed his left hand and found several broken bones. The PA was able to position the broken bones without surgery and put the hand in a removeable plastic cast. It was a hard shell with foam lining. He had partial use of his fingers. The PA manipulated his kneecap, which hurt like hell when he moved it, but declared there was no break. There was a dilly of a bruise, however, and he had a decided limp. Out of habit, he tried running past the checkout station and out of the building as the clerk yelled at him to stop. It was a stupid thing to do, since the cop had stayed with him through the entire process and had no trouble chasing down the limping runner. The cop put him on the floor with a little more force than was absolutely necessary. The cop stood him up and marched him back to the clerk, who was incensed that he had tried to skip the paperwork. He spent forty-five minutes filling out forms to get Medicaid to pay for the visit. Crusher really wanted some meth but, of course, the cop was right there watching him.

They got to the jail a little after four in the morning. During a more thorough search, they confiscated the meth tablet he had in his pocket and took away his belt and shoelaces. He was taken to a cell with several drunks and living-under-the influence types. He passed out on a cement bunker built onto the cell wall; his arm was his pillow. When they woke him, his hand was throbbing along with his knee and his forehead where he had hit the door the night before. If he had seen a way at that moment, he might have considered suicide. The police took him from the jail to a courtroom at 8:15 am. He had to wait for his case to be called with a fair number of drunks and aggravated battery cases before him. It gave him a chance to catch up on a little more sleep. There were no witnesses against Crusher, and he hadn't done any physical damage to the bar, so the judge let him go with a warning to leave town. "I really should hold you for the methamphetamine in your possession. Since we would have to prove its identity and hold and feed you until we had the results, I think it's better you get the hell out of Tucson. Get out of my courtroom and get out of town."

Another cop gave him a ride back to the bar where his car was parked. This cop repeated the warning. "If we find you around town today or in the future, we'll arrest you for vagrancy and throw you back in jail."

Crusher stopped at a fast-food joint for a cup of coffee and headed east on I-10. He didn't know it, but he was only about half an hour behind Aden and Steve. *If they grabbed more than a couple of hours' sleep, they shouldn't be that far in front of me.* He put his foot to the floor and started looking for motorcycles.

After crossing into New Mexico, he thought he saw them. The road had run straight northeast for the last fifteen miles and now made a gentle curve to the east.

He spotted a motorcycle several miles in front of him as it started around the curve. He stepped on the gas pedal and thought about ramming them or just running them off the road. Too much traffic for him to get away with either option. Maybe he could force them to stop. Otherwise, he would have to follow them to wherever they were going. As he started to speed up, he looked at his gas gauge, sliding towards empty. *Shit!* He had left Tucson without filling up and totally ignored the gauges and speedometer since. Now he needed fuel. After he rounded the curve, the town of Lordsburg appeared, and he spotted a sign for gas not too far off the highway. That old saying was right—God does protect fools and drunks. He swung onto the off ramp, cutting in front of several other cars, and crossed under the freeway and into the gas station, beating another car to a gas pump. Crusher ran his debit card through the reader and started pumping gas. He knew he had been pushing his junker hard, so he thought he'd better check the oil. He was below the safe mark, so he headed into the office/sales room to buy a quart. As long as he was stopped, he might as well eat, so he picked up a couple of candy bars and some chips. He would wash them down with energy drinks. A road map seemed like a good idea, so he swiped one covering Arizona and New Mexico. By the time he was back on the road, he figured Aden, if it was Aden, was close to an hour, meaning seventy-five miles, ahead of him. Well, at least he knew he was heading in the right direction. He would catch them when they stopped for the night, probably somewhere in New Mexico.

Reaching Deming, he decided it was too early for the asshole to want to stop. *What the hell was his name?* His glimpse of the motorcycle had showed him that Aden was staying with the guy. Crusher hoped she would try for another job tonight. His map showed he was headed for a good-sized city called Las Cruces. It was a little early for them to stop, but it would be a good place for Aden to find a singing job. He would look for the two of them there. If he didn't find them, he would try El Paso. He checked his gas and continued east on I-10.

Fourteen

Aden and Steve reached Las Cruces about 5:30 that afternoon. Steve pulled off I-10 onto University Avenue, noticing several motels nearby. The business district seemed to be on the north side of the street, with university buildings starting on the south side and continuing south. They cruised down the street looking for a bar with live music. Something within walking distance of the motels would be perfect. Steve told Aden it was both a military town and a university town. Holloman AFB and the White Sands Missile Range was just across the Organ Mountains to the east and lots of soldiers took their liberty in 'Cruces. They had a choice, either here or Alamogordo. For a weekend they might drive down to Juarez, Mexico. Another audience source, New Mexico State University, was also here, with an enrollment of around 25,000.

About five blocks from the freeway, he spotted a tavern advertising a band playing that night. Pulling into the parking lot, Steve said, "How does this look?"

"Well, it's worth a try." She looked at the advertisement beside the door. "Looks like three guys, a guitarist, piano, and bass. They might like a female singer."

They went inside. It was a cleaner, mirror image of the Happy Hideaway... bar down one side with tables down the other. Aden said, "Well, I'd feel right at home in here." A small stage and dance floor were in the back. Aden asked the bartender, "Is anyone from the band here?"

"They usually come in around six. Don't start playing until seven. Can I get you anything?"

Steve checked his watch. "Might as well wait. I'll have a Coke. Aden?"

"Well, maybe a glass of wine. Do you have a nice red?"

"We got a Cabernet Sauvignon, a Merlot and a Chardonnay."

"I'll have the Chardonnay." She looked at her watch. "We can talk to the band and then find a room for the night. Okay?"

"Yeah, that will work. I saw a couple of motels near the highway. We can get two rooms and then I'll run you back here if you get a gig. I'll take the bike back to the motel and walk over. Then I can have a couple of beers."

"About that. I'm thinking we only need one room. I mean we've already slept together twice," she said with a gentle smile, pressing herself against him for a brief moment.

"Works for me. And I think I see a guitar player coming from the back room."

A man about their age or maybe younger carried a guitar case up to the bandstand. He was wearing a western shirt, jeans, boots and a straw hat. It was almost Aden's costume/uniform but in better condition and not as well filled out. Aden walked back to talk to him.

"Hi, are you part of the trio?"

"Hi yourself. Yeah, I'm Richard Bills. You a student here?"

"No, just got to town. I'm Aden Carlow. Could you use a female singer in your group? I also play the guitar."

"Um, I don't think so. We're all students at NMSU. The bar doesn't pay us. We get whatever is left in the tip jar. Splitting the money four ways instead of three we'd be losing money."

"Are there any bars around here where I would do better?"

"No, most places around here have pretty much the same setup. You'd be better off in El Paso."

"Well, looks like I'll just be passing through. Since I'm here, I could do a couple of songs tonight for free. You could see how the crowd likes it. Maybe if it's a hit you could think about adding a woman to your group."

Richard laughed. "We get lots of offers. You wouldn't believe how many students want to perform here. But if you want to sit in for a couple of songs, you're more than welcome. Maybe one of the other guys can suggest other bands that work here on other nights that might be interested, if it doesn't work out with us."

"That sounds fair. What time do you want me?"

"Be here about eight and you can sing a couple of songs. If it goes over well, you can stick around and sing in our other sets if you want. What are you going to sing?"

Aden suggested some songs and Bills agreed. "Unless the guys in the band have other ideas."

Aden and Steve rode back to a motel a few blocks away and checked in—one room, ground floor. When the manager wasn't watching, Steve rolled the motorcycle into the room. "It's in the way but I don't want to take a chance. Crusher is still following you and might spot it parked outside."

"Surely he's given up by now."

"He seems to have a strong attachment to you. I think he's a stalker."

"Well, I don't understand it... he's only known me for two days."

Steve changed the subject. "Do you want to eat now or later?"

Aden checked her watch. "Let's eat and then clean up. Afterwards I'll change into my uniform, and we'll go to the bar. Assuming you want to come with me."

"Sure, your performances are growing on me. I'll be your groupie."

They ate a quick meal in the cafè attached to the motel and went back to the room. While Aden changed in the bathroom, Steve mused, "Hey, if you didn't want to use your real name you could use your initials. Acey, or Acey Deucey, the sailors' game."

"What are you talking about?" She came out of the bathroom in her torn jeans and tied-up cowboy shirt. She was carrying a plastic bag containing the boots and straw hat. She was still wearing her sneakers.

Steve whistled. "Lookin' good. I was just saying if you wanted to use a stage name, you could use a nickname, Aden Carlow, A C, Acey, or Acey Deucey."

"Huh, I kind of like it. Maybe I'll try it out. And thanks for the thought." She held up the plastic bag. "Although I could walk the two blocks in these heels, I choose not to. I'll add the rest of the outfit when we get there."

Steve grabbed her guitar case and they headed for the bar. The evening was pleasant, still warm and calm. "You're lucky we missed the windy season. Last month we would be fighting a thirty-knot tail wind."

"After riding on the bike, that doesn't sound like much. How fast were we cruising today?"

"About seventy-five. I wanted to get you here in time to check out some bars for your playing. I guess it was a fairly smooth ride if you managed to fall asleep so easily."

"Thanks. When I wasn't sleeping, I thought we were going a little faster. Carrying the guitar upside down was a smart idea. The wind doesn't bother it at all."

"Yeah, wind pressure is a function of the square of the velocity. It's getting pretty strong by seventy miles per hour. It would be a strong force on the guitar neck if it stuck up. That's also why I suggested the leather jacket."

"You're going to make a fine engineer. You rattle those facts off like a real nerd. I still can't believe I was sleeping for so much of the ride."

"You've become a skilled rider. But as for the wind blast, I speak from experience. One time I had a girl ride with me from Albuquerque to Fort Sumner to watch a motorcycle race. She was wearing a cotton shirt, and her shirt sleeve tore off on the ride. She hitched a ride back in a car." He thought about how mad Sandy had been with him that day. Not a good idea to think about Sandy.

They got to the bar a little before eight. The band was on stage and in the middle of a song. Richard spotted them and waved at Aden. He pointed with his chin. Aden took her guitar and headed for the back room where musical-instrument cases were scattered along the wall. She sat the guitar down, shrugged out of her jacket and changed into her boots and hat. When she got back, the song was over, and Richard motioned her to the front of the stage. "We'll play another couple of songs and take a break. After the break, why don't you lead us off with, say three songs? We'll see how the audience likes them and go from there. The guys liked all the songs you suggested, so we can decide on the ones for the next set during our break."

"Works for me. Thanks for the chance."

"No problem. Incidentally, I like your outfit. You'll have most of the crowd on your side before you even start."

"Uh, thanks." Aden walked away with Steve. "I don't know if he just paid me a compliment or he's hitting on me. On the other hand, I did wear the clothes to attract attention."

"Let's grab a table and see who watches you and who watches the show." They sat near the middle of the room and Steve noticed a fair number of the men in the audience did turn to look at her. The two were impressed with Richard's guitar playing. Whether doing fill-ins between phrases or playing an instrumental riff, he was all over the neck of his guitar. The piano added a distinctive jazz feeling to the songs.

During the break, Steve held the table while Aden and the band moved to the back room and decided on the songs Aden would sing. They agreed she could have any money thrown in the tip jar during her performance.

She came back before the band returned. "I think this will be fun, but clearly this isn't the town for me. Too many good amateurs willing to work for nothing."

After returning to the stage, Richard told the crowd, "We're going to wander away from our usual song set to bring you a special treat. In her first appearance in Las Cruces, Acey Deucey!"

Aden looked at Steve and grinned. "Thanks for the idea, I always look for an edge." She climbed onto the stage and grabbed her guitar.

Fifteen

Steve was enjoying watching Aden as she sang John Prine's "Angel from Montgomery." His attention was toward the stage and he didn't notice Crusher walk in. The meth-head's idea about how to find Aden turned out to be not-so-dumb. He knew the biker wanted to get to Florida and, if Aden was still with him, she wanted to find a place to sing. He was certain the two would ride until late afternoon and whatever town that put them in, the singer would try to find a job. He studied his map and decided that would be in some town called Las Cruces, New Mexico. He got to town about six o'clock. After pulling off the highway, he used his smart phone map to locate bars. He found several along University Avenue, some advertising live music. The street was near his location and it seemed like a good place to start looking for Aden, then spread out if he didn't have any luck. He drove past several motels and checked out the parking lots for a motorcycle, but didn't spot any.

He was afraid that Aden had found his $40,000. The bitch was going to run away from him and spend it on herself! He had to get it back before she had a chance to spend all of it. If any was missing, he most assuredly would take it back as a pound of flesh.

It was a little early to start looking for Aden; the music probably wouldn't start until eight. He found a local café and had a bite to eat. He had his back to the door and didn't see Aden and Steve ride past him as they looked for a motel. Afterwards, he stopped in the first bar off the highway which had no music but was a pleasant place to wait for the search to begin.

Crusher had worked his way through three bars before stepping into the right one. After seeing Aden on stage, he spotted Steve sitting at a table near the stage and a blind fit of rage swept through him. He started to push through a standing crowd near the bar. He would put a hurt on the bastard that would teach him to butt out when dealing with Crusher. As he took a step forward, his hands curled into fists, except the cast on his left hand wouldn't allow it. It reminded him of the whipping he had taken the previous night, the whole baton pounding flashing into his mind. Maybe the last rational cell left in his brain made him stop and think.

Aden was on stage; he was in the right place. They couldn't get away from him. She would leave the bar by the front door; he would be waiting outside where there would be no crowd. He slowly turned and limped out, cussing under his breath the woman with the baton. His car was parked on the opposite side of the street where he could look directly at the bar. He settled down in the front seat with a clear view of the establishment and watched customers going in and out. A small envelope from the glove box called to him. He opened it and poured the contents into the palm of his hand. A quick rush came over him as he snorted the powder. He slouched down and watched the door of the bar.

Sixteen

Aden's set was popular enough that the band had her do an encore. They told her to stick around if she wanted to and they would have her sing three songs in the next set. She was flying high when she sat at Steve's table. "Good set," Steve said. "What now?"

"They told me I could do another couple of songs in the next set if I wanted to. I don't want to stay around this town, but since we're here I would like to sing a couple more songs. If you want to go back to the motel, I'll meet you there later."

"No, I'll stick around for a while." He surreptitiously checked his watch, recognizing it would be another late start tomorrow. "Would you like something to drink?"

"I guess a Coke, It's so nice to be asked to do a second set. I'm amped."

Steve ordered the soda for her and another beer for himself as the band broke into a fast dance melody. "Would you like to dance?"

"Sure, I didn't know you could dance."

"My two step is the only dance that puts your feet in danger. The rest of the time, I just stand there and shake."

"Oh, this I've got to see." They got to their feet, and she held his hand to lead him to the tiny dance floor. Aden thought she would fall down laughing when Steve started shaking and swaying to the beat. Aden had a much more refined rhythm as she swayed to the music. The other dancers recognized her as the singer and started applauding her dancing. She made some interesting moves, showing off her body, and curtsied at the applause. The crowd loved it.

"Wow! I didn't realize I was dancing with a professional."

"Hardly, but I have always loved to dance."

About that time the band segued into a slow foxtrot. Aden moved into Steve's arms. They started in the standard ballroom position with his left hand holding her right hand and his right hand on her bare back as he guided her around the floor. Soon Aden moved closer, and it turned into more of an embrace than a dance. They were standing still, just swaying to the music, when she whispered, "Damn the second set. Let's go back to the motel."

"Grab your gear and we're out of here."

Aden gave him a quick kiss and before he could react, she slipped out of his arms and headed for the back room. Soon she returned wearing her sneakers with her leather jacket over her shirt. She carried her guitar case slung over one shoulder and had a bag with her boots and hat. Steve took the guitar from her as she waved at the band and they walked out the front door.

Seventeen

Out on the street, Aden and Steve turned toward the motel. The sidewalk and street were empty, leaving them alone to enjoy each other's company and the warm night. With arms around each other's waist, looking more at each other than where they were going, they didn't notice Crusher on the other side of the street as he watched them walk past. He stayed still, just following them with his eyes, waiting until they were half a block ahead of him before getting out of his car and trailing them. He thought about staying behind them to find out where their motel was, but his knee was bothering him, and he could see the guitar case right there in front of him. All he had to do was grab it and run. Better to do it before they got farther away from the car. He stepped up his pace.

They must have heard his footsteps. Just before he reached them, Steve looked back to see who was coming up behind them. He and Aden were facing each other as Crusher caught them. The big man seemed to go berserk, barreling between the two and knocking them apart as they fell to the sidewalk. Steve felt himself going over backwards but managed to twist around, catching himself on his hands and knees, protecting the guitar with his body. The guitar stayed on his back. If Crusher had continued the attack on Steve, he probably would have won the fight. Instead, after one kick to Steve's ribs, he grabbed at the guitar case, trying to wrestle it off Steve's shoulders. With the cast on his left hand, he fumbled the grab and stopped to get a better grip. Another kick to Steve's ribs and he slipped the strap off one shoulder. He jerked on the case and it rolled Steve onto his side, allowing Crusher to slip the strap off the other shoulder. He turned to run, but Aden was climbing to her feet and got a leg in front of Crusher, tripping him so he fell headlong, throwing the case in front of him as he reached out his arms to cushion his fall. The guitar gave a loud 'bonk' as the box hit the concrete.

Steve winced at the pain in his ribs, but got his feet under him and stood. When he saw Crusher on the ground, he quickly ran to him and grabbed Crusher's shoulder. He rolled him over and landed a punch on Crusher's nose. Kneeling on Crusher's chest and pinning him to the ground, he grabbed Crusher's arms and looked him in the eye. "You son of a bitch! That's the last time you sandbag me."

Crusher's nose was bleeding as Aden grabbed his hair and pulled his head around. "Why are you still following us? And why do you want my guitar?"

"You bitch, I know what you're doing. I'll follow you all the way to hell if I have to. Just give me the damn guitar." He tried to free his arm to swing at Steve, but he had no leverage and Steve was able to hold him down.

Aden ran to the guitar and picked up the case. "Crusher, why do you want the guitar? I know you don't play. Are you just trying to get back at me for leaving you?"

Crusher's head fell back and he seemed to lose consciousness. Steve let go of his arm and tried to check his pulse on his throat.

Crusher used the opportunity to punch Steve in the chest and push him off. He rolled over and, before Steve could stop him, he was on his feet making a lunge at Aden.

"I'll be damned! He did it again!" Steve managed to grab a foot, causing Crusher to lose his balance and go down on hands and knees. Aden backed away. Steve grabbed Crusher's ankle and then his belt and quickly pulled himself on top of Crusher, pushing him down flat on the sidewalk while pulling his arm up behind his back. "Stay down, you asshole. What's this all about?"

"I know what you're doing! You want it all for yourself! I'll see you in hell first. I'll follow you anywhere you go. You can't get away from me!"

Aden looked at Steve. "What's he talking about? What do we do with him?"

Steve thought about it. He looked both ways up and down the street. There were no cops or pedestrians on the street. Just as well... he didn't want to get the police involved. He probably should have.

Twisting Crusher's arm higher behind his back and holding it there, Steve pulled Crusher to his feet. "Where's your car?"

"Go to hell, asshole!"

Steve pulled Crusher's arm up higher."Where's your car, dammit! I'll tear this arm off."

"Uhh, down the block." He pointed with his other hand to the car across the street.

"Walk!" Steve pushed him off the curb and the two walked down the street to his car.

Aden followed behind. "What are you going to do with him?" she asked.

"Giving him a time out. Probably not the best option, but it's this or call the police."

At the car, Steve told Crusher to open the trunk. "I can't reach my keys. They're in my right front pocket." Steve was holding Crusher's right arm.

"Shit! Don't get any ideas from this." He looked at Aden. "Grab his keys."

Steve secured his hold on the arm with both hands as Aden reached into Crusher's pocket and found the keys. She pulled them out and opened the trunk lid. "Okay, climb in."

"Climb in the trunk?"

"You can spend time in the trunk or in the jail. Your choice. Makes me no never mind."

Crusher laid down in the trunk and Steve slammed the lid. He took Aden's arm. "Let's hurry, I don't know how long that will hold him.

"Does he have air?"

Steve wound up and threw the keys onto the roof of the building where the car was parked. "Oh sure, that thing is not air tight. It won't hold him long. He'll either get the trunk lid open or he might be able to break into the back seat. Let's go." They started running.

Eighteen

It took Crusher some time to maneuver himself to where he could start kicking at the trunk lid; it made his knee hurt more. He had to hand it to the car; it was stronger than he expected. After several minutes of kicking, he had accomplished nothing. He took a deep breath, then remembered his back seat folded down. He had to turn himself over—not easy at his height with his legs folded to fit in the width of the trunk—and feel around for the seat-back release. Even with the seat-back down, the space to slide through was a tight fit. He finally wormed his way through and climbed out of the car. He looked up and down the street... no sign of Aden and the asshole. He thought about what to do next.

He knew they were staying somewhere near the bar, within walking distance. He knew the direction. He would wait until morning, listen and watch for a motorcycle leaving the area. He felt smug as he got his spare key from the magnetic holder under the fender, pulled a U-turn, drove to where he had noticed several motels and checked the parking lots for a motorcycle. When he didn't find one, he circled back to where he could keep an eye on all of them and settled down to wait.

Nineteen

Meanwhile Aden and Steve had made it back to the motel, one of whose parking lots Crusher would soon be searching. They were both shaken up by the attack. Steve made sure all the blinds were closed and the door security was engaged. Aden exclaimed, "I thought you were being paranoid bringing the motorcycle in here. Now I'm glad you did. I don't understand what's going through that guy's mind. Clearly, he is not that attracted to me. I don't know why he wants the guitar. It's nothing special and he doesn't play."

"Let's look at the guitar."

"Okay." She unzipped the case and handed Steve the guitar. As she had said, it was a good, middle of the line acoustic flattop with some electronics added so she could play it through an amplifier. Steve got the flashlight out of the Beemer's tool kit and tried to look inside using a small mechanic's mirror. He didn't find anything. Aden looked in all the compartments in the case but didn't dig down under the string packages and guitar strap, so they didn't find the money. Steve handed the guitar back and Aden zipped the case shut.

Aden asked, "So what now? We know he'll be looking for us in the morning. How do we get out of here?"

"I guess we have to take him at his word. It doesn't sound like he's giving up. So, we're going to have to get off Interstate 10. We'll ride the secondary roads from here. I know this screws up your plans. Do you want to keep going?"

"Oh yes. I don't want to stay here. This isn't a town where I can find a singing job and support myself." She shuddered. "I don't know what he has planned, but I think I'm safer with you. Unless you don't want to be involved. I would understand if you told me to buzz off."

"No, for several reasons I want to stay together. First of all, I like your company. Two, I also think you're safer if you stay with me. And don't beat yourself up over this situation—it isn't something anyone expected or planned on." Steve laughed. "I don't know why I think I'm any smarter than he is. He's blindsided me three times now and I still feel the hurt."

Steve had noticed an old road atlas that Kruzick had stuck in one of the saddlebags, probably something he acquired for planning his own trip home. That would have been before he shipped over. He dug it out and opened it to the pages showing the entire United States. Finding Las Cruces, he started checking roads. There was one red line that stood out for him. "This is the latest plan. Looks like US 82 will take us where we want to go. Of course, it hits a town every twenty or thirty miles, but it goes in the right direction. So, the plan of the day is, I'll sneak out early in the morning and look for Crusher's car. If it's out there, we'll wait for him to leave. If it's not in sight, we'll take off and head north and east for Alamogordo. When we're sure we're clear of Crusher, we'll decide what's next.

"Alamogordo. That's a funny name. What does it mean?"

"Fat Cottonwood. I guess it was named after a grove of big cottonwood trees in the area. The town's mainly supported these days by a nearby Air Force base. We better hit the sack so we can get an early start."

When they turned out the lights and fell into bed, neither was in the mood to explore the feelings they had started developing earlier. Aden realized she was feeling traumatized from the latest encounter with Crusher. Three nights in a row he had attacked her, well, her and Steve. *Why would he want the guitar?* She drifted off to sleep when her thoughts moved on to Steve. She was happy he wanted her company. Steve lay awake most of the night waiting for Crusher to break down the door.

Friday

At about 7:00 am, Crusher snapped out of a doze when he heard a motorcycle start up around the corner from where he was parked. He realized he hadn't looked for motels on the side street. Quickly starting the car, he followed the sound. It was fairly loud but by the time he turned the corner it was around another corner and out of sight. At the next corner there was a solid line of rush hour traffic, so he wasted a minute before making the right-hand turn. He stepped on the gas and cut around several cars as he tried to catch the motorcycle. The bike was leading him back to the street he had been parked on which led to the freeway. It looked like they were trying to get an early start and stay ahead of him. Two stoplights later, he made it to the on-ramp of I-10 headed east. He had a glimpse of a motorcycle, by now almost a mile ahead of him, as he drove through the heavy, going-to-work traffic. The machine was far enough away that he couldn't see any details of the motorcycle itself; he was sure he saw two riders. Working bouncer's hours, he wasn't used to the early morning work traffic. For the moment he was bottled up in the same lane the motorcycle was in... at least they were both going the same direction.

Somewhere along the way, he found himself merged into the traffic on I-25 southbound.

Crusher fought his way forward through the closely-packed cars, chasing after the motorcycle. Short glimpses ahead showed him he was getting nearer. He was startled to see a road sign announcing the next city was El Paso coming up in fifteen miles. He cut in front of a semi, forcing the driver to hit the brakes and let loose a string of cursing and honking. Finally, Crusher got a good look at the motorcycle he was chasing. It had two people on it, but he didn't see a guitar case. It was a Harley-Davidson, not Aden and Steve. He pounded the steering wheel and checked his watch... a little after eight. He had to go another five miles before he found an interchange where he could turn around.

When he got back to Las Cruces and the area of the motel , it was almost nine o'clock. He had watched for Aden and Steve going the other way as he returned to Las Cruces but didn't see them. The next step was a tour of all the parking lots of all the motels in the area. No sign of the motorcycle or Aden. His only chance was to find them along I-10.

Twenty

Steve got up just after seven and had a quick look up and down the street. No sign of Crusher. He got back to the room as Aden was coming out of the bathroom. "Good morning. Are you as hungry as I am? Let's get out of this part of town before finding a place to eat so Crusher doesn't run into us on the street. I looked around outside, no sign of your nemesis. "

"Very funny. I'm laughing inside. Actually, I'm astounded you know the word."

"I been around."

"Yeah, all the WestPac dives, I'll bet."

"I'm astounded you know that word."

"Ha! Half the women in The Happy Hideaway were WestPac widows. The band told me all about them and where the term came from."

"Yeah, some of the brown baggers on the *Sterett* had problems when we got back to the States. A couple of guys had started divorce proceedings by the time I mustered out."

"What's a brown bagger?"

"The Navy pays a basic allowance for subsistence. Normally it's paid to the chow hall. If you're married, the money is paid to the family, called comrats. That means a married man has to pay for his meals if he eats in the chow hall, so he brings his lunch in a brown paper bag."

They were fed and on the road by eight-fifteen. Steve took them a little bit north on I-25 to the US70 intersection and they headed east for the San Augustine Pass over the Organ mountains. Shortly after starting east, Aden asked, "I see all these signs on the businesses, why is everything named 'Jornada' this and that? What's that all about?"

"This area is the south end of the *Jornada del Muerto*. Some folks think it means journey of death, but it's actually journey of the dead man. This is part of *El Camino Real de Tierra Adentro*, the road from Mexico City to Santa Fe. Story goes that a man in Santa Fe was sentenced to death for some crime, probably something to do with the Spanish Inquisition. This was in the sixteen hundreds. He escaped and with the help of an Indian guide, he made it this far, trying to get back to Mexico. One version of the story goes that when they got to somewhere around here, the Indian killed him and took all his possessions. Or he might have just got sick and died. Since he was already sentenced to die, they called it the journey of the dead man." Steve looked at all the houses and businesses expanding on each side of the highway. "Now you might call it 'journey of urban sprawl'."

"You have some strange stories in this state."

"I'll bet all states have similar stories. In fact, isn't Washington the home of bigfoot?"

"Touché. But that story is used to scare kiddies into being good. Many cultures have a boogie man."

"Adults are mean. Or is it just parents?"

"Depends on your definition of mean. Crusher is mean."

"And let's hope that's the last time we hear that name."

Their path was a straight climb all the way to the San Augustine pass through the Organ Mountains. At the crest, the highway did an S curve before taking them by a pullout to a site overlooking the descent and valley to the east, but they didn't stop. "What did we miss?" Aden asked.

"Not much. Looks like the Army has put a rocket on display and then you have the same view that we now have of the Tularosa Basin, which is the valley floor between here and the Sacramento Mountains way over to the east." They went off the crest and followed the road downhill to the northeast past the White Sands National Monument and Holloman AFB. About an hour after leaving Las Cruces, they were passing through Alamogordo. "Now we get to some good motorcycle country. We cross the Sacramento Mountains."

"Well, take it easy on the curves. I'm still not used to the way this thing leans."

"I'll try not to scare you. I've never figured out why people think that's funny."

"Thank you."

Near the north end of Alamogordo, they found the intersection with US 82. From there they started climbing through the bare, desert landscape toward High Rolls, a village in the Sacramento Mountains where the landscape started getting a little greener, with piñon and juniper spread among the creosote and mesquite bushes. The road carried them through a valley, climbing and winding through the hills until, after the road made a one-hundred-eighty-degree turn, they were in Cloudcroft, 8,700 feet above sea level. Steve looked at his watch and decided it was too early for lunch and was about to ride on when Aden said, "Let's stop for a cup of coffee or something. I need to stretch my legs."

"Okay." He found a coffee shop and they went in. He told the waitress, "Coffee and milk for me," turning to Aden, "how about you?"

"I'll have the same thing combined in an iced caffe latte." They sat and talked. "I like this greener scenery. Things were getting a little too brown for me on the ride from Las Cruces. What's next?"

"We get back to the brown, I'm afraid. There's not much green between here and Texas. Then there will be lots of green farms."

"Farms? I thought Texas was all ranches."

"Yeah, I think that's mostly in south Texas and the panhandle. West Texas is mainly farms and oil fields. We'll ride by some cattle ranches along the way. There used to be ranches in the Tularosa Basin we just crossed, but the Army gobbled up all the land." He finished his cup. "Let's ride on to Artesia and stop for lunch."

US82 had enough curves in it to make it interesting for Steve without scaring Aden as they made it out of the mountains and back to the plains. Blue grama grass covered the land in sparse clumps and fair-weather cumulus clouds floated in the blue sky. In Artesia, the highway became the main street. They rode along to the center of the town until Steve spotted a Mexican restaurant. "How about Mexican food?"

"Again? You had Mexican food yesterday. But sure, I like tacos."

"This will be different spices than west coast mex. Make sure you get your salsa on the side so you can control it."

They pulled into the parking lot. "Yeah, you gave me that lesson in Las Cruces. You're saying you've burned out your taste buds and require spicier food."

They went inside and found a table. After ordering Aden's chicken tacos and more green chile chicken enchiladas for Steve, they were talking about the ride through the mountains when a forty-something fellow with a cowboy hat and a paunch stopped by the table and hitched up his pants.

"Howdy, little lady. I saw ya ride in on the back of that scooter. You look kind of windblown. Why don't you dump this loser and ride along with me in that Lincoln Navigator out there?"

They looked out the window at the big, black SUV parked where the fellow was pointing. The man's proposition to Aden hit Steve like a bombshell. "Hey! You're pushing in here with no invitation. Piss off."

"I ain't talkin' to you, sonny. Butt out." Steve started to stand but Aden put her hand on his arm and pulled him back down. "...and where are you going?" she said in sweet tones. Steve was wondering what the hell? Would she consider getting off the bike and into the dude's boat?

The character turned back to Aden. "Anywhere you want, sweet cheeks. I see you got that there gee-tar, we can go somewhere and make sweet music together. If you play your cards right, there could be some money in it for you. I gotta oil patch down south a ways. Does purdy well. I do like to spread the good times around."

She grinned at him like a sly Cheshire cat. "You're an oil man?"

"Sure am, raised around the fields in Odessa. Been wildcatting in the Permian Basin. Had some good strikes. That's how I can afford that beautiful vee-hicle out there."

"I'm guessing you're a Texan?"

"You guessed that one right. I suppose you could tell by my manly figure and my silver tongue. Where you from?"

"I'm from Washington State and I don't think we have a lot in common."

"Hell, that's okay. I don't wanna talk to you anyway. We can get comfortable in the truck and not have to say a word. That Lincoln has air conditioning, reclining seats, a music system that'll pull in anything from Hank Snow to Morgan Wallen."

She patted his stomach. "I guess you need a vehicle that big to hold that potbelly of yours." She turned to Steve. "Do you know what SUV stands for?"

"What's that?"

"Stupid Ugly Vehicle." She turned back to the Texan. "I've had better pick-up lines from high school students. I think you'd have better luck if you stick to women your age and IQ. What made you think I'd be interested in you?"

The man, looking astonished, took a step back. "I got lots a money." Her words soaked in. "Sorry, didn't know I was talkin' to a bitch." He looked at Steve. "She's all yours, junior. I'd knock some a that west coast crap outta her."

Steve stood up, but Aden grabbed him by the arm. "Sit down. You would hurt him, and he'd cry. Then he'd call a cop. It's not worth getting in trouble over dumb words."

Steve let go a short laugh. "Reminds me of a New Mexico governor from many years ago… he had a quote that's still popular around here, *Poor New Mexico, so far from heaven, so close to Texas.*"

Aden laughed as the Texan turned red and stomped off. She put her hand on Steve's arm. "Piss off? What are you, British?"

"Yeah, I don't know where that came from. It conveyed the message."

She laughed again. "So, I'll never know what I'm missing riding in a Lincoln Navigator. Well, we've got air, but it's not conditioned, we do have music… could you put a reclining seat on the Beemer?"

"For you, I'll try it, but you'll have to hold the guitar on your lap."

"Forget it then. It has been nice to stretch out my legs and interact with the local gentry. Switching subjects, you haven't said where we're going today…"

The food came before he could answer. She thought the salsa was too hot, but she liked the sopapillas with honey that came with the meal. "Let's see, we'll gas up here. Then we'll follow US 82 to Lovington, about fifty miles, then angle northeast to Lubbock, Texas. That's about three hours and will be our next gas stop. From there I was thinking of Wichita Falls, another three hours and then we'll probably feel like stopping for the night." He checked his watch. "We should be in Wichita Falls by six o'clock. Maybe look around a little for a music spot."

"Or do some sightseeing, I don't have to play music every night. We can take life easy."

Between Artesia and Lovington, they crossed the dryline, the line that separates the desert air from the great plains. The temperature stayed about the same, but they could feel the humidity rising and the air becoming muggy. The mugginess continued climbing the further east they rode. The landscape was slowly changing as well. The change in flora was really apparent in Texas. As they left Lovington, the creosote bush and mesquite had slowly given way to huge crop circles of irrigated land. After crossing into Texas, they passed field after field of irrigation circles stretching out as far as they could see. Passing through Plains, Texas, Steve could look down the highway running straight ahead for thirty miles with nothing to break the vista but telephone poles and old windmills. It reminded him of looking out at the horizon at sea. As they rode east, the skyline of Brownfield's buildings appeared to rise out of the ground. Brownfield was where the highway took off northeast to Lubbock.

The stop in Lubbock was a short one. They found a truck stop where they gassed up and had drinks. Steve had his traveling combo, a cup of coffee and a glass of milk. Aden wanted a large Coke to go so she could sip it on the ride. "I think my shoulders are getting stronger. Carrying the guitar isn't the chore it was when we started. And I don't notice the weight of the helmet anymore."

"Good. Sounds like you're getting acclimated. This really is a great bike to ride. I'm going to hate going back to my CB."

"CB?"

"My Honda CBR 500. Everything gets a nickname."

"So, what's this machine's nickname?"

Steve grimaced. "Besides Beemer? BMW calls it Shifthead. Probably named by some German that doesn't speak English. You can imagine how that gets mispronounced. They added a feature where the intake cam shifts to a more aggressive profile for higher power settings."

"Huh? I don't know what that means, but I take your point on the name.

"In general, BMW motorcycles are called Beemers and the cars are Bimmers. The Beemer was a British nickname since they already had the Beezer, which was a BSA. That company has since gone out of business."

"I get it, you have to know the language to play the game. It's the same with music. You have to know the common progressions and licks for the usual keys."

"Licks, huh? I guess you're right. Every hobby and vocation has its language. Changing the subject, we have a choice to make."

"I like choices. What is it?"

"I've been thinking. I sorta promised you some big cities on the ride. On the next stretch of highway, we will come to a fork. I know the saying is when you come to a fork in the road, take it. But do you want to go to Dallas or Wichita Falls? There's a considerable difference in size and population."

"You're right, that's quite a choice. Do we have to decide right now?"

"No, the fork in the road is about two hours away. You have that much time to decide."

"Why do I get to decide?"

"Just because I told you we would ride through some major cities. I won't tell you my choice, so I don't influence your decision. I don't want you to think you're a captive on this trip; you have choices."

"Okay, I'll think about it while we ride."

"You ready to go?"

"Sure, let's hit the road."

From Lubbock it was one small town after another. The road was in good condition, four lanes with a wide divider between the opposite-bound lanes. They would lose the divider when they passed through the towns where the highway became the main street. The land started out covered in farms and cultivated fields.

That ended a couple of miles from the shallow canyon of the White River. The area on both sides of the river was a little too rough and tumble for farming, covered with natural flora, dry stubby grasses and scattered bushes, all over the sides of the canyon. A few miles past the river, it was back to crop circles until the road swung southwest. While they were still looking at fields to the north, wild stunted trees and bushes were taking over the land to the south, finally covering both sides of the road.

An hour after leaving Lubbock, they were passing through Dickens. The area was all unimproved land. Some cattle were grazing along the highway. "There's your ranch."

"What?"

'You wanted to see a ranch. There's one."

"I've seen more animals than that in a kiddie zoo."

"Well, who knows how many are over the next hill."

"There aren't any hills. This land is as flat as a pancake."

"It's not flat. A friend of mine that lives near here dropped a ball one day and it rolled clear to the Gulf of Mexico."

"Oh, very funny. You should do an act. If I ever get my own show, you can open for me."

A little after five, Steve said, "We're almost to the fork. Which way?"

"How far is it to Wichita Falls?"

"About fifty miles."

"And Dallas?"

"About a hundred and fifty."

"Let's go to Wichita Falls. I want to find a motel with a pool and try to cool off. This climate really has my ass dragging. I could phrase that more elegantly, but it wouldn't indicate my true feelings."

"You got it, lady. I have to say I feel the same way. Wichita Falls it is. That was my choice, incidentally."

Twenty-one

They made Wichita Falls a little before six. Now the highway had frontage roads on either side. Steve got off onto the frontage road so he could stop when they found a gas station or restaurant. The streets were busy with going-home traffic. Although there were some businesses along the highway, they noticed lots of neighborhoods backing up to the road. Finally, Steve spotted a gas station with a nice-looking diner nearby. He took the exit to McNeil Ave. and turned under the highway to the station. As he shut off the ignition he asked, "So, you don't want to try to find a gig tonight?"

"No, by the time we eat, it'll be too late and frankly, since we crossed into Texas I feel like a wet mop."

"Yeah, get used to it for the rest of the trip." He pulled out his phone to check the weather. "The thermometer says ninety-six, the humidity is about the same. It really drags me down when I come over here."

"There's a restaurant down the street. I'll bet it's air conditioned. Let's check it out. I want something besides a hamburger or Mexican food tonight."

"Okay, we'll gas up, eat, then find a motel, maybe do some sightseeing."

When she got off the bike, Aden took off her leather jacket saying, "Ride slow tonight, I'm going to melt if I wear this jacket." As she stored it in a saddlebag, Steve gazed admiringly at her in jeans, T-shirt and sneakers. For a moment he got lost in the reality of her smiling face and feminine air. Steve shook himself, paid for the gas and they rode the block to the restaurant.

It was air conditioned and had a wide selection of dishes. Steve went for the baby back ribs and Aden had the salmon Caesar pasta salad. The waitress kept pushing iced tea at them, but Aden wanted wine and Steve stuck to water. He couldn't really tell the difference between iced tea and water, and the water was free. The restaurant did sell drinks to go, so Steve bought a couple of beers to have at the motel.

He realized he was enjoying not worrying about Crusher. He was pleased that neither of them had mentioned the character since this morning, although he must have been lurking in the back of Steve's mind. He discreetly studied Aden and thought she seemed more relaxed and carefree. He was certainly enjoying her company today and he wasn't going to spoil it by bringing up a bad memory. They were discussing doing some sightseeing and the waitress overheard. "You should go see the falls."

"Where are they? I'm surprised you have waterfalls here on the plains," Steve said.

"The original waterfall the town is named after was destroyed in a flood in the 1800s. The town decided to build a new waterfall since the tourists expected to see one. Just take the street out front east to I-44 and head north for a ways. Ya can't miss it. There's motels near there as well."

"The original waterfall was destroyed in a flood?"

"Well, it was only five feet high. The flood turned it into a bunch of rapids."

"The town is named after a five-foot-high waterfall?" Aden asked.

"Well, they had to call the place somethin'. What'd you expect? Texas ain't exactly hilly, being part of the great plains."

"Can't argue with logic like that. Let's check it out."

Back on the Beemer, Aden put the guitar straps over her T-shirt and got ready to ride. Steve held the machine up as she climbed aboard. The modern falls should truthfully be called a fountain but was certainly spectacular. The city had built a series of waterfalls divided into three cascades flowing down a fifty-foot hill; the water was surrounded by lush vegetation on each side. It sat facing the river and, a passerby told them, the water was recirculated. A little more peaceful sightseeing and Steve started looking for a motel.

They had left the waterfall and were cruising down the street when a couple of bikers on Harleys pulled up on either side of them. Steve waved hello; the two didn't respond. "We seem to have attracted some motorcycle gang members. Wonder what they want?"

They looked Aden over carefully. One pointed at the guitar and yelled, "Do you play?" He was wearing a beanie helmet and sunglasses, although the sun was down. The other had headgear that looked like a World War 2 German helmet. "Where are you going?"

"We're looking for a motel," Steve yelled back. He couldn't tell if they understood the muffled sound coming out of the full-face helmet. Aden unconsciously took a better grip on Steve.

After a while, the beanie-helmet guy said, "Follow us." Two more bikers rode up from behind and joined the group. Aden and Steve were trapped in the middle.

Steve started to slow down, but the riders behind started to close in. One of them put his foot out, pushing on one of the

Beemer's saddlebags. Steve opened the throttle so the box wouldn't get bent and the whole group accelerated and matched his speed. The leader yelled, "Just stay with us!" and slowed down again to the speed limit.

Aden asked, "What's going on?"

"I think we've been kidnapped. I don't know where they're taking us."

The riders, all wearing vests over their leather jackets embroidered with "Master Links MC," stayed tight around the BMW. Steve had to stay alert to match the turns to other streets.

"What's a master link?" Aden asked.

"It's the link in a motorcycle chain that can be taken apart to allow the chain to be removed from the bike. Or, conversely, the link that holds the two ends of the chain together. Ironically enough, most of those motorcycles have a belt drive rather than a chain."

"What do we have?"

"We have a shaft drive. Entirely different concept." The 'we' came as a pleasant surprise to Steve. He didn't know if he was reading too much into it, but he had been subconsciously hoping Aden would consider them a 'couple.'

By then, the sun was down, and they were riding through an open area at the edge of town. Soon they turned into an unlit, dirt parking lot with a dimly lit building sitting at the back of the lot. A neon sign over the door said, "Rarin' to Go Saloon." Lots of Harley Davidson motorcycles were parked near the building. "Yeah, we're in the midst of a motorcycle gang. Stay close." They parked with the newcomers and climbed off.

The rider that had asked him where they were going came over as Aden and Steve pulled off their helmets. He was approaching middle age and had a week's growth of beard. Tall and wiry, he projected an air of confidence. Steve could see some sort of tattoo on his neck. He looked at Aden and said, "Wow!

You're the singer? Great! I'm Gary, incidentally. I kind of run the place." Steve noticed the embroidery on his vest read "President."

"Okay, I'm a singer but I wasn't planning on singing tonight. Why have you brought us here? What do you want?"

Gary ignored her. He looked at the license plate on the Beemer. "You guys traveling from California? Come on in and tell us about it." He put a hand on each of their shoulders to usher them inside the bar. Steve stopped to lock up the helmets in the saddlebags. "Good idea, never know when some thief is lurking around here."

It was a dimly lit room filled with smoke, not all of it from tobacco. The walls were covered with girlie posters, neon signs, and motorcycle parts. Judging from the conditions of the parts, they had been taken from wrecks. At least it was air conditioned. Steve started to perk up in the cooler, drier air. Several pool tables were on one side of the room with a bar running down the other. Some tables and chairs were back against the far wall. It looked like about ten men were standing at the bar or sitting at the tables with four or five women mixed in. All of the pool tables were occupied with both men and women playing. It was a relaxed-looking crowd. The club members saw Gary escorting the two strangers into what was clearly their bar, but didn't seem upset.

"Well, what are you waiting for? Give us a song," Gary said.

"A song?" Aden responded.

"Sure. You didn't think we brought you here just because of your pretty face."

"Where did you see my face?"

"At the waterfall. We happened to be passing by when you guys were walking back to your scooter. Carrying a guitar like that, we figured you must be a professional. Let's see what ya got."

Aden started to say no. But as she looked around at the bearded, stone-faced riders watching her, she wondered what would happen if she didn't cooperate. Did she really have a choice? She got out her guitar. Unexpectedly, a club member showed her where she could plug into an amplifier and set up a mike for her. Steve noticed there was a large set of drums and an upright piano already there. This seemed to be a very musical gang. The crowd gathered round as she tuned and plugged in. Surprising Steve, she broke into a fast version of an old Hank Snow song, "I've Been Everywhere." The crowd loved it and the whistles and applause rang out. After she sang another song, two of the bikers broke out a fiddle and a bass guitar. Sticking with standards they all knew, the concert continued for some time. The crowd grew as the evening wore on. Now Aden was playing to a packed house.

Gary was sitting with Steve. "How about a beer or something stronger?"

"No, thanks. I don't drink while I'm riding. I have a couple of beers in my saddlebag. I'll have them when we get a motel room."

"You don't drink when you're riding? Never?"

"I bought my machine from the widow of a guy who had a couple of drinks at a poker game and died on the ride home. It's never seemed worth it to me to break the rule."

"So, do you smoke? Anything?"

"No. As an athlete, I wasn't interested in high school and the Navy was totally against weed. I never tried cigarettes."

Gary smiled. "Do you eat hay?"

"Hay! What? No."

"Hell, you aren't fit company for man or beast." He rolled a joint and asked, "Is this what you guys do? Just travel around and pick up jobs wherever you happen to be?" After lighting the joint, he offered it to Steve.

"No, thanks."

"More for me." Gary took another hit.

"I'm just out of the Navy and kinda killing time until school starts in September. Aden is just starting a singing career. She had some trouble in San Diego so she joined me in my travels."

"Thank you for your service. Where are you headed? And what kind of trouble?"

"Florida."

"Florida? What's Florida got that we ain't got here in Texas?"

"The owner of the motorcycle I'm delivering."

"It's not your bike?"

"No, I'm doing a favor for a friend in the Navy. He got shipped to Japan and I'm taking his bike to his brother in Florida."

"That's a lot of riding. Wouldn't I-10 be faster?"

Steve grimaced. "That's the trouble. Aden managed to pick up a stalker. He's looking for us along I-10."

"You've met some interesting characters."

"Not to mention tonight. This is our first kidnapping."

Gary chuckled. "You're our first kidnappees. Feel free to leave anytime you want to. But I don't think Aden's ready to split just yet."

They both looked up at Aden and the band. They had picked up a mandolin and a drummer, along with a lead guitar player.

Gary grabbed a girl walking by. "Wanda, dance with Steve. He needs the experience."

Wanda looked like a girl to give someone experience. She had long brown hair falling below her shoulders, a white, long-sleeved top leaving one shoulder and her midriff bare, skinny jeans and high heels. Her face could have been the face of an angel or devil. Steve had no idea what Gary was talking about, but the girl grabbed his hand and pulled him to the dance floor. She really got into it and Steve was having fun while he danced. Steve looked at Aden to see if she was watching. She was. He was enjoying the dance, but was disconcerted the way the girl was all over him. At the moment it was a crowded dance floor and Wanda and Steve were pushed together as the dancers moved to Aden's cover of "Crazy." Wanda certainly put her all into the dance; it felt as if she had eight arms. When Aden did a fast number next, Wanda showed that she could have been (or maybe was?) an exotic dancer.

Wanda joined them when Steve sat back down with Gary. "That's quite an experience. You have a very musical club."

"Yeah, the band plays at several bars around town. How did it go, Wanda?"

"He's a dead-end kid. No problems."

Steve wasn't sure what she was talking about. Meanwhile, Gary was motioning for another biker to come over. When the fellow got close, Gary motioned with his chin at Wanda. The man walked around behind the woman and placed his hands on her shoulders. She reached up and squeezed his hand, after which he walked away.

Gary turned to a blonde who was shooting pool. "Sophie, why don't you give Aden a break and do a couple of songs?"

"Let me make this shot first." She lined up the shot and made two balls at the same time. She threw the cue stick on the table and sauntered to the stage area. Aden shook hands with her, sat down with Steve and was introduced to Wanda as Sophie started a torch version of "Cry Me a River."

"Wow!" Aden professed. "She's really good. She's got twice the range as me." Sophie segued into a song called "Black Coffee," one Aden and Steve were not familiar with. "She sure has the voice for the blues."

Gary yelled, "Sing something happy." The sounds of "Under the Boardwalk" filled the room. Apparently, it was something she did often... everyone joined in the chorus singing the two parts.

"She has a great voice for all the songs. So why did you want to hear me?"

"To find out if you have a great voice, too. And you do. It's just fun to mix up the sounds occasionally and it was fun to, as Steve put it, kidnap you. You should have seen your faces when you got off the bike."

"Well, if that's the way you get your kicks, glad we could help you out. But I've had enough. I want to go now."

Gary acted like he hadn't heard her. He waved another biker over, who walked up and handed Gary an envelope. "But you've been a good sport about the whole thing, so here's two-hundred dollars for your trouble. I hope you have a pleasant journey to Florida." He handed her the money and stood. "Let's give our guests a big hand as they continue on their journey through life." Everyone gave Aden a standing ovation as they stood. While Aden put her guitar back in its case, Steve automatically reached for the key, although the motorcycle had remote keyless starting. He felt a moment of despair when he didn't find the remote.

He stopped. "My remote is missing."

"I'm sorry, what?"

He was frantically searching the rest of his pockets. "The remote for keyless starting is missing. I must have dropped it during the dance."

Gary looked annoyed for a moment and then yelled, "Everybody look for Steve's remote unit to start his motorcycle. He can't leave until we find it." People started searching around the tables and along the bar. After a few minutes one of the men called out, "Here it is. It got kicked under a pool table." He handed the unit to Steve and Gary, who again placed a hand on each of their shoulders and escorted them to the door. They didn't make it.

As they neared the door, it suddenly opened and a squad of uniformed, helmeted policemen hurried in, about half carrying M-16 style rifles and the rest with shields and batons. The man in the lead, wearing sergeant's stripes, yelled, "Gary Cain, you're under arrest!"

Gary, without hesitating, let go of Steve's shoulder, grabbed Aden's arm and, placing a hand on her back, pushed her at the sergeant. She stumbled into the man and the two fought to stay on their feet. Gary bolted for the back rooms as Steve was thrust aside and all the bikers formed a barrier between the police and Gary. The sergeant pushed Aden off to the side and led a charge to break through the obstacle of bodies. Chairs were being thrown; batons were swinging. The cops with rifles stayed in the back watching that no firearms appeared. Steve helped Aden up off the floor and they crept behind the bar, out of sight.

The fight went on for some time, but slowly the police were getting all the bikers down on the floor with plastic ties restraining their hands and feet. Soon the Master Links and their ladies were all stretched out on the floor. When the fighting finally stopped, the cops began searching the bodies and the building. The police created a pile on one of the pool tables with lots of pistols, knives and bags of drugs. One officer was photographing the accumulation. Gary had not been found. The police had officers stationed at the back door before the raid started so it wasn't apparent how he got out. When the ruckus settled down and the bikers were being searched, Aden and Steve climbed to their feet with their hands in the air.

Several guns were pointed at them as the action stopped and a cop holding a night stick walked over. "Who are you?" the sergeant asked.

"I was doing a singing gig here. We were just about to leave," Aden said. The two slowly put their hands on the bar.

"You're not members of the Master Links?"

"No. We're traveling through town. We just met them tonight."

"Do you two have that strange motorcycle out there?"

"If you mean the BMW, yes, that's ours. We're traveling to Florida," Steve added.

The sergeant had been listening and motioned to the officer with the night stick. "Get their names and addresses and search them and the motorcycle. If everything is copacetic, let them go." Steve didn't argue with the sergeant; he could see how their presence looked to the cops. After a female cop patted down Aden, a patrolman got a little more familiar with Steve than he was comfortable with. The female cop went back to more productive duties and the male cop opened Aden's guitar case. But after shaking the guitar to see if anything rattled, and taking a cursory look at the case, he handed the guitar to Aden to put away. He took them outside and started going through the saddlebags.

Outside there were more cops doing mob control, stopping several reporters from barging into the building. The lights and sheer number of police cars had attracted a mob, half of them glad to see the raid and the other half claiming police brutality on the poor children just trying to have a nice, quiet evening. Other cops were talking on radios and cell phones. All the police vehicles had approached silently with their lights off, but now their red and blue lights were causing a confusion of colors sweeping the dark parking lot. This was obviously a big deal in the community.

Fortunately, Aden and Steve were able to hold everything coming out of the saddlebags as the cop rummaged through their belongings. He wanted to read all the sayings on Steve's T-shirts. Finally, he told them to put everything away and waited impatiently for them to store the clothes he had scattered around. Once they were through, he took them back inside.

The scene was much the same, but a little more order had been restored. Anyone found with drugs was booked and removed to a van for transport to jail. The guns were a bigger problem. The police had to run a records check to see if the gun holder was a felon or had any other reason that they could not have a firearm. Almost everyone in the bar had a pistol and it was going to take a fair amount of time to find out if they were all legal.

The escort cop found the sergeant. "They're clean, Sarge. What now?"

The sergeant looked them over. "They're not part of this raid." He turned back to Aden and Steve. "So, how did you get involved with this bunch?"

Aden answered, "They surrounded our motorcycle and led us here. They saw the guitar I was carrying and wanted to hear me sing. The evening was quite peaceful until now."

The cop showed no emotion and said, "Well, you got lousy timing. Where are you going now?"

"We're looking for an inexpensive motel."

"You'll find some good motels back down this road a couple of miles. Good luck." He led them outside and shut the door.

The two stood still for a moment catching their breath. Finally, Steve laughed. "You get me into more trouble! That was weird. The whole evening was weird. Actually, the whole trip has been weird. Good set, though."

"Thanks. This whole scene scared the hell out of me. I'm still not sure what that was all about. I guess we'd better get out of here while we can. Let's go. And don't be blaming the nuttiness on me. I'm beginning to think you attract weirdness."

Steve found a motel near the falls and pulled into the parking lot. The name was MJ Hotel, but it was the standard, motel style, two-storied row of rooms looking out on the parking lot with an office at the entrance. A small swimming pool was in the parking lot. Before getting off the bike, he asked, "One room or two?"

Aden hugged him tighter and put her chin on his shoulder. "I think we know each other well enough by now to stop asking that question."

Twenty-two

It was late enough that the desk was not manned. Steve rang the bell, and a fellow came out of a back room to register them and give them a key. They had a room on the second floor and, without a worry, Steve left the motorcycle outside. He carried in the saddlebags, and they checked out the room. Aden asked, "Was that unusual, Gary stopping us?"

"Oh yeah. It's never happened to me before. It must be you. Maybe they were bored and looking for something to do. He said we were their first kidnappees. I talked some to Gary. He seemed like a nice guy, but I wouldn't trust him as far as I could throw him. That money they paid you is probably from selling drugs or guns or both."

"I'd throw it away, but I can't afford to." She changed the subject. "So, you found a motel with a pool. Thank you. It's getting late but I'm going in." She took her bag into the bathroom and came out wearing a pair of cut-off jeans and a T-shirt. "I wish I'd brought a swimsuit but I packed light."

Steve was admiring her legs. It was the first time he'd had a good look at them. "I think you'll be okay as long as we don't make too much noise. I don't have anything to wear in the pool. I'll watch."

"You could wear your BVDs. At this time of night, I don't think we need to worry about onlookers."

He thought it over. "Why not? Let's go." He pulled off his shirt, boots and socks, and the two walked down the stairs and into the pool area. It was surrounded by a chain-link fence to keep the youngsters out, but the gate was open. Steve looked around, but there was no one outside. He slipped off his jeans and quickly lowered himself into the pool. Aden followed without making any noise.

"This feels wonderful," she said as she floated up to Steve. The pool was shallow enough that he could stand on the bottom with his chin out of the water but deep enough that they could actually swim from end to end. Most of the lights in the motel windows were dark, so they kept the noise down. They quietly played around for five or ten minutes until a car drove into the parking lot, its headlights sweeping over them.

They stayed still until the car's occupants had gone into their room petting and touching with their arms around each other. "I've had enough, the water is getting cold." Aden whispered.

"I'm ready to quit." Steve grabbed his pants and Aden's hand and the two ran for the stairs and into the room, giggling all the way.

Steve called, "Dibs on the shower. I want to wash off whatever the kids have added to that pool," as they came through the door. He turned around to look at Aden, appreciative of the wet T-shirt that was practically invisible. She was a truly beautiful woman. He knew his wet BVDs were probably nearly transparent and, seeing her, started to get an erection. He quickly headed for the bathroom but wasn't shocked when the bathroom door opened and she joined him in the shower. "I also want to wash off the remnants of the pool and decided not to waste time or water," Aden said. Steve turned toward her as he thought to himself that in the old movies this was where the camera would slowly pan away.

Saturday

Steve was being rocked from a sound sleep. As he emerged from the deep sleep state, he wondered what kind of a drill they were holding on the ship. Steve never was really awake until he'd had a cup of coffee. He finally realized it was Aden waking him up. His first thought was that she could have awakened him in a more interesting manner. He found he had his arms around her and asked, "What's wrong?" He looked at his watch. Four thirty-four.

"I think I hear the motorcycle. Could someone be stealing it?"

Steve got out of bed instantly, looking out the motel window. He couldn't see the parking space, so he opened the door and ran out onto the balcony. The Beemer was not where he had parked it. "Shit! The bike's gone."

He went back into the room and fumbled through his pants for his phone to pull up the GPS location app. He normally kept it set to report every eight hours, now he switched it to every two minutes. It showed the machine on Magnolia Street a few blocks away, heading south. He quickly called nine-one-one and was finally connected to the police. "Third precinct, Officer Crandall, how may I help you?"

"My motorcycle has just been stolen. I know where it is. I have a tracker on the bike and its location shows on my phone."

"Okay, give me your name and address and what kind of motorcycle are we looking for?"

"I'm Steve Luce at the MJ Hotel, room two-one-two. It's a BMW R1250GS with a California license plate." He gave them the plate number. "It's headed south on Magnolia Street approaching Kell Boulevard."

"I'll broadcast a be-on-the-lookout notice and we'll call you if we have any luck."

"Have you got someone in that area that can look for it right now?"

"Uh, it's not clear if there's a patrolman in that area. Give me the best phone number to reach you and I'll get back to you."

Steve gave him the phone number, although he understood nine-one-one automatically recorded the phone number calling them. The cop hung up.

Aden was pulling on her jeans. "Do you think it's Crusher?"

Steve thought about it. "No, he would be trying to get into the room. And he couldn't get the bike started."

Steve was beside himself. To come this far, get away from Crusher and then have this happen. He got dressed and was wondering what to do next when there was a knock on the door. A patrolman was standing outside. Steve checked Aden; she was up and dressed. He opened the door wide. "Come in. Are you here about the theft?"

"Yes, I understand it just happened. I need to get a description of the motorcycle."

"As I told the policeman on the phone it's a BMW R1250GS, predominately black. It's got a windshield and saddlebag mounts. I've got the saddlebags here." Steve gave the cop a full description and license number then pulled out his phone and looked at the app. "Right now, it's turned onto Kell Boulevard heading west."

The cop didn't seem to take in that last part. He finished writing in his notepad and said, "Okay. We'll get out a bulletin to all patrolmen and keep a lookout for it."

"Or you could just go over to Kell Boulevard and arrest the bastard."

"What?"

"I said you could go to Kell Boulevard and arrest whoever's got the machine."

A sneer broke out on the cop's face. "It doesn't work that way. Everybody thinks they can do a better job than us catching crooks. We have developed a protocol over the years that has proven to get the job done. We'll take your information as a 'tip' and act on it, along with other leads we develop. You'll hear from us when we have something concrete to report." He closed his notepad, said goodbye to them and left.

Steve was fuming. He knew damn well within a few feet where the motorcycle was but couldn't get the police to listen to him. He noticed it had been stationary for the last two reporting periods. If it was still for four minutes, it was probably parked. "Shit! I guess if you want something done right, do it yourself. Can you drive?" he asked Aden.

"Of course. What are you thinking?"

"We'll find a car, maybe the manager of this motel will rent us his for a short time. And we'll go get the bike."

"Is that wise? You're dealing with someone who steals vehicles. Incidentally, I thought you needed that remote key in your pocket to start the bike. How did they get it going?"

"That's a good question. I look forward to asking the bastard just that. As far as dealing with the thieves, I hope I don't have to. According to the location program, the thief has stopped moving. If we can get there quickly, maybe I can steal the machine back."

"Where is it?"

"Looks like it's on the west side of town. It's only about fifteen miles away."

"Why don't you try the police one more time. If it isn't moving, they can go pick it up."

He thought it over. So far, the police didn't seem that helpful. "Okay, one last time." He made the call.

"Third precinct, Officer Crandall, how can I help you?"

"Steve Luce again, Officer Crandall. I can tell you where my motorcycle is. It isn't moving, you can go and pick it up. Probably catch the thieves at the same time."

"Sure, where is it?"

"It's on the west side of town, south of US 82 on a street named Grove Lane. It's at the south end of the street."

"We'll check it out. We'll get back to you."

"Thank you. I'll expect to hear from you."

"You stay put. Don't try anything on your own. You'll just be in the way."

"Uh... sure. Please let me know what's going on."

Time seemed to be flying—it was after five o'clock. Aden suggested they get something to eat. Steve wasn't that hungry, but he agreed; they had to do something. The sky was still dark; a cloud cover had moved in overnight. It added to the gloomy mood as they walked to a diner next to the motel. It was empty at that time of the morning, so they got good service. After a breakfast he really didn't taste and several cups of coffee, Steve called the police station again. " Third precinct, Officer Dover, how can I help you?"

"Hi, this is Steve Luce, I wondered if there is any word on my motorcycle theft yet."

"Uh, I'm not quite sure what you are talking about."

"I phoned in a stolen motorcycle report about four-thirty, a cop came by and took notes. About five I called again and gave you the location of the motorcycle according to my GPS locator app from my phone. Officer Crandall said they would get right on it."

"I'm sorry. Officer Crandall's shift ended, and I don't see any paperwork here about a motorbike. Do you want to file a report?"

Steve had heard about seeing red. In his case he was afraid he was going to black out. He hung up the phone and settled back in his chair. "Son of a bitch! This cop couldn't find any sign of the paperwork on the theft. He asked me if I wanted to file a report. Let's get out of here."

They walked back to the motel and went into the office. "Are you the manager?" Steve asked the girl behind the desk.

"No, can I help you?"

"My motorcycle was stolen out of your parking lot early this morning. I know where it is. Do you have a car I can rent for an hour to go and get it?"

"Well, that's not a service we usually provide."

"Is robbery part of your usual service?"

The girl looked shocked. "Excuse me." She walked into the back room and they heard her yell, "Daddy! You're needed out front." She came back with an older man who needed a shave and who was stuffing his shirt tails into his pants. He was the one that checked them in. "Help you?"

"My motorcycle has been stolen from your parking lot. I know where it is. I have an app on my phone that shows me its location. Can I rent your car to go get it?"

"I'm sorry to hear about your problem. How long would you need the car?"

"Just an hour or two. It's about fifteen miles away. I don't think I'll have any problem getting it back."

"Well, I guess we owe you some sort of help. Did you report it to the police?"

"Yes. They have been less than helpful."

"Sorry to hear that, but not surprised. They seem to think we're here to serve them. Yeah, I'll let you use my car. No charge."

"Thanks. I promise to return it in the same condition it's in now."

The manager laughed. "You could do a lot of damage and still keep that promise. Here ya go." He handed over the key and pointed to where the 10-year-old Chevy was parked.

Steve thanked him and headed across the parking lot as he checked the location finder again. "C'mon, they won't stay there forever." A check of the GPS showed that the motorcycle hadn't moved. Steve's fear was that they had discovered the sending unit and removed it from the frame. Kruz had done a good job of hiding the unit, but nothing is perfect.

When they got to the car, Steve thought for a moment and handed the keys to Aden. "Here, you drive. You did say you have a license, didn't you?"

"Yes. I'm a good driver. Why am I driving now?"

"You'll have to drive the car back when we find the bike. And I haven't really driven a car in over three years. In my present mood, I better not start now. I'll watch the GPS app and give you directions."

"That will work. Get in." She took the keys and sat in the driver's seat. Steve got in and directed her south to US 82 and back west where they had first ridden into Wichita Falls. Aden proved to be an experienced driver; she anticipated other drivers' moves and knew when to stay back when the idiots insisted on having the whole road. It was a little early for the going-to-work traffic, so the streets were relatively empty. The sun was up but it was a gloomy, cloudy morning, the gray light giving everything a washed-out effect.

They drove to the outskirts of the town and actually passed the point shown as the location of the motorcycle while looking for a chance to get across the highway and onto the other frontage road. Aden finally found an intersection leading to a county road running parallel to the highway and passed under the highway to head back east on the side road. They continued until the locator unit indicated the machine was just to the south of them. Aden stopped the car and Steve got out for a better look.

"There's a house about half-a-mile south." He looked at the road in both directions. There were houses spaced about a quarter mile apart along the road. "I think we have to go back to that dirt road we just passed." He checked his locator unit one more time and walked around to Aden's window. "Why don't you go back to the road we passed and drive slowly toward the house. I'm going to walk across this open field and try to sneak up on it. You stop when you're about halfway there and wait to see what happens. I'll either be riding back or running back."

Aden reached behind him and pulled his head in the window, planting a substantial kiss on his mouth. "Good luck and be careful. If you don't get the motorcycle back, that's too bad. But it's not worth your life or limbs."

"Gotcha. You stay out of trouble yourself." He grinned at her and started walking toward the barbed-wire fence stretched along the road. It was in bad shape, with most strands sagging or missing and easy to cross over. Then he was walking across a field covered in weeds and stunted trees. It was a ten-minute walk to get near the house. He stopped behind a small tree, deciding how he should approach it. *Damn the police!* He shouldn't have to risk his life when the cops were trained to handle situations like this. They had the manpower and firepower to get the Beemer back safely with no one hurt.

Steve saw that the road ended at the driveway of the house. It was clearly a residential dwelling, but there was absolutely no sign of human habitation. The yard was entirely bare dirt, no trees or bushes of any kind. At least the fields around the house had weeds growing on them. The house faced east with the garage on the north side of the building. A window about midway down the side was dark. That probably meant it wasn't covered. There were no signs of life around the place, so he quietly made his way to the window. He eased up to it and slowly moved to where he could look inside. It was crusted with a thin layer of dust and mud which filtered the light but did allow a hazy view of the interior. He first looked to see if anyone was in the garage. After making sure no one was in there, he took a better look around at the contents. A number of dark shapes were scattered around on the floor. He decided they were cardboard and wooden boxes of various sizes. As his eyes adjusted to the gloom, he spotted the Beemer parked near the garage door. He checked carefully. Yes, it was Kruz's bike. The front was obscured by boxes piled on the floor, but he recognized the saddlebag mounts and California license plate.

The next step was how to get it? He would have to open the garage door. *Was anyone inside? Was the door locked?* He tiptoed to the front corner and peeked around. There were no vehicles in the driveway and no noises came from the house. Maybe whoever had ridden it there had someone pick them up and left. He walked over to the garage-door latch and twisted it. It turned. The door handle was not locked but a gentle tug showed something holding the door closed. Then Steve spotted a sliding bolt lock on the side of the door, secured with a combination lock. The lock looked familiar somehow. Again, tiptoeing over he checked it out. It was the same brand as the one Steve's high school had used. Schools must buy them by the bushel. He remembered how easy it had been to defeat this particular brand. He held the lock in his left hand and pulling on it slightly, tapped it on the side with his knuckles. Nothing happened. He tried it again, harder. Again, nothing happened. He looked around and found a fist-sized rock. He held a slight pull on the lock and hit the side with the rock. Nothing. He stopped to think about it. Trying one more time, he hit the other side of the lock and it slipped open. He was in.

He wondered how loud the door rollers were. If anyone was home, would they hear the door going up? Maybe he'd better have a look around before opening the door. As quietly as possible he walked around the house, but all the blinds were closed so he couldn't see anything inside. He tried putting his ear to the doors but didn't hear anything.

Back at the garage, Steve slowly started raising the door. It was going smoothly, and he had it about three feet up when suddenly someone behind him said, "I wouldn't have taken you for a lockpick, but I was impressed when you opened that lock. Damn, you just don't take a hint, do you?"

He spun around. "Gary! How the hell did you get out here? The cops had that building surrounded."

"On your Beemer, actually." Ignoring the real question of how he got out of the building, he added, "I'm strictly a Harley man myself, but I admit that is a very smooth ride. But I can't let you take it back. Get away from the door." He showed Steve the pistol in his hand. He held it in a manner showing complete confidence that he knew exactly what he was doing, standing far enough back that Steve couldn't grab at it. Steve let the door roll closed. "Now what am I going to do with you?"

"How did you know I was out here? Did you hear me?"

"In this day and age, why would you not look for cameras?" He pointed at a security camera mounted on the underside of the eaves. "I've been watching you since you walked up. Where's that pretty woman you travel with?"

Steve felt like slapping himself and saying "Duh!"

"Why are you out here? What's going on?"

"Among other things, I'm waiting for the buyer of your BMW. I know it isn't your bike, but I'll keep referring to it as yours. It keeps the conversation simpler. Anyway, we were going to follow you to your motel and steal it during the night, but the cops interrupted that plan. I... happened to be on foot after the events of the evening and was passing by your motel when I saw it in the parking lot. It seemed to be a serendipitous moment. I had the remote for keyless starting in my pocket, so I grabbed it and came out here."

"You have a remote?" Steve felt in his pocket and felt the remote unit Kruz had given him. "How did you get a remote? BMW gets big bucks for a spare unit, and you have to prove it's your bike. And you didn't know about the bike until last night."

"Or you can order a blank one on eBay and have a club member with a degree in computer science duplicate it. I've had a blank one for some time... just needed a bike to program it to. We were making a copy of yours when you thought you lost it at the bar. I am amazed you found your way out here. Clearly there's a location transmitter on the bike that I didn't find. That's on me. Which brings me back to my original question, what am I going to do with you?"

"You could let me get on the bike and ride out of here. No need for anyone else to know about this. We're leaving town as soon as we can be on our way."

"Well, someone else already knows about this. We had a buyer lined up before we invited you and your lady to the clubhouse. He's meeting me here this morning. I'm afraid letting you go is not an option. Come inside." He motioned for Steve to walk in front of him as he kept a distance between them, too far for Steve to attack him. Inside, Steve looked at the empty rooms. Clearly no one lived there but there was a table with a monitor showing the areas surrounding the house and a computer with an internet link. He didn't see any other furniture.

"What's going on here? Selling that bike can't be a major moneymaker for you."

Gary laughed, clearly wanting to talk. "No. I'm not that interested in selling your machine. I'm trying to recruit the buyer into the club. He doesn't have a motorcycle, but he said he always liked the BMW products. We prefer hogs, but nobody's perfect. He has a great reputation as a hacker and is knowledgeable about bitcoin. Bitcoin is handy for transferring funds but a lousy way to save money. This guy knows how to move funds in and out quickly. Plus, maybe... uh... liberate bitcoin from people stupid enough to store their money in a bitcoin savings account. We've been after him for some time, but your Beemer sealed the deal.

"Anyway, I decided to steal your bike when I saw it parked at the falls. You looked so smug walking around with that great chick and that over-the-top motorcycle. I wanted to piss you off, show you how the rest of us live. I called the recruit and asked if he would be interested in a GS1250, and he said yes. That's when we corralled you and took you to the clubhouse.

"There's a tunnel running from behind a refrigerator in the basement and ending in the woods off the property. I used that to escape the clubhouse, then started walking to another building we own, as luck would have it, not far from that motel you picked for the night. We keep a spare bike stashed there. I was taking my time, making sure there weren't any cops around before I got out on the streets. Imagine my surprise when I cut across the parking lot at the MJ Motel. Finding your machine at a time when I needed a ride to get away from the fuzz was pure luck. You just keep showing up at the wrong place. When I got here, I called my buyer and now I'm waiting for him to show up. I offered the machine to him at half what I assume it cost. What did your buddy pay for it anyway?"

"I don't know exactly. He got a bonus for shipping over; that's what he used to buy it."

"Doesn't matter, just curious." Gary motioned for Steve to sit in the middle of what would be the living room. Gary threw Steve a couple of plastic zip ties. "Put those on your ankles. Loop them together." When Steve finished, Gary pulled them tighter and had Steve put another couple on his wrists. At least he had his hands in front of him. Gary settled on the floor with his back against the wall. "We'll wait together. As I said, where's your girlfriend?"

"She's back at the motel. No reason to get her involved with this."

Gary thought for a moment. "So how did you get out here?"

"I borrowed a car from the motel manager."

"Where is it?"

"Up the road about a mile."

"So that is where Aden is. I'll have to take care of her after we finish the transaction here."

"She's not part of this. I drove out here alone."

"I don't believe you. If you got the bike back, you'd need a way to get the car back to its owner. She drove you out here."

"So, what is this place? Thinking of going domestic?"

"No, just a convenient warehouse. I don't mind telling you because I know you won't be telling anyone. I've had this place packed full with product many times before moving it out to the sellers."

"Guns or drugs?"

"Both. Why limit ourselves? We've even run some women through here who thought they had found a better life. Unfortunately, they were wrong."

A vehicle out on the driveway interrupted the conversation. A door slammed. "That has to be my buyer. Don't move." Gary stood as the doorbell rang. He opened the door and two characters in greasy jeans and unbuttoned, long-sleeved shirts over dirty T-shirts walked in. Neither had shaved in a day or two and their hands were greasy. One gave off a faint odor. They looked around the empty room, taking in Steve sitting on the floor.

"Where's this twelve-fifty GS?" the less smelly one said.

"In the garage. Practically brand new, just ridden here from the coast." He turned to the other fellow. "I don't believe I know you."

"I'm with Dale. I drove him out here. If he doesn't buy it, I'll drive him home."

Gary pointed at Steve. "That's the previous owner. He can tell you how well it runs."

"Shit, he's not supposed to be here. This is gonna be a problem. He's seen us. He can describe us to the police."

"It won't be a problem. He won't be talking to anyone."

"I don't know," Dale said. He rubbed his face. "I thought this was a simple business deal. Now it's getting fucked up."

"It's not your problem. In fact, it simplifies things." He pushed Steve over on his side and reached into his pants pocket. "Don't get any ideas that I like you. I just want your remote." He left Steve on his side and turned back to the buyer. "I'll take you out to the garage and show you the bike. We can make the deal there.

The buyer looked at Steve as if sizing up a trussed-up pig. Finally, he said, "You're gonna take care of this character? We won't be involved?"

"That's right." Gary nudged Steve with the toe of his boot. "This is my problem. Nothing for you guys to worry about. Let's finish the transaction in the garage. You can look over the machine." They walked out to the garage, leaving Steve to struggle with his ties.

As he looked around the room for something, he tried twisting and pulling on the ties. All he accomplished was rubbing his wrists raw; there were no loose knives laying around and no glasses or bottles to break. Suddenly he heard shouting in the garage. Gary yelled something Steve didn't understand and then there was silence.

Footsteps were coming back into the house. He watched in horror as the buyer came into the room. He was sweating and his shirt was torn. He was holding a large pocketknife and Steve watched him snap it open. Steve could hear cars turning into the driveway, doors were slamming. "You do have a way of getting where the action is, don't you, Mr. Luce?"

"Huh? What happened? How do you know my name? What's going on?"

The buyer opened the front door and several uniformed police officers came into the room. "The perp is handcuffed and lying in the garage. My partner is with him. He may be unconscious; he was uncooperative." He walked over to Steve and cut the restraints off his wrists and ankles. "I'm Officer Schmidt. You don't know me, but I did a checkup on you after you gave your name at the Master Link raid, and I read the report from the officer you talked to this morning. The theft at the motel sounded like Cain taking a chance to grab an escape vehicle. I had told him in passing that I like BMW vehicles. He decided it was a good chance to get me involved with the gang. Well, after last night and today, there won't be a gang." He put the knife away and looked at the torn shirt. "This undercover grind is hard on clothes. I made the mistake in the garage of mentioning your girlfriend and Gary smelled a trap. Fortunately, he fumbled pulling out his pistol, we were able to ah... subdue him. Your information was invaluable in locating him. We didn't know about this site. You've done the Wichita Falls police a big favor."

Steve stood up, rubbing the raw spots on his wrists. "Glad to help. You mean when I was getting the runaround from your phone clerk you were working on getting out here to arrest Gary?"

"Yeah, sorry you decided to take things into your own hands. You know you would have been in big trouble if I hadn't shown up."

"You got that right. You could have given me some indication you had things under control. That last cop I talked to acted like the whole episode was being buried. In fact, he made your department look like incompetent fools that didn't give a damn about a citizen's problem."

"Yeah, it sounds like we need to work on our communication with civilians some. Right now, the question is what do we do with you?"

"How so?"

"By rights, we should take your statement and hold the motorcycle as evidence of the theft. We would search it, fingerprint it, anything we could think of to tie the machine to Gary Cain. No telling exactly when you would get it back. I don't think you would like that scenario."

"You're damn right I wouldn't! I'm sure the trial won't be for months. But you sound like there's an option."

"Happily for you, we don't need the motorcycle as evidence. In some ways this incident today just muddies the water in the case we've built against Cain. And we owe you for the, um, runaround we gave you. I don't need your statement about a motorcycle theft. We have plenty of evidence against Gary on other charges. He's going away for years. My chief says if you just ride away, no one will stop you."

Steve thought it over for two seconds. "I'd like to get the remote units from Cain. Then I'm out of here."

"Let's go get them and you can be on your way."

They walked into the garage where several cops had Gary up and sitting on a box, his hands cuffed behind him. Steve looked at him and grinned. "I told Aden I wouldn't trust you as far as I could throw you, I'm sorry you proved me right."

Gary snarled. "Fuck off, loser. All I wanted from you was your Kraut motorcycle."

"Well, you didn't get it for long." The police had all of the contents of Gary's pockets laid out on another box. Steve picked up the keyless remotes from the pile and showed them to Officer Schmidt. Schmidt indicated to another cop to raise the door and Steve wheeled the machine out. Outside he put it on its stand and did a walk around. He didn't see any damage and got ready to ride. His helmet was back at the motel; he hadn't thought to bring it. Gary's helmet was sitting on a box in the garage. "Hey Gary, can I borrow your helmet?"

"Eat shit and die, you bastard. No, you can't borrow it."

Officer Schmidt laughed. "Go ahead, Cain won't need one for fifteen to twenty years."

Steve strapped on the helmet. "You don't have head lice, do you?" Gary just snarled. Steve asked, "So, I'm free to go?"

"Yeah, have a nice trip and try not to think too badly of Wichita Falls." He held out his hand. "Good luck and have a safe trip." Steve shook it and fired up the bike. About a quarter mile down the road, he found Aden parked where she had a view of the house. She had started the car and had it in gear.

"Oh! I didn't recognize you with that funny helmet. What was going on down there? I saw Gary take you inside and called the police to report that you were being abducted and they told me they had units on the way out here already. Then I saw that old pickup drive up followed by the police. What happened?"

"That guy in the pickup was an undercover cop. I'll never bad-mouth this police force again. They had the operation planned all along, they just didn't share that info with me. Gary's under arrest and we're free to be on our way."

"Good. I'll follow you back to the motel. We can drop off the car and pack up. This seems like another town we should not dawdle in. Wrong town, I know, but let's get the hell out of Dodge."

"Did you know that phrase came from a TV show?"

"You're kidding."

"No. My parents used to watch a TV western called *Gunsmoke* that was set in Dodge City. The hero's line to the bad men was, "'Get out of Dodge.'"

"Amazing."

"Of course, but your idea is right on target. C'mon."

Twenty-three

After thanking the manager for the use of the car, they changed clothes and packed up. Steve had a T-shirt that said, *Coffee, the WD-40 of adulthood.*

Aden read it and laughed. She asked, "Are you really all right? You were in there quite a while, and it looked like Gary had a gun."

"He did. And I'm embarrassed. I thought I was sneaking around the house and all the while Gary was watching me on the cameras planted around the house. I can't believe I didn't look for them."

"What did Gary tell you once you were inside?"

"He said they were only interested in the Beemer all along. They had promised one to a recruit they were trying to get to join the gang. That woman I was dancing with is obviously a great pickpocket. She got the remote out of my back pocket and they made a copy while you were singing. They were going to steal the bike except Gary had the remote in his possession and the club members had nothing to do with the theft. Gary just happened to be walking by and saw the bike in the parking lot. He tried the remote he had, and it worked."

Aden was silent for a moment. "You didn't feel Wanda's hands on your pants?"

"Ah, no. It was crowded and we were getting jostled a lot."

"Sure. That was probably part of the scam."

"Well, that explains why Wanda said I was a dead-end kid."

Aden laughed, putting the incident behind them for the moment. "So, what's your plan of the day?"

Steve hauled out his road atlas and followed the course of US 82 across Texas. "You're in luck. Today I'm taking you to Paris. Are you ready for fashion and The City of Lights?"

"Paris? *Haute couture?*"

"Yeah, I don't know if we'll find Paris, Texas very *couture* but it will be *haute*." Aden groaned. "And that's where we're going. It's near the Arkansas border. We'll stop there for gas. Then on to Texarkana, which splits the border. After that, we enter Arkansas where we'll head for El Dorado. That's about five hours of riding; we'll see how we feel when we get there. Again, I feel I should apologize. I promised you big cities and we're going in between the most prominent. We'll be north of New Orleans and south of Atlanta. But we'll hit several mid-sized cities."

That's okay, mid-sized seems to be working for me. I have no complaints. I'm starting to like the secondary roads. The scenery is better, and we've certainly met some interesting people.

"Yeah... I'm finding there's a limit to that."

Saturday morning had started out gray and cloudy. It still was, but Steve's outlook was much brighter. He was feeling really great when he left Gary's house, but his mood began to sink as the adrenaline wore off. He would change that with more food. His appetite came back, and he wanted a good second breakfast so they wouldn't have to make a long stop for lunch. Steve asked the office manager if the truck stops along US 82 had any good cafés, but he recommended a better place just around the corner, not much farther than the café where they had eaten their first breakfast in town. It turned out to be a great choice. During a big meal, Steve gave Aden a further account of what had happened in the house. She was horrified that he had come so close to being killed. After breakfast they headed south to pick up US 82 where it continued easterly towards Jolly and Henrietta. It was a divided highway, two lanes each way, which made it nice, no oncoming traffic, and the road was in good condition. They watched the clouds darken and were a little concerned about the weather.

The morning overcast didn't clear and seemed to be turning gloomier. It looked like they might get their first rain of the trip. Steve asked, "Do you have anything to cover up your guitar case? I'd hate for it to get wet."

"No, I didn't think about rain. We spent so much time in the desert, the thought of rain never occurred to me. Silly me, being from Washington I should have expected it. What can we do?"

"I'll stop when I see a place to get off the highway and check the saddlebags. Maybe there's something we can use to cover it up." There were frontage roads, but no place to exit until they got to Jolly, about three miles out of the city proper. They turned into the Jolly Travel Center as a light rain began falling. There was a canopy over the gas pumps, so Steve stopped at a pump and filled the tank; it took all of half a gallon and added a dollar-seventy-five to his credit card. While they were stopped, Steve dug through the saddlebags, but the only thing he found that was waterproof was Kruz's rainsuit. He had thought he might wear it, but it was clearly too small for him. He should have known when he thought about Kruz's size. He handed it to Aden. "This will probably fit you better than me. In fact, it may be too short on you if it fits Kruzick. Try it on while I check inside."

He ran into the travel center and asked if they had any big plastic bags. "Bags? What for?"

"We need to wrap up a guitar case we're carrying on a motorcycle. Anything waterproof would help."

The manager said, "Let's try in the café." He went into the back room and came back with a long piece of plastic about three feet wide. "This was wrapped around a box of steaks we just received. That's all I could find."

"This is perfect. Thank you very much." Steve ran back through the now heavy downpour, and they wrapped up the case. Aden donned the rainsuit which almost fit. She would stay dry, and it certainly didn't pinch. Steve hoped his leather jacket would keep out most of the weather. He made sure the windshield was in the highest position so the airflow would go over them. They made all their preparations and headed out under a dark sky with water standing on the highway. The wind built up behind them and pushed them on their way, but Steve kept the speed down so they wouldn't hydroplane.

It was about an hour later that the hail started. By then, the sky was really dark, and the wind had picked up. Steve kept a lookout for cover and when he got to Muenster and the highway became the main drag through town, he spotted a drive-in café. An awning to park under ran out from the building and an additional awning covered additional parking rows on one side of the parking lot. The place was empty. They pulled under the awning and ran for the building as the hail increased in density and size. Steve noticed most of the hailstones had become golf-ball size and were shattering when they hit the pavement. Lots of cars were going to be damaged around there.

There was no customer area inside the drive-in building. The two found themselves standing with a couple of carhops and two cooks watching the downpour. One of the kids had watched them pull in. "That's a cool bike, mister." She looked at the two of them, "Where ya'll from?"

Aden answered. "We started in California. We're headed for Florida. What's with this weather?"

"Boy howdy, looks to me like a twister comin'. None has ever hit the town but this sure seems like the weather for it. It'd be good if'n you could get that 'cycle inside somewhere. Fact is, I don't much trust this building we're standin' in." Steve paid attention to the walls and saw a construction of sheet metal over a light steel frame. The carhop pointed toward the back of the drive-in. "There's a machine shop just behind us. It has concrete-block walls and garage doors. I bet they'd let you wheel the 'cycle inside. I'm gonna head there myself when the hail slows down."

Steve could tell the wind was still picking up. If it got too strong, it would blow the BMW off its kickstand. "Can I ride straight back to the shop from here?"

"Yeah, it's just at the back of the parking lot. Its front is on the next street over. It's a lot more good for stout than this tin building."

Fifteen minutes later, the parking lot looked like it had snowed when Steve ran out to the Beemer. The hail had died down to small pellets about the size of rice mixed with a steady rain when he fired up the bike and headed for the machine shop. The bike was fine, but he could see dimples beat into the aluminum awning by the hail. When he crossed from the paved parking lot and dropped into the muddy area behind the shop building, he pulled up, checking his path around the building. The only thing there was a well-muffled diesel, evidently powering a generator. As he looked at the path to the front, a man opened the back door and came out to meet him. He checked the diesel before saying, "Hey, you better get off the street. I'm purdy sure a twister's comin'!"

"Can I run my motorcycle into your work bay until it passes?"

The man looked at the darkness to the west of them. "C'mon," he said. He started walking around the building, Steve let out the clutch and followed him. Meanwhile Aden and the teen came running up. Aden wore her helmet and carried Steve's; the carhop had a pair of roller skates in a plastic bag. "Boy, I'm glad we're not wearing our skates today," she said.

The front of the building included a tall, roll-up garage door next to the front door. The man went in the front with Aden and the car hop following him, and soon the garage door began rising. Steve wheeled the motorcycle in, leaving muddy tracks across the cement floor, and immediately the door closed. It felt good to be out of the steady rain.

A work pit about five feet deep sank into the concrete floor about a car-length in from the garage door; metal stairs at the far end led down into it. The man's pickup truck was parked to the right of the pit with an additional space large enough for a vehicle to the left. Continuing to the left of the open space was an office. The front and side walls of the building formed two of the office walls. The inner side and back walls were framed up from two-by-fours and sheet rock to form the office area. A low roof over the office served as a storage area; scrap metal objects could be seen piled up on top and jutting over the side. The building's front door led into the office, which had a glass window and door leading into the work area. A second window faced the street next to the front door.

Steve got the motorcycle parked and looked around. Most of the shop space was filled with metal-working machines, lathes, mills, and welding equipment. Metal tables were aligned along the walls. Lights were hanging low over the machines, most of them turned off, leaving the ceiling in darkness. The rest of the walls were solid concrete blocks. The clear space near the garage door was large enough for a truck to be parked on either side of the pit or over it. The pit itself would be useful for working under trucks or oil-rig equipment brought in for maintenance or alterations.

The building had fiberglass insulation glued to the walls. It was strictly utilitarian; no effort had been made to cover the paper of the insulation. It was not that big, except for the office, just a large single room. It had only one floor, but the ceiling was about twenty feet above them, allowing plenty of room for big projects. Steve noticed a chain hoist hanging over the pit. It was mounted to a slide that traveled along an I-beam running across the room and attached to carriages riding on I-beams down each side of the building so the hoist could be moved to any point in the room.

The man that let him in held out his hand. "I'm Carl Flusche. I think we're gonna get hit by a twister." Steve shook his hand and introduced himself and Aden as he looked him over. Flusche was probably in his fifties, about five-foot-nine with a slender build and dark yellow hair going gray. He wore glasses and had heavily callused hands.

Aden asked, "Is there a season for twisters?"

Carl gave a sarcastic laugh. "The politicians in this state say there is no such thing as climate change or global warming but, for some reason, we are seeing more tornadoes during the regular season, which is now, and some during the rest of the year when we didn't used to get them at all. The ones now seem to be stronger than in the past. Actually, we've never had one in Muenster, but after today I don't think we'll be able to say that anymore. Hope the wife stays okay, she's usually here working on the books, but she stayed home today to keep an eye on the dogs and the house. I called her a little while ago and she said she had everything battened down. Let's go up on the roof and see what's coming."

Carl led the way up a set of stairs, almost a ladder, to a hatch that opened onto the roof. The roof was composed of steel trusses attached between the walls and covered with planks and tar paper. A coating of tar and gravel covered the outside of the roof. Like all flat roofs, it was actually concave, holding a shallow pool of water in the middle. Steve could feel the roof vibrating slightly as they walked across it.

They were on one of the tallest buildings in the area, allowing a good view of the countryside for miles around. The rain had stopped for the moment and the sky was a patchwork of ragged clouds of various shades, ranging from light gray to almost black. There was a lot of almost black. The overall effect created an ominous feeling of disaster. Carl pointed to the south and said,

"Yep. Look there. Two of them, by God!" Almost due south of them, a couple of funnel clouds were popping in and out of the cloud layer.

Steve had a funny feeling. He didn't believe in premonitions but, taking in the situation, it looked like he had a good chance to get killed just when things were looking up. He grabbed Aden's hand. No one said anything as they stood there watching. The funnel clouds were on parallel paths and obviously moving in the general direction of the town... the one on the right seemed to be sliding to the right. The path of the one on the left didn't seem to move left or right; it was obviously heading right at them. The one on the right was dipping lower and lower. Neither one had hit the ground, but they were getting closer to the town and the ground.

"The left one is going to go right over us," Aden said.

"How do you know?" the carhop asked.

"I've been watching it in relation to that windmill out there on that farm to see if it moved left or right. It doesn't move at all. That means it's coming right for us. If it hits the ground, it will strike us."

About that time, the rain picked up again, blowing into their faces in the increasing wind. "C'mon," Carl shouted and led the way back down the stairs.

Steve checked out the room for a more secure place to protect the motorcycle. Carl suggested, "Why don't you put the bike between two of the lathes? They might give some protection if something, like a wall, starts collapsing."

The carhop said, "What about us? What protection do we have?"

"We'll get in the pit and wait it out. I'm still hoping for a near miss. The twister on the right was sure 'nuff headed to the right. I'm thinking the one on the left will follow it. If we're really lucky, those funnel clouds won't touch down."

Steve was really worried about the $25,000 motorcycle. They hadn't discussed it but, knowing Kruz, there was no insurance on the machine, and he felt responsible for its condition. He pushed the bike between two lathes and looked around to see what else he could do to protect the machine. Several 2 x 12 boards and some 4 x 4s were leaning against the wall, so he grabbed two of the 4 x 4s and laid them along the length of the lathes he was parked between. The 4 x 4s on the head stock and tail stock formed a support taller than the bike once he lowered the windshield, allowing him to bridge the space between the lathes and over the bike with the 2 x 12s. A dirty canvas tarp Aden found lying on the floor went over the boards and motorcycle. It was long enough to drape to the floor at each end. With any luck, the cover would give protection from falling debris. As he straightened up from draping the tarp, Aden picked up one end and placed her guitar, still in its case and plastic wrapping, under the tarp, leaning against the bike.

The rain and the wind continued to increase in strength as the travelers and the carhop made their way into the pit. The floor was filthy with a dirt and oil mixture. No one wanted to sit so they stood waiting to see what was going to happen next.

The carhop looked like she was about to lose it—her face was developing a blueish tinge as she held her breath. Steve nudged Aden and pointed at her with his chin. Aden put her hand around the carhop's shoulder and said, "I didn't get your name."

"I'm Mary Belle. Do you think we're safe?" A strong gust of wind rattled the garage door, and she grabbed Aden's hand and clung to it as they listened to the noise increasing outside. "Maybe I should go home. My mother won't know where I am." She started to walk to the steps.

Aden kept a strong hold on Mary Belle's shoulder. "Maybe you'd better stay right here. If you go out now, the tornado will catch you in the open. Give your mother a call."

"Oh, right." She pulled a cell phone out of her pocket and dialed. "Hi, Mom. I'm at Mr. Flusche's shop. We're gonna wait here for the twisters. Oh yes, we saw two funnel clouds coming toward us. I'm purdy sure they're gonna hit the ground. Should be here right soon. Okay, we'll stay put. Yes, it's a solid building. Okay, love you." She hung up. "She said to stay put and keep down."

"That's what we're doing. Your mother probably has experience with tornadoes."

"Yeah, she grew up in Oklahoma, so she's been in a few."

Steve realized he had been hearing a roaring noise building up. He asked, "Am I hearing a tornado?"

Carl was searching around the shop for something to sit on; he stopped to listen. "Damn straight you are! We better get down lower in this pit." He handed a couple of wooden crates to Steve, dropped into the pit and sat on the floor obviously more worried about the weather than his pants.

Steve set the crates on the floor and offered them to Aden and Mary Belle. Mary Belle sat down but Aden just moved closer to Steve and grabbed his hand. He didn't say anything but hoped to get some circulation through it later after she released it. He crouched down and got Aden seated on the crate. The four of them listened to the roar getting louder. "Sorry I doubted you," Carl said. "I think one of those things has us zeroed in. It sounds like it's coming right at us."

"Think this building will stand the wind?"

"Who knows. It ain't somethin' that gets tested when a structure is built. There's rebar and poured concrete in the walls, so I think they will stand. I'm not so sure about the roof."

Suddenly the air pressure dropped noticeably. They felt it in their ears. The sound increased as if they were inside a wind tunnel. "Shit! It's right over us!" Carl said. Steve grabbed Aden and squatted lower in the pit. He looked at the ceiling just in time to see light coming in between the planks.

"I think your weatherproofing has blown off the roof." As he said it, the boards began to disappear. One second a plank was there and the next second there was an empty space. Then a whole section of planks was gone. The wind swirled in above them, bringing rain in a spray that seemed to come from everywhere. The walls seemed to be shaking as one end of a truss broke loose from the wall and came swinging down, bringing some planks with it. More debris fell as they all ducked deeper into the pit. Some of it was rocks and items picked up by the tornado, but some of the concrete blocks vibrated off the top of the wall, shattering as they hit the floor. Aden grabbed Steve and buried her head against his chest. She had her fists clenched tightly in front of her face. Steve put his arms around her, squeezing tightly.

"Ow!" Mary Belle said. Steve looked at her; she was holding her hand against her hair. Blood was dripping out. He moved her hand to see a torn scalp bleeding profusely. A large chunk of concrete block stained with blood sat on the floor.

"Shit! We have to stop the bleeding. What have we got for a bandage?" When no one moved or said anything, he slipped free of Aden, removed his leather jacket and peeled off his T-shirt. He moved Mary Belle's hand so he could see the wound and the blood flowing heavily through her hair. Mary Belle looked at her hand, started screaming and tried to stand. Steve grabbed her by the shoulders and pushed her back down in the pit. He shook her and said, "Stay still. I need to bandage your head." She stopped screaming and grabbed Aden's hand. Steve pulled out his pocketknife and cut and tore a couple of strips off the shirt.

Aden said, "Let me help." She disentangled her hand, took the part of the shirt that was still in one piece and folded it into a pad. Steve had a strip ready as she put it over the wound. He wrapped the strip around Mary Belle's head and tied it in place. The other strip made the bandage more secure. For now, there were no more signs of bleeding, Steve thought it was probably just soaking into the shirt. They all huddled together and waited for the tornado to pass. He put his jacket on over his bare skin. "How do you feel?" he asked Mary Belle.

"Uh, like I'm gonna throw up." She bent over and tossed her cookies at her feet. "I'm sorry. I don't feel good."

"Sit tight, you might have a concussion."

Suddenly Aden screamed. Steve looked where she was staring and saw the chain hoist sinking down on them. With the walls shaking, the weight of the I-beams running along each side were pulling the trusses loose. The whole system of trusses and I-beams suddenly fell.

Steve pushed Aden and the others against the back wall of the pit and out of the path of the chain hoist and its I-beam. The beam hit the cab of the pickup, smashing it down several feet and breaking off the driver's side mirror, which came flying into the pit. The other end of the cross bar and the I-beam landed on the roof of the office, breaking through the roof and tearing a path several feet down the wall. The pickup and the office supported the I-beam, leaving it hanging several feet over the pit. The chain and the hook fell into the pit and slapped hard against the pit wall.

"Anyone hurt?" Steve asked.

"I am," Mary Belle said.

"We know about you. Anyone else?"

Aden grinned. "I might have a bruise from hitting the wall, but it beats the alternative. Thank you for the shove. I thought that beam was coming right down on top of us."

"Yeah," Carl said. "Thanks for getting us out of the way. That mirror or the hook would have done some damage if they hit someone."

The sound seemed to go on for hours as they huddled in the pit. Carl said, "This sumbitch is either really slow or really big. Most twisters pass over in about a minute." No one was timing this one, but it seemed a long time until the sound diminished, and the walls stopped shaking.

When they were sure the tornado had passed, they stood up and looked at the shambles of the machine shop. The roof was gone with most of the trusses caught on various tables and machines. The I-beam with the hook was supported by the smashed truck and the crushed office walls. Most of the roof components, laying across tables and metal-working machines, were about four feet off the floor, less in some places. Some of the trusses were bent over the machines and worktables, twisted and hitting the floor. Judging from the number of concrete blocks torn off the top of the walls, Carl had been cheated in the wall construction. The rebar and concrete filler hadn't been installed clear to the top. Many of the concrete blocks that the trusses attached to had come loose and had fallen onto the floor where they shattered into shrapnel-like fragments flying over the interior of the room. That's what had hit Mary Belle. With the entire roof gone, a steady rain was falling, soaking everything and everyone in the shop.

The four climbed out of the pit and Carl went to the door to look out. Steve ducked under the fallen trusses and went to the motorcycle, expecting to find broken fiberglass and dented metal. A portion of a bent truss was near the floor just missing the 2 x 12s. Concrete fragments and rocks picked up from the ground were scattered across the tarp. He cleared everything off the tarp and got it and the planks off to uncover a shiny, undamaged bike. It really looked out of place among all the debris. He could feel the tension drain from his body as he looked at the unblemished tank, fenders, and windscreen. The only flaws on the bike were the bugs splattered on the fairing and windscreen, the raindrops running off the tank and seat, and the mud on the tires and fenders from the trip across the field. His muscles slowly started to relax. Aden checked her guitar and found it in one piece as well. He put the tarp back over the bike and guitar to protect them from the rain.

When they walked outside, what he could see of the town looked like a bomb had gone off. The four of them marched around the side of the building and looked where the drive-in had been. The metal building and awnings had disappeared, with pieces scattered down the street. He could see several people lying next to the stove and refrigerator, no longer surrounded by walls. One person was trying to get up. People up and down the street were coming out of wherever they had been hiding and checking out the destruction. They were moving like sleepwalkers. The tornadoes were funnel clouds once again. The whole system was continuing north.

As they watched, an ambulance pulled into the drive-in's parking lot. Aden took Mary Belle's arm. "C'mon, let's get you some help." They walked across the parking lot as the ambulance crew placed a body on a stretcher. "Can you help this girl? She has a head wound; she may have a concussion."

"Yeah, let's see." An EMT sat her down on the tailgate of the ambulance, looked at the bandage and checked her vital signs. "You better come along with us," she said.

Aden asked, "Aren't you going to check the wound?"

"No, we've found it's better to wait until we get to the hospital to remove the bandage. It looks like you got the bleeding under control. That's the main thing. Good work."

"Did both tornadoes touch down?" Steve asked.

"Yeah, we got a lot of destroyed homes from the one to the west. The one that came over you was bigger but didn't have as many buildings in its way."

Two more people were helped out of the nearby ruins, both with obvious injuries, and the ambulance was full as it headed back to the hospital. Mary Belle had to sit on the floor. Steve and Aden walked back to the machine shop where Carl was ducking under trusses and checking his machines. "Well, as I said, the walls stood up for the most part. I'm gonna sue the bastards that didn't run the rebar and concrete clear to the top. I'll add a stronger roof next time."

"We never had much of a chance to talk. I guess this is your shop?"

"Yeah, I designed the building, had the walls and roof run up. I did the plumbing and electrical and started business about three years ago." He looked around. "Been doing pretty well up until now. I'll work on anything, but I mainly build and refurbish oil well equipment."

"You had a nice shop. I take it you're gonna rebuild?"

"Oh, hell yes. No damn twister is driving me away from my business. I suspect my insurance company is gonna be busy with all the businesses around here, but they'll do right by me. You want a cup of coffee?"

"You have coffee here? Now?"

"Not yet, but I can brew up a pot. I don't see any loose wires." In several places, the insulation had been torn loose from the walls, exposing conduit running around the building. "The electricity should still be working."

"I saw several power lines down outside. You think the power is on?"

"I doubt it. I've got my own power."

"Your own? How do you do that?"

"When I built this place, the town wanted a shitload of money to attach to the power grid. I think they were trying to gouge me because I was competition for the mayor's nephew. For what they wanted for a year's electrical service, I bought and run this place on my own generator. So now they've had three years where I paid no electric bills to them at all.

"When I was outside just now, I checked over the diesel and generator. It quit running during the storm when the intake got blocked, but I cleared the blockage, and it looks like it should work. Just to be on the safe side, why don't you two stand outside while I fire it up?"

"Okay, let me move the bike out first." Carl had installed the garage door himself and supported the garage door rails with struts standing on the floor rather than hung from the tall ceiling. The two men removed several roof trusses off the top of the rails. Fortunately, the rails were not bent, and they disconnected the garage door from its opening machinery so the two of them could push the door up. Steve cleared a path from the motorcycle to the front door and pushed the bike outside. He had to sit on the machine to balance it and lay flat on the gas tank as they passed under each truss. He enlisted Aden's help to push as he balanced the five-hundred pound machine with his feet. Aden grabbed her guitar and followed Steve outside. "Fire it up," Steve yelled. They soon heard a diesel motor start, the sound coming from behind the shop. As Aden and Steve stood out front waiting for something to happen, an electric light lit up in the office, shining brightly. The electricity was back on.

Carl walked around the building—it was faster than trying to fight his way across the shop floor with all the trusses down—and they all walked into the office. It was a typical office with two desks and half a dozen filing cabinets. A drafting board with several designs taped to it stood against the outer wall.

Steve had wondered why they didn't shelter in the office before the twisters hit since it had its own roof. When he entered the office, he saw several places in the ceiling where concrete blocks had fallen through and falling trusses cracked the single layer of plywood. Broken bits of concrete and some of the items stored above the office had fallen through and covered the floor. The fallen I-beam protruded into the room, but it was high enough that they could maneuver under it. They had been better off in the pit away from the walls. Now the office provided some shelter from the rain. They just had to stay away from the holes in the roof. Carl started a pot of coffee with water from a thermos on the desk. "You two had enough fun for the day?" he asked.

Aden laughed. "I don't think I could get used to living in an area with tornadoes. Why do you stay?"

Carl thought it over. "I grew up here. Every place has something wrong with it. Where you from?"

"Washington state. You're right. I remember earthquakes, wildfires, floods and volcanoes. I take your point, it's what you're used to." She turned to Steve. "What's the biggest problem in New Mexico?"

Steve started to say, "Texans," but changed it to, "Forest fires. Both natural and man-made. We get several each year." His jacket was beginning to feel clammy, so he dug a T-shirt out of a saddlebag and put it on. This one read, *I can explain it to you, but I can't understand it for you.*

Carl read it and said, "Ain't that the truth." He poured them cups of coffee and indicated the powdered cream and sugar on the shelf. "So, what are you going to do now?"

"What do you mean?" Steve asked.

"You look like you're just passing through town, am I right?"

"Yeah, we're headed for Florida. Seems like we're having a lot of trouble getting across Texas. If we hadn't stopped, we would have missed the whole storm."

Aden said, "Of course it was hailing like crazy when we stopped."

"Good point."

"If I was you, I'd get out of here now. The way those two funnels were spaced they probably did more than twice as much damage as one twister. I'll bet a good portion of the town is gone. You won't find much in the way of gas, food or accommodation. Not to be unfriendly but, at this point, you're just in the way."

Aden said, "I feel like we should try to help someone."

"Everyone will need help. There's too many. We'll be months, hell, years, getting back to normal. You'll just be in the way here and you can take better care of yourselves down the road."

"Anything we can do for you before we go?"

"No, I think I'm done for the day. I'm gonna lock up, head home and see how my wife and house are holding up. I need to think about the things I need to do here. Go on. You will just be two more mouths to feed here."

"Well, hell, I guess you're right. You think the road's open?"

"Yeah, once you clear the debris in town. I'll bet an hour down the road there's no more rain."

"That would be nice," Steve said. He finished his coffee and looked at Aden. "We might as well go. You ready?"

"It makes sense. Thank you for the shelter." She gave Carl a hug.

"You're welcome. Now get outta here."

Steve started to wipe off the seat, but then realized it was still raining and his pants were already soaked through and through. Aden was still wearing the rainsuit, she had only her wet hair to show for the ordeal. She produced the helmets and shouldered the guitar case.

"Wait." Carl led them back into the office and supplied a towel for them to dry their hair before they put on their helmets. They would feel much more comfortable, Carl told them. "You're almost at the east side of town. There shouldn't be much wreckage to cause you trouble. Good luck." He shook their hands and the two rode out onto the street and around the block to the main road.

Twenty-four

They turned east and, after dodging some minor rubble, were out of town in a few blocks. Other than the rain and crazy clouded sky, there was no sign of the tornadoes. Traffic was light as they made their way through Gainesville and Whitesboro. By Sherman, they had run out of the rain. The skies remained cloudy. Aden asked, "What time is it?"

Steve looked at the instrument panel. "It's about noon. Getting hungry?"

"No, it just seems like it should be much later. I guess that's because the day feels like it started last night at the Rarin' to Go Saloon. It seems like an awful lot of excitement for one day. Can't you arrange to spread out the emergencies over a longer time period?"

Steve laughed. "I know what you mean. I'd be happy if there were no more emergencies at all. It seems to me we should be in good shape. I mean what else can happen?"

She looked back. "I still feel like we're running out on them."

"I know. But Carl is right. We would be more of a hindrance than a help. Boy, I have no desire to go through one of those again. My dad grew up in Oklahoma. He tells tales of stopping the car out in the country and lying down in the bar ditch awaiting a tornado to blow past. I never expected to be in that situation myself."

"What's a bar ditch?"

"That's Okie for borrow ditch. They dig a ditch on either side of a road and use the dirt, or borrow, to build up the roadbed."

"My education increases every day."

"You are sadly lacking so many of these details."

"I'll bet you can guess at my response to that statement."

"I'm impressed by your eloquence in not saying it." She lightly bopped the back of his helmet.

"What does, or did, your dad do for a living?"

"He's a house painter. Not really house, the company he works for does mainly corporate work. New buildings and such. He's a foreman. How about your parents?"

"Dad has a welding business. He does some welding, but mostly he sells supplies to others. Mom helps with the books. I'm so grateful they started saving my tuition money just after I was born. They clearly wanted me to continue my education. I think Dad hoped I would take over the business but, even if I don't stick with singing, the welding business is just not my cup of tea. I take it you don't want to be a painter?"

"Dad has told me many times he didn't want me to be a painter. He was pushing for college, but he thought I'd get a scholarship to pay for it. It would have been a mistake for me to start right out of high school. By the time I graduated, my ideas about school and my girlfriend were all over the place. I would have gone through several majors and probably still not graduated. Now I know what I want and what I have to do to work toward it. How did you decide on a major?"

"Oh, after high school I was where you are now. I've known what I wanted to do since junior high. I made the right choice for and I enjoyed working in the discipline. I just decided if I want to do a bit of traveling and see something of the country, this is the time to do it. You know, before settling down."

"You don't think you'll be a singer forever?"

"I may always be a singer, but I won't always use it as a way to make a living. For now, it's fun but it's obviously not going exactly as I pictured it. There are so many great amateur singers I guess you have to meet the right people to do well in the business."

They were quiet for a while, each thinking their own thoughts. Once again, they were riding through grasslands, with stands of trees dotting the landscape. Small towns were scattered about every ten to fifteen miles. They made it into Paris about two in the afternoon. After gassing up, Steve found a barbeque café on the main drag and pulled in for lunch. "I hope you like meat," he told Aden. "This probably isn't the place for vegetables." He was wrong; they had a good selection of grilled veggies with barbequed ham that Aden enjoyed while Steve had pork ribs with a sticky, tasty BBQ sauce along with grilled corn on the cob. They could hear other customers talking about the tornadoes back at Muenster. The storm had continued north along I-35 towards Ardmore, Oklahoma.

The two of them tuned out the talk and concentrated on each other. It was a good chance to unwind and talk about their actions that morning. Aden started. "I was impressed how you managed yourself all morning." She stopped him when he grinned and started to say something. "I'm talking about after we got up. Of course, it was stupid to walk in on a possible killer, but you certainly have your passions."

"Yeah, not my finest hour. I was afraid whoever had the machine would take off somewhere and we would never find the bike again. With people like that, it was stupid to not look for cameras around the house."

"And you should have had a better backup plan. All I could do was call the police. If they hadn't already been on their way, how would you put it? You would have been in deep shit."

"Can't argue with anything you've said. I guess I didn't really believe we'd find the right place or the bike."

"Well, you survived it and did much better after that. When we encountered the hail and the tornado, you anticipated the problems and solved some of them before they happened. I think I was in shock when the concrete hit the girl. You immediately looked for something to use for a bandage and stopped the bleeding. Then you got us out of the way of the falling beam."

Steve could feel himself blushing. "You're the one that spotted the beam falling. I just did what anyone would do."

"No, I looked at Carl when Mary Belle was struck. He froze, just as I did. She could have bled to death if you hadn't been there. Just as I froze when the beam fell."

"Sooner or later, you would have responded. I've just had more training in handling emergencies." He thought of all the drills on the *Sterett;* they practiced every day and night. As a fire controlman responsible for the electronics, radars, computers and ancillary equipment, he hadn't worked much with the deck crew, certainly not with the black gang in the engine room. Those were the rates that had the most injuries. But he had been involved in first aid to a boatswain's mate who fell off the mast while helping Steve replace a co-axial connector on a radar antenna. Boats had a compound fracture of his leg. The corpsman had to apply a tourniquet to stop the blood. Steve helped get the sailor onto a Stokes stretcher and watched a team of corpsmen carry the man to sick bay. "Onboard the ship, we had drills day and night to keep us on our toes. I've just had more practice than you in responding to something unusual happening. There's a saying drummed into us in the Navy, probably all branches of service, 'Lead, follow or get out of the way.' In other words, don't just stand there."

"Be that as it may, I'm glad you were there." She reached across the table and took his hand. "It's nice when someone I'm interested in turns out to be the real thing."

"Don't put me on too high a pedestal; I'll hurt myself when I fall."

"I'm sure that will happen, but not today."

Steve looked at his watch. "And if we don't make some mileage today, we'll never get to Florida."

"That's okay. I'm starting to enjoy the trip. So where are we off to?"

"I think... hope... we're well rid of Crusher. I changed my mind about riding through Arkansas. When we get to Texarkana on the Texas / Arkansas border let's ditch US 82 and cut south to Shreveport, Louisiana. We can make better time on I-20." Steve checked his watch. "I think we can make it by five. Maybe you can find a gig tonight."

"Oh! I'd almost forgotten about that. I don't know how late we'll want to stay up after getting up so early this morning, but let's see what happens."

Out on the highway again, they found the same scenery of eastern Texas, green fields with scattered woodlands of small trees. Heat and humidity. They made Texarkana about four-thirty, cutting down the west side of the city and along the south side to I-49. About five-thirty they were in Shreveport.

Steve had no idea where he was going; the map on the motorcycle's display helped tremendously. He knew he wanted I-20. The map took him to I-220 where he turned onto that heading east. It took him north and east across the Red River, eventually swinging south and intersecting with I-20. That put them on the east side of town, so he headed back west, passing Barksdale AFB. It seemed like a good place to look for a tavern catering to airmen, so he pulled off onto a local road running through a business area. Sure enough, he spotted a sign for the Lizard Lounge. It didn't look like the kind of place that had live music—at least there was nothing advertising it—but he pulled into the parking lot and stopped. The two of them walked into the place and looked around. The room wasn't a dive, it was clean and about half full with the low hum of a quiet crowd sitting and drinking. There were quite a few more young men than women or couples, probably from the Air Force base. The lounge obviously didn't have a band or a dance floor, so it didn't look promising.

Aden walked to the bar and asked the bartender, "Hi, would you be interested in some live music?"

"Let me get the manager." He wandered off.

Soon he was back with an older woman. She looked the two of them up and down. "Hi. You want to sing a few songs?"

"Yeah, I do mainly country with some ballads thrown in. I could set up a tip jar."

"Just you?"

Steve laughed. "I have the musical ability of a crow, but Aden is very good. I just schlep the equipment around."

The manager looked at the crowd. "Why not? This is about as good as it gets in here. Maybe you can stir them up. What do you need?"

"Just a place to set up. I've got a small amp and microphone in my bag. They're battery powered."

"Ah, yeah. How about over by that wall. Let's give it a shot."

"I'll just change into my stage outfit."

"Wait, what's that?"

"Oh, just a different pair of jeans and shirt."

"Okay, I just don't want it turning into a stripper act."

"No problem." Aden grabbed her bag and headed for the restroom while Steve unpacked her amplifier, mic and cords; all in different pockets than the one with the money. Aden had the perfect equipment for this room. She had a small amplifier, battery powered, that created enough sound for the bar where there was no dancing. A rickety microphone stand came out of another pocket. Before she came back, he had the guitar and mic ready along with a tip jar sitting in front of the mic stand. He added a couple of dollars to the jar to make the point. He was sitting at a table near the music setup when he noticed the crowd stirring and showing interest—she was back, in her torn jeans, bare-navel shirt and boots.

The manager looked her over and said, "Well, I'd say you're borderline, but you wouldn't get arrested on the street, so go ahead."

Aden checked the guitar's tuning and sat on a chair Steve brought over. "Hi folks, I'm Acey Deucey. I'll be playing some songs for you. If you have any requests, please tell me. I'll be glad to play anything I know."

She broke into a Johnny Lee song, "Looking for Love." The single men were definitely listening. Steve watched them leaning forward to catch the lyrics. At the end of the song, the applause was loud. A few songs later, the tip jar was starting to fill and a steady stream of men, and some of the women, were making requests for favorite songs. One couple was dancing between the tables. At the end of an hour, Aden took a break, came over to Steve's table and sat down.

The manager walked up, looking pleased. "Well, you're drawing them in. You're keeping the ones that came in early, and the crowd is increasing. Can you do another set? How about a drink for both of you on the house?"

"Thanks," Aden said. "Sure, I can do more sets. I'll have a soda water. Steve?"

"I'll pass for the moment. Can you recommend a motel near here? And a place where I could get some food?" he asked the manager.

"Sure, the motel across the street. It ain't fancy but it's clean. There's a café next to it."

Steve had been worrying about their gear, still on the motorcycle. He looked at Aden. "I'll go check us in and come back. I'll take a beer when I get back."

"You got it. Tell them I sent you. Maybe they'll give you a break on the price."

"What's your name?"

"They wouldn't know it. I just know the clerk comes in for a belt before work."

Steve rode across the street to the motel and got a room. There was no price break. He checked out the room and unloaded the bike before walking to the café. Aden had asked him to pick some sort of salad for her. He got that and a roast beef sandwich for himself and walked back to the bar.

It looked like he got back just in time to rescue Aden. She had attracted a couple of admirers who were hanging around while she sang. They were trying to outscore each other telling whatever the Air Force calls sea stories. Aden told them to sit down, she was working. One was persistent—he headed for the table where Aden took her break and seemed startled to find someone sitting there. "Sorry, buddy, that table is reserved for the entertainment."

Steve looked at him. "I know."

About that time the waitress showed up with a beer. "The bartender said to give this to you. No charge."

"Thank you. And tell the manager thanks."

Now the airman looked really confused. "Why do you get a free drink?"

"The manager likes my fascinating personality."

The airman sat and turned his attention back on Aden. Steve started to say something but decided to wait to see what would happen when Aden finished her set.

The set ended about half an hour later. From the applause it was obvious the crowd liked her, and she was getting great tips. She had a smirk on her face when she walked up. "What's this then?"

"Your admirer decided to join us."

"I'm flattered. Are you stationed at the base?"

"Yes. I'm a mechanic working on the A-10 Warthog."

"Warthog? That's the name of an airplane?"

Steve broke in. "The official name is Thunderbolt 2, but when the first aviators saw it, they called it the Warthog and the name stuck."

"Yeah, what he said."

"Well, it's been interesting talking to you, but we're leaving soon, so you better go back with your buddies."

He still tried to buy her a drink and join in their conversation. Aden told him, "Thanks for the drink offer, but I've already had my limit. If I drink any more, I won't be able to play."

"Oh, I don't believe that. You play and sing great. If you don't want a drink, how about I take you out for dinner after your next set?"

Aden indicated Steve. "Well, thank you, does that include my boyfriend?"

"Of course not. Your boyfriend? He just walked in!"

"Well, you whose name I do not know, don't have all the facts. It was a good try, but you struck out."

"Sorry, dude. I just stepped out to arrange our room for the night. No, you're not invited over for a drink."

He looked Steve over. "You look like Air Force, are you stationed here? What's your rank?"

"Air Force! I just got out of the Navy, which doesn't have ranks. My rate would have translated to somewhere around major or lieutenant colonel."

"You were an officer?"

"No. But I feel my rate would have equaled those Air Force ranks."

The guy could tell he was losing the battle but wasn't giving up. "Navy? What happened, did you lose a bet?"

"Yeah, my buddy bet me he could convince an airman that the word 'gullible' is not in the dictionary. I told him nobody in the Air Force is that dumb."

The airman seemed to be stuck for something to say. "Better quit now before you say, 'oh yeah?'" Steve told him.

Aden jumped in. 'Now, now, boys. Let's play nice." She turned to the airman. "Thanks for the compliments, but as you see I've made other arrangements."

The fellow sat there for a second, then got up and walked back to a table with two other men. Steve tried not to watch, but saw the others laughing at their buddy. The guy stood tall and looked like he was saying, "At least I tried."

The manager came over with a soda water for Aden and a shot. She looked at Steve. "I don't know what you like to drink, so I took a chance. This one is bourbon… if you prefer scotch I'll switch it." She turned to Aden. "Would you be interested in performing here on a regular basis? We could work something out, I'm sure."

Aden shook her head. "Sorry. We're just passing through town. I'm afraid this is a one-time thing." She looked at her watch. "I will do one more set, if you want."

The manager looked around at the full bar. "Yes please, this is going to be our best night ever. I may have to find someone else to play here. If you come back this way, please stop in."

Aden ate her salad before playing the next set. Steve turned down the shot and drank his last beer of the night as he watched Aden and her happy audience. She got a huge ovation at the end, so she closed with an encore. He congratulated her as he helped carry her guitar and equipment across the street to the motel. Aden was obviously feeling on top of the world. "Well, that went better than any night I've ever had. That was the first time I've played strictly by myself. Maybe I better start doing that for all my gigs."

"You had a good night all right. That tip jar was stuffed. You are obviously a hit with the Air Force crowd."

"I've always been a fan of the military." She started going through her tip jar. "Well, I can buy you breakfast in the morning and pay for my own meals tomorrow. That two hundred from the bikers was a godsend. They paid me two hundred while trying to steal your twenty-five-thousand-dollar motorcycle. I think they had a sense of humor." She looked at the money again. "But I don't believe I'm going to get rich doing this."

"Hey! As long as you enjoy yourself."

They were tired from the extra-long day, but they sat talking long enough to show that they weren't just interested in jumping into bed before they jumped into bed. Aden's warmth and sensitive touch surprised Steve; his intense physicality seemed to be all Aden wanted. They blended together seamlessly. The next morning, it was a fairly late start to continue the trip.

Twenty-five

Sunday

Steve donned a T-shirt that said, *My people skills are just fine. It's my tolerance toward idiots that needs work.* Aden looked at it and commented, "I'm sensing a theme to your T-shirt captions."

"Yeah, I probably need to expand my comments on the world."

He knew it was silly, but he went out to check on the Beemer. It was beginning to seem normal that something would have happened to spoil their trip. But the machine was right where he left it.

At breakfast, Aden had her usual question. "So, what's the plan of the day?"

Steve had the road atlas handy to answer the question. "Looks like Jackson, Mississippi is about two hundred miles; we'll plan to gas up there. With this late breakfast, that's a little early for lunch, maybe stop in Meridian for a lunch break. Then we'll leave I-20 and take US 80 east to Montgomery and stop there for the night. That will put us into Mayport sometime tomorrow."

"Then we'd better get on our way." She stood as Steve left money on the table for the breakfast.

The outskirts of Shreveport seemed to go on forever. They didn't get into the countryside until they passed Minden. The interstate was faster than the smaller highways they had ridden, with less dense traffic, straighter stretches and no towns to slow them up. The towns still appeared every ten or fifteen miles, but the road bypassed them. Steve had heard of small towns complaining the freeways bypassed their speed traps, and thought of all that money they were losing. He laughed to himself. The day was clear and bright. They had left the clouds far behind in Texas and the sun seemed to take full advantage of the clear sky. Steve could really feel the humidity. The land was green with tall trees rearing up on each side of the road. Around twelve o'clock, they crossed the Mississippi River at Vicksburg. It seemed like a milestone, but they didn't stop.

"You can add another state to the places you've been. Welcome to Mississippi." By one o'clock they were in Jackson, gassed up and ready for the road.

Before climbing on the bike, Aden asked, "Do you want something to drink?" She was headed into the shop attached to the gas station.

"I'll come in with you. I don't know what I want." It was the usual highway shop, everything from beer to Twinkies. Steve found a coffee pot and a stack of cups and decided to go with his usual, helping himself to the pot. He also looked through the refrigerator section and found a small container of milk.

Aden, holding a can of soda, looked at his purchases. "Milk? The only time I've seen you drink milk is while we're riding. Something special about it?"

"It's a trick I picked up from an old motorcycle shop owner. I find that on the road it quenches my thirst better than water. It's about the only time I drink it."

She said, "Well, let's see if you know what you're talking about. I'll try it." She returned the soda and grabbed a container of milk.

At the checkout counter, a scruffy-looking man in dirty coveralls and a cap with a slogan that read, "I'd rather be an American than a Democrat," was paying for gas and a can of snuff. He looked them up and down and said, "You two on thet motorbike out they'a." He was short, with a week's growth of whiskers, a deep red face and neck and he was dipping snuff. He opened the flat can he'd just bought, took a pinch out of it and placed it inside his lower lip while cramming the can in his hip pocket.

"Hi. Yes. We're passing through."

"Why ain't ya ridin' a Harley? Why that German shit?"

"It isn't mine. I'm delivering it to its owner in Florida."

"Huh. I notice you from California. That's a sorry state. Nothin' but queers and spics."

Steve didn't feel like getting in a fight. "If you say so." He should have stopped there. "The bike's from California, we're not."

"Where you from?"

"New Mexico."

"That's just as bad. They kill babies in New Mexico. You must be a Dem'crat." He spat a brown stream into a cardboard coffee cup he'd picked up from the counter.

"No, I'm an independent."

"Same thing. If you ain't a 'publican, you ain't shit."

Steve thought it over, but he couldn't resist. "You mean if you are a Republican you are shit?"

"No! You puttin' words in ma mouth. Why don't ya jes' get the hell outta here!"

"Works for me. We're leaving as soon as I drink this coffee."

Steve pulled out his wallet to pay for the drinks but the redneck grabbed his arm and turned him around so he could read the saying on the shirt. "Wha's that mean?"

"Huh? Get your hand off my arm." He jerked away.

The fellow removed his hand and pointed at the text. "Wha's that sayin' on yer shirt talkin' 'bout?"

"It's just a funny saying."

"Wha's funny 'bout it? Sounds like you think we're all idjits."

"Not everyone. Just someone looking for a fight for no reason."

Aden put her hand on his arm. "Remember that old saying about wrestling and pigs, let's get out of here."

Steve paid for the drinks, and they walked out as the redneck glared at them. They were standing by the motorcycle as the redneck walked out to a battered, muddy Toyota pickup. Steve couldn't let it go. He yelled across the parking lot. "I guess German equipment is no good but Japanese trucks are okay."

The redneck stared at him. "Get out of here, you commie fascist."

"C'mon man, you can be one or the other. You can't be both."

The redneck flipped him the bird and climbed in the truck.

"So much for Mississippi being the hospitality state. I don't understand people like that. They go out of their way to find something to fight about. I'm sure us being on a German motorcycle or where we're from doesn't affect him at all. Incidentally, what old saying are you thinking of?"

"I think it's Russian, 'don't wrestle with pigs. You both get filthy, and the pig likes it.' I think it's the environment. They're raised in a household where they're both masters of their domain and downtrodden by 'the man.' That confuses them and they never learn to think critically. But you shouldn't keep taunting him. No telling what he'll do."

"Thank God, we won't see him anymore."

Out on the highway, the two settled into their riding posture, Steve sitting upright, his arms resting gently on the handlebars, Aden keeping a light hold on his hips. The windscreen forced the slipstream over their heads with just enough breeze flowing around them to keep them comfortable. The traffic was light as they cruised at seventy.

The interstate was two lanes in each direction, sometimes separated by a grassy center section and sometimes by a solid stand of trees so the oncoming traffic was hidden. The inside shoulder was paved about half the width of a vehicle lane with a lane's width of grass beyond the shoulder before the trees started, where there were trees. The outside shoulder was paved a full lane's width, wide enough for a vehicle to pull off and stop if needs be. Rumble strips were built in on each side of the traffic lanes. A line of tall trees formed a thick forest beginning back from the shoulder retreated and advanced towards the road up to thirty feet leaving pockets of grassland between the road and the trees.

Steve was almost daydreaming when he checked his rearview mirror and noticed a large cloud of blue smoke about a mile behind them. He was thinking that you don't see that much anymore, clearly a vehicle with a worn-out engine, but when he looked closely, he saw a battered, muddy Toyota pickup emitting the cloud. It looked a lot like the redneck's pickup from the gas station. The truck was traveling noticeably faster than the traffic, Steve estimated about eighty or eighty-five. He watched it pull into their lane about a half-mile behind them. "I think we have a problem," Steve said.

"What's that?"

"That asshole from the gas station is coming up behind us."

Aden turned around to look over her shoulder. "You're right. He's coming up fast. You think he's chasing us?"

"From the way he switched lanes to get behind us I'd say so."

"What do we do?"

"Stay away from him." Steve kept switching his attention between the traffic ahead and the truck coming up behind them. When it closed to about a quarter-mile, he started accelerating up to the pickup's speed. He sped past several cars and a semi-trailer and lost sight of the redneck behind the traffic. When he got to an interchange, he quickly slowed down and turned off the highway. He rode about fifty yards down the road before turning around and heading back and stopping before the interchange. They were in time to see the pickup pass by, sounding like the driver had the throttle pedal to the floor.

Steve pulled over to the side of the road and cut the engine. He checked his watch. "We'll give him ten minutes to get away and then continue. I don't know if he's after us, late for a meeting or always drives that fast, but it didn't look good."

Ten minutes later, they started down the interstate again. Steve held the speed down, thinking he would let the redneck run away from them. The two of them watched the shoulder and the roadside in case the redneck realized he'd passed them and tried to get behind them again. Half an hour later, they spotted the pickup parked on the shoulder. As they passed the truck, Steve saw the redneck sit up and, in the rearview mirror, watched him pull back on the road. He pushed the motorcycle up to eighty and began passing cars, weaving through the light traffic.

As they approached another interchange, an almost new, red pickup came down the entrance ramp. Steve had switched to the inside lane to give the truck room, but the driver sped up, passing the motorcycle before pulling in front of the bike and slamming on his brakes. Aden screamed as Steve instinctively hit the brakes and swerved to the left-hand shoulder, missing the truck by inches. He opened the throttle and was accelerating as he pulled even with the cab.

The driver, a younger version of the first redneck, had the weeks' worth of whiskers but cleaner-looking clothes. He was holding a phone to his ear and glaring at Steve. Suddenly the driver jerked his steering wheel over and swerved to the left to hit the motorcycle, but Steve had just enough time and speed to pull ahead of the truck, still riding on the shoulder. "Shit! He's got help now. That guy tried to kill us!"

He kept the throttle open, pulling back onto the roadway after passing a couple of cars and keeping his speed up. In the mirror he could see the red pickup weaving, looking for a break in traffic to come after them. It was a newer, bigger truck, obviously in better shape than the first redneck's. Steve worked his way to the outside lane and looked for an interchange but there was none in sight. The map display showed the next one ten miles ahead. Traffic had slowed slightly and bunched up enough that both lanes were blocked in front of them. Steve had to slow to the speed of the cars, all doing about seventy. In the mirror, he watched the pickup weaving through the traffic and catching up with them. The driver came up behind him traveling like he had an open road. The truck was about fifty yards behind them when Steve sandwiched the motorcycle between two cars in the inside lane. He watched the truck force its way up alongside in the outside lane.

Steve had learned in a driver's education class that you should keep a minimum of two and a half seconds between you and the vehicle in front of you. At seventy miles per hour, that's two-hundred and fifty feet. Right then, he was almost on the bumper of the car in front of him. He hoped the car behind him didn't back off, allowing the pickup to get in behind them or lunge sideways at them again. He was debating whether he could ride up the middle between the two lanes of traffic, when the driver behind him decided he was too close and slowed down. The pickup driver took advantage of the opening and swerved toward them. Steve quickly shifted to the inside shoulder and sped up as the truck came after them with its left wheels on the shoulder. The driver lost control for a second going over the rumble strip and bumped the car Steve had been tailgating. The pickup bounced back and both vehicles swerved back and forth across the lane several times before the drivers got them under control. Fortunately, Steve had pulled on forward, still riding on the narrow shoulder. After passing several cars, he found a spot big enough to squeeze into the left-hand lane. After a few seconds, an opening appeared in the right-hand lane, and he switched to it. The traffic was slowing for some reason; they were traveling at sixty miles per hour. He looked ahead at the solid lines of cars and trucks that prevented him from pulling away from the rednecks. This was dangerous riding. He was either on the throttle or the brake. He saw no way to get completely away from the murderous pickup trucks. He thought about riding out onto the grass beside the road but was afraid the pickups would follow and ram them.

The traffic in front of Steve was packed too tightly to weave through, and the older pickup had caught up with his buddy and the two were forcing their way through the line of cars, honking and bullying the drivers. The motorists near the pickups seemed to sense something was wrong and slowed down, spreading out, allowing the trucks to work their way up behind the motorcycle.

The red pickup driver closed up, tailgating a car in the inside lane which put him next to the motorcycle's rear wheel as the first redneck finally made it directly behind the bike. Steve eyeballed the pickup in his rearview mirror and when it accelerated to bump him, his only choice was to turn to the right. Steve rode onto the shoulder and opened the throttle. Fortunately, this outside shoulder was a full lane wide. The older redneck jerked his steering wheel to the right to stay behind the motorcycle but went too far and got his right wheels off the pavement. He slowed down, losing distance, before forcing his way back onto the shoulder.

Rocks and gravel thrown up by the traffic were scattered across the surface of the shoulder. It made the ride rougher as Steve used the opportunity to accelerate and pass several cars before working back into the traffic lane. He used some of the redneck's tactics to open up opportunities to speed up, weave around the cars and trucks and put some distance between the two of them and the rednecks, as Steve now thought of them. "Are you okay?" He asked Aden as he pulled back onto the roadway.

"Can you get off the freeway? This is crazy," Aden said. "Those assholes are nuts. What do we do now?"

"Sorry, I'll try to take it easy. But I have to keep ahead of them. I'm afraid if I stop on the shoulder, they will just accidentally ram us. I'll try to keep some cars between us and them. The map shows the next exit is about six miles. We'll do what we have to do until we get there. We need to stay in survival mode."

The traffic had thinned out a little and was now scattered loosely along both lanes as they wove back and forth through the cars, SUVs, and big trucks sharing the road. Steve kept a lookout for police cars. Naturally there were none now that he wanted one. A couple of miles further on, the traffic in front of them started to bunch up again. Steve and Aden were sitting at the back of the pack when Aden grabbed his arm. "I see the trucks coming up."

In the mirror, Steve saw the two trucks side by side. That would make it a lot harder to dodge them. There was no choice. Steve pulled onto the outside shoulder and passed a couple of cars. The traffic slowed down to fifty miles per hour, and cars were practically bumper to bumper, bunched too tightly to allow Steve to cut back onto the traffic lane. The forest bushes and branches came down to the shoulder and hung over its outside edge, reaching for the motorcycle. He felt trapped with cars on the left and tree branches on the right.

Redneck number one pulled onto the shoulder behind him and stepped on the gas. The red pickup moved into the right lane at the back of the pack to block Steve from switching back.

The highway was making a gradual right turn, preventing Steve from seeing very far around the shoulder. He did spot an opening in the traffic about five cars ahead. If he could get to it, he could take advantage of the opportunity to get back on the highway. He sped up.

Steve checked his mirror and saw the redneck closing in on him. It didn't look like the motorcycle would make it to the opening in time. He shifted his gaze forward as they continued around the turn—just in time for the view to open up and show him a semi parked on the shoulder. He had a fast glimpse of the driver changing a tire. It was too close for him to stop, so he downshifted twice into fourth gear and opened the throttle full, something he hadn't done before. The bike leaped forward and almost threw the two off the seat as it responded to the extra power. Steve estimated the distance to the break in traffic and decided they were not going to make it. He aimed for the space between the truck and the cars.

And then a good thing happened. The driver in the car next to him apparently heard or spotted the motorcycle. He stepped on his brakes, giving Steve a chance to swerve left. Steve jumped into the lane and roared past the semi. The mirror showed him the redneck's pickup crashing into the corner of the semi-trailer and spinning into the traffic on the interstate. The rear of the pickup missed the car that had let Steve in and hit the one behind it. That threw the two vehicles into the car in the inside lane. The whole freeway came to a halt, blocking the red pickup from chasing them.

Meanwhile Steve had a new problem. He hit the brakes to slow down to the traffic's speed as he watched the cars ahead of him coming to a halt. A fender bender blocked the outside lane, forcing everyone to switch into the inside lane. Steve continued braking hard, almost stopping, before forcing his way into the other lane amid honking and shouting from the driver he cut out. Then they were past the collision, and he could cut to the outside lane and wave the driver behind him to go on. As the car came up beside him, he took both hands off the handlebars and made a namaste sign. The driver scowled as he made the bird sign and went on his way.

Aden asked, "Should we stop to help?"

"No. Those hillbillies will blame everything including the Civil War on us. There are plenty of folks there to help. Our best bet is to get out of here." He waved acknowledgement to the car that let him into the lane, then sped up slightly to pull away from the scene.

Twenty-six

"Where are we?"

Steve checked the map on the display. "We're near a town called Forest. Want to stop?"

"Oh yes. I want to stop." He could feel her hands shaking as she held on to him.

He found the exit for State Road 35, took it and made the turn north into the town. He passed a Walmart and a Wendy's and found a local café located half a mile on up the road. As he pulled in, his worry was that they'd stopped too close to the crash site but, clearly, Aden needed a break and the freeway and the rednecks were probably stuck for several hours. It would take the state police to straighten that one out. In fact, he thought, they shouldn't dawdle too long. After they talked to the rednecks, the police might be looking for them as the instigators of the collision. He took off his helmet and waited for Aden to climb off the bike. She was just sitting there with one foot on the ground. "Are you okay?"

"No." She removed her helmet, climbed off, and stood looking at the motorcycle. "Let's get a cup of coffee and I'll give you a chance to talk me out of never getting back on that thing."

"You're thinking of jumping ship? Here?"

"I'm thinking this is a foolish way to travel. I was scared shitless back there. I was sure we were going to die. If that car hadn't backed off and let you in, you were aiming at a three-foot opening between, literally, a rock and a hard place." She thought for a minute. "When we passed that first guy stopped on the shoulder, we should have gotten off at the next exit and looked for secondary roads to ride like we did for Crusher. Then we could have avoided the whole chase."

"Right, that idea didn't occur to me until after we met the red pickup. By then it was too late. Well, I won't try to talk you out of getting off here, but I'll listen to you while you talk it out."

The two went into the café and ordered coffee. Aden's hands were still shaking as she tried to pour cream into her cup and Steve had to admit he was having the shakes from waves of adrenaline pumping through his body. Finally, Aden spoke up. "I don't think I can go any further. I've never been in a situation like that, and I don't know how to handle it."

"I don't either. I've never had anyone try to kill me before. And that's what they were doing, trying to kill us. I'm sure they would say they were just trying to scare us, but their actions were attempted murder. I can't say your reaction is wrong. I don't know if getting back on the bike would help you or make your feelings worse. What do you want to do?"

"Well, I just know right now I can't get back on that motorcycle. I don't know what to do. Do you think it would do any good to go to the police?"

"I get the impression that around here those assholes are the good ole boys and we're... outsiders. I'm afraid somehow it would turn out to be our fault. I know from listening to some of the Southern boys on the ship that they stick together. They're nice as anything until something doesn't go their way." Steve's mind was racing. He didn't want to lose her. What to do? He could wait there with her and give her a chance to think things over; did she really want to leave him? He didn't have that much experience reading her emotions, but clearly, she needed time to calm down, even then she might not get back on the bike. "I can call you a cab to take you to the bus station. You could catch a bus to Mayport and meet me there. Would that work?"

Aden was also thinking. *Do I want to stay with this man?* He had put her in some dangerous situations, granted, most of them had been of her making. He did get her away from Crusher but at what cost? Was this the life she wanted? He had his future mapped out, but would that include her? What the hell was she doing? She needed time to think, but he expected a decision now. She would give him one. "Let me check something." She pulled out her phone and started flipping screens. "Actually, I have an Uber app on my phone, and they have Uber in this town. I'll use that. I think I'll get a room here for the night and tomorrow I'll decide where I want to go, what I want to do. I know right now I don't want to ride on that motorcycle, so I think it's best that you continue on. You have commitments. When will you get to Mayport?"

Steve hated to hear she wanted him to go on without her but checked his watch and conjured up a mental image of the map. He figured, riding alone, he could cut down to Mobile, Alabama and be there by three-thirty. That would put him back on I-10. Pushing it some, he could make it into Mayport by ten o'clock tonight. "I can get there tonight. I'll unload the bike tomorrow. I can stick around a couple of days if you think you might head that way."

"That soon? You have really been holding back for me, haven't you?"

"Not really. I wouldn't have missed our trip together for anything. I'm glad we met. I've enjoyed every minute we've been together, and I hope this isn't the end of our... friendship, relationship, whatever the hell we've got. I hope, somehow, we stick together."

Aden thought about what he was saying and what her situation was. She was going to be alone in a place where she didn't know anyone; she was low on funds with no transportation. Kind of the situation she was in when they met. Her heart was saying to keep Steve in her life but was that probably her brain unconsciously telling her *Keep Steve as an ace in the hole.* It probably wasn't fair to Steve, but she realized how much she had come to depend on him since they met. "Uh, why don't you give me until Wednesday. Where would we meet?"

"Probably the bus station in Jacksonville, unless you can afford to fly, and I don't even know what airlines they've got around here. You've got my phone number. Just give me a call and I'll pick you up some way. Actually, you can always give me a call whether or not you come to Mayport."

"Okay, let's leave it at that. If you don't hear from me by Wednesday... make it Thursday, I'd need time to get there, and I need at least a day here to get my wits about me. Anyway, if not by Thursday you probably won't hear from me."

That sounded to Steve like she already knew she'd be blowing him off. She was just letting him down easy. He steeled his mind to the fact that he wasn't going to see her again. "All I can say is never say never. I hope you change your mind. How are you fixed for money?"

"Pretty good at the moment. The tips in Shreveport were the best I've had."

"Will they cover bus fare to Florida?"

"I expect so. Buses are cheap, right?"

Steve was dazed by the situation and at his feelings. He was pissed at the rednecks for igniting the split and annoyed at Aden's prevarication. He felt a good thing had been ruined and she just couldn't bring herself to say so. Feelings of gloom washed over him as her words telling him to go sank in. To Aden, it showed on his face as impatience.

He peeled fifty dollars off his much-diminished roll. "Just in case. Better safe, etcetera." He stood up, thought about kissing her, decided it wasn't the time. "Goodbye for now."

"You're going now? No more talk?" That was faster than she'd expected.

"Why prolong it? What else is there to say? You need some time to think things through, I actually have a job to finish. I hope to see you later. I hope you find what you want."

He was going. She stood up. "Thank you." A dozen things to say raced through her mind, "Goodbye." She wouldn't look at him, but she hugged him tightly. He headed for the cash register and paid for the coffees. Not having any smaller bills, he added a five-dollar tip. Too much for the bill but he didn't care. He just wanted out.

The waitress picked it up and said, "Thank you, that's a nice tip. You two on that motorbike? Where ya headed?"

"Oh, Meridian to Mobile to Mayport. Just me." He pocketed his wallet.

The waitress ignored the last part. "Be careful in Meridian. The whole town is a speed trap. You might be tempted to take the 145 highway to US 45, but there's no way a motorcycle could get through there without a ticket, or more than one."

"Thanks for the tip." He laughed. "A tip for a tip. Works for me." He bobbed his head at her and strode out the door. He was putting on his helmet when he remembered Aden's clothes in the saddlebag. He grabbed her duffle bag—she had her guitar with her, so this was everything—and took it inside. The interlude made everything seem anticlimactic. Back on the bike, he headed south to the highway. It already seemed lonely without Aden holding on to him. He swallowed the thought, decided he better concentrate on the road and tried to put his mind back on the trip. As he turned east on the interstate for Meridian, he looked both ways for roving pickup trucks, but he was all alone in the eastbound lanes. Luckily, he knew, the two he was interested in were not going anywhere anytime soon. He just hoped they didn't have any more friends.

Twenty-seven

Aden spent the rest of the day in Forest trying to calm down. She used the Uber app for some calm transportation. A late model Kia with a black driver showed up and was happy to tell her about the town. She asked him to recommend an inexpensive motel. As he drove, she looked at the various businesses scattered along the road and asked about any live music places in town. "There's not much. About half the bars cater mainly to blacks. A few beer joints have music, but they are really rough. They have chicken wire around the stage so the musicians can't get hit by bottles. They still get beer thrown on them."

"Um. Can I get a bus from here to Mayport, Florida?"

"Uhh, yeah. There's a gas station where the buses stop. Where's Mayport?"

"I guess near Jacksonville."

"While you can get a bus that will end up in Jacksonville, I doubt it's a direct route. Probably have to go through Atlanta."

"Well, maybe tomorrow." She wasn't sure where she wanted to go, but now wasn't the time to decide.

After checking in to the motel, she went for a walk. It felt good to be stretching her legs, so she picked up the pace. It was mainly a commercial neighborhood, several fast-food joints and car dealerships. She had noticed many of the fast-food cafés congregated near each other. Most buildings were stand-alone. It seemed to have everything a town needed but was obviously a small town. *No place to play and sing* hopped into her mind. Several good ole boys drove by whistling and shouting at her, but no one stopped. She decided it was probably a nice place to live but too small a town for her needs. That left her with choices to make... where did she want to go? She could get out of the south where they had tried to kill her, go to Mayport and connect with Steve or maybe Meridian would have a place where she would like to work. She realized some of those choices weren't mutually exclusive.

Shreveport and the previous two nights had made her feel she could find work as a singer. Now she wondered if she had just been extremely lucky. The problem was, she was missing Steve. She was shocked how much she missed him. She hadn't expected him to up and walk out on her just because she told him to. His support had helped build her confidence, and seeing him sitting in the audience had become important to her. It was odd how quickly it had become natural to talk over her ideas and plans with him. She wanted to talk to him now, go over her choices. Clearly, whatever she wanted to do, it wasn't going to happen here in Forest. She decided she would take the Uber to Meridian in the morning and see what the music scene was like there before she made up her mind about the future. She had worked up a muck sweat in the high humidity so, after stopping at a KFC for something besides a hamburger, went back to her room for a shower, to wash out some underwear and practice some songs.

Twenty-eight

Back on I-20, Steve pushed the bike up to seventy-five and engaged the cruise control. He was amazed at the response and performance of the bike and realized he had almost never ridden it by himself. When he lost nearly half the passenger weight, the effect on performance was noticeable. Judging from the light traffic, the collision with the rednecks and the semi had not been cleared. He used the opportunity to make up time.

The day was hot, nearly ninety, and the high humidity must have been about the same. A few clouds floated in the dark-blue sky. His leather jacket was too hot to wear but he hated to ride without it. He remembered a friend in high school who had taken a spill without a leather jacket. He had come off the motorcycle and skidded on his back, grinding off the muscles down to the ribs. The body took so much energy repairing the back muscles, all his hair had fallen out. He was bald for about a year.

He thought over what he had said to Aden. Was he strong enough making his feelings known? He really wanted to hold her again, but had little hope that she would show up in Mayport or New Mexico. He decided he'd better get his mind on the trip.

A road sign told him he was twenty miles outside of Meridian where he would gas up and head south on US 45. He figured two hours for the Meridian/Mobile ride. For part of the distance, the speed limit was sixty-five and the rest was fifty-five. So far, he hadn't gotten a ticket, and he didn't want one. His plan was to ride the speed limit until someone who looked like a local passed him and then ride at the local's speed. So far that had worked.

He spotted the sign lowering the speed limit as he entered Meridian. He slowed down and watched for a gas and a fast-food joint off the highway. After gassing up and grabbing a burger, he kept checking his phone to see if Aden had called, but of course she hadn't. He finally put the phone away and got ready for the ride south. He was on his way when he saw the 145 cutoff the waitress had warned him about. It did look like a time saver, but he stayed on I-20 until he could turn directly onto US45. His plan for the ride seemed to be working as far as staying within the speed limit. He passed several highway cops, but none of them paid any attention to him. He hadn't counted on the towns, though. There was one about every twenty miles. The speed limits were often out of sight behind a bush or tree. So far, he'd found them all, but it slowed up the travel.

He got caught in a small town where he didn't even catch the name. The speed limit sign was behind a large bush, and he saw it just as he rode past. "School zone—15 MPH 9:00 am to 3:00 pm." Steve hit the brakes but a patrol car with its lights on was rolling out of an alley as he started slowing down. He pulled to the curb, put the bike on its stand and stood taking off his helmet.

At least the cop was polite. "Sir, you were doing thirty in a school zone."

Steve knew it was useless to argue. "Yeah, sure. Out of curiosity, where's the school?"

"It's around the corner on State Street. We take protecting our children very seriously where they cross the street here coming and going to school."

Steve looked around; there was no one in sight. "So, what now?"

"Sir, the fine for thirty in a school zone is one-hundred-fifty-three dollars. We can go to the courthouse, and you can pay the fine or I have a self-addressed envelope. You can put the money in it, and I'll watch you put the envelope in a mailbox. If you don't have the cash, we can find an ATM."

Steve sighed, kissed the money goodbye and started counting. He didn't have enough ones. "Can you break a ten?"

"No sir. I don't make change."

Steve looked around. "Let's go over to that coffee shop and I'll get the change. There's a mailbox there as well."

The cop thought it over. "Okay, we can do that."

Steve started to get back on the bike, but the cop stopped him. "Sorry sir, I think we better walk to the coffee shop."

Steve stopped, got off the bike. "Makes me no never mind." They walked the block to the coffee shop where Steve bought a cup of coffee, got his change and put the fine in the envelope the cop gave him. The cop watched him drop the envelope in a mailbox and said, "You're nicer about it than most folks who I stop. I'll give you a heads up—there's two more... speed traps between here and the city limits." He told Steve how to spot them as they walked back to the motorcycle.

Steve said, "Thank you," and stood on the sidewalk sipping his coffee. As he watched, the radar unit in the cop's car gave a warning signal and the cop put on his lights and stepped into the street to stop a car coming toward them. The driver clearly hadn't seen the speed limit sign and hadn't even tried to slow down. When the car stopped, the cop checked his radar unit and walked to the driver's window. He had his hand on his gun. When the driver rolled his window down, the cop said, "Sir, you were doing thirty-seven miles per hour in a school zone."

"Shit! I'm surprised this podunk town has a school." Steve recognized the accent as East Coast, but he wasn't familiar enough with them to locate it any closer. "How 'bout I give you twenty and we forget it."

The cop straightened up and said, "How about I take you to jail, yes we have that too, for trying to bribe a policeman and you can cool off until you decide to pay the fine."

The driver calmed down. "Okay. So, what's the fine?"

"As I was telling this gentleman, the fine for thirty-seven in a school zone is one-hundred-seventy-two dollars and fifty cents. We can go to the courthouse, and you can pay the fine or I have a self-addressed envelope. You can put the money in it, and I'll watch you put the envelope in a mailbox. If you don't have the cash, we can find an ATM."

"Shit! Let's find an ATM."

"We can walk to one just down the block."

As the two talked, the radar unit buzzed again. The cop looked up at a pickup truck doing about thirty. The cop and the driver waved. "Local driver?" Steve asked.

"Yes sir, the locals know to watch for children. We don't have any problems with locals."

"Right." Steve knew better than to point out the hypocrisy.

After the two walked off, Steve checked his watch. The cop had two speeders in less than twenty minutes. He didn't know how normal it was for the town, but he realized that worked out to 900 bucks an hour, give or take. The town was making money off its speed limits. No wonder the towns didn't like the freeway. Thanks to the cop's help, Steve made it out of town without another ticket.

He was in Mobile by four o'clock. As he was coming into town, he spotted a Shell station and stopped for gas. Then it was time to find a fast-food joint for a quick meal. He spotted a Mexican restaurant, but he'd learned the food was not what he was used to in New Mexico, so he kept looking. He finally spotted a place offering seafood to go. That whetted his appetite, and he pulled into the parking lot. It was strictly a take-out café, so he ate his shrimp sandwich and coleslaw outside at a picnic table in the shade. One teenager looked the bike over but didn't say anything to Steve.

Soon he was back on the Beemer. US 45 was taking him through a commercial neighborhood. It was a four-lane until he passed I-65 when it shrank down to a two-lane. It was now called St. Stevens Road. He followed it to a five-way intersection and rode out on Springhill Avenue.

His online navigation system was earning its money for him in this part of town. He turned onto Broad Street, which led him south to a roundabout that looked like it would take him to I-10, but the map display said to continue south. The display finally turned him onto Texas Street, and he headed east. The instructions worked and, several streets and turns later, he was on I-10 east.

The first surprise was entering a tunnel. It took him under the Mobile River, emerging on a spit of land between the river and Mobile Bay. The next surprise was the bridge across the bay, about seven miles of travel over water. He spotted the *USS Alabama* off to his right at its memorial park. It would have been nice to stop and go through the old battleship. He wanted to compare its fire control system to the systems he worked on. If Aden were with him, it would have been fun to explore through the old ship together. Well, another trip.

By then, it was five o'clock and he put the cruise control on seventy and headed east. He realized his estimated time was off and it would be eleven when he got to Jacksonville. He would stop there for the night. A little before six, he crossed into Florida and was in Pensacola. Looking at the clocks on buildings, he realized the time zone had changed, and it was now a little before seven o'clock. It would be midnight when he pulled into Jacksonville. He looked around for signs of the Naval Air Station but a sign pointing south showed he was too far away to see it.

After crossing Escambia Bay, the road swung a little north again before trending east through lots of residential areas and towns. Finally, he broke out into open country with grass and scrub trees on both sides of the road. The cars and SUVs thinned out a little, but traffic was still fairly heavy with semis going in both directions. He stopped for gas about eight-thirty just south of Mariana, the halfway point between Mobile and Jacksonville. As he pulled into a gas station the temperature really hit him. Even two hours after sunset, the temperature was in the eighties. The humidity didn't help either. He wondered what the heat index was. He stripped off his jacket while having a quick cup of coffee and a glass of milk at the diner. Then it was back into his jacket and helmet, and he was off again. He thought about stopping in Tallahassee at a Cracker Barrel for dinner but decided to tough it out and kept riding.

About ten o'clock, he saw a sign for the Monticello rest area and thought about calling it a night but he was less than two hours from Jacksonville, so he pressed on. It was eleven-thirty when he found a cheap motel just before riding into Jacksonville proper. He fell into bed and hoped the air conditioner didn't keep him awake. His thoughts turned to Aden as he was drifting off to sleep. Would she show up? He didn't think so. It seemed to him she was too likely to head back west or meet someone with a car. He remembered how she was ready to quit the trip in Tucson and thought about the Texan with the big Lincoln. She wasn't interested then; would she be now? It was a much more boring ride by himself. She had added the spice to the trip. He was thinking about calling her when he fell into a deep slumber.

Twenty-nine

Monday

Sleeping on a lumpy bed and listening to street noises all night long convinced Aden she wanted to go somewhere else. Meridian seemed like a reasonable start. A fast-food joint serving tasteless breakfast sandwiches convinced her she had made the right decision. She finished her coffee as she texted the Uber driver.

In Meridian, the driver dropped her at a slightly nicer motel than the one in Forest. She noticed it was near a couple of lounges that were advertising bands. After lunch she walked to the nearest one and asked for the manager. "Hello, little lady, what can I do you for?"

"I noticed you have a band. Do they need a singer?"

"You'd have to ask them. They come in around seven. What kind of songs do you sing?"

"I'll try just about anything. Mostly Country and Western."

"Hmmm. Don't know if that will fit. About all this band plays is bluegrass. You're welcome to try. As I said, the band gets here about seven. Come back then."

"Thanks, I will." She left the lounge and tried several more in the neighborhood. She received no better encouragement. She got the impression it was local boys only. She decided to go back to the first one at seven. She spent the afternoon listening to and practicing bluegrass songs, not the sort of thing she was familiar with.

Thirty

It seemed like something was missing when Steve awakened alone in bed. He knew what was missing and wrote it off as he packed up and rode across town, following the signs to Mayport. He found a café along Mayport Road and had a good breakfast, after which he called Frank Kruzick. "Logistics, Petty Officer Kruzick speaking, sir."

"Frank Kruzick, Steve Luce here. I've got your motorcycle to hand over."

"Motorcycle? Oh! You're Larry's shipmate. I really haven't given this much thought. Ah, let's get together this afternoon. Where are you?"

"I'm here in Mayport. I can meet you anywhere you want. I plan to stay around for a couple of days."

"Do you have a motel?"

"Not yet. Any recommendations?"

"Yeah, and it's a good place to meet." He told Steve about a hotel on Mayport Road just outside the naval station gate. They agreed to meet about six o'clock, or eighteen hundred, as Frank put it.

Steve found the hotel, as the Floridians seemed to call their motels, and checked in. It was located in a scenic setting with palms and greenery all around. Florida was certainly greener than California. After unloading his gear off the bike, he consulted his watch; it was still morning, and he decided he wasn't going to just hang around the room all day. The bike was still his until six tonight. It was showing the evidence of a hard ride and really needed cleaning. He found a do-it-yourself car wash and spent an hour getting the grime and insects off it.

Afterwards, he took a ride to the beach. Riding along Seminole Road led him to a public parking lot on 35th Street with access to the beach, and he opted to stop there. An hour's walk in the sand felt really good. He enjoyed watching the ships going in and out of the St. Johns River, just to the north of where he was walking. It was mostly commercial shipping, but he did watch a destroyer clear the breakwaters and head out to sea. It didn't make him miss the Navy, but he could feel the nostalgia. He was loosened up and in a mellow mood when he got back to the bike and headed out to find some lunch. Some aimless riding took him to a café advertising, "Watch out! You can get crabs here." He stopped and went in.

After lunch, he did some sightseeing, and it was about three o'clock when he got back to the motel. He had just walked in and was debating turning on the TV or taking a shower when there was a knock at the door. *Did Frank get off early?* was going through his head as he walked to the door.

He unlocked the deadbolt as he twisted the doorknob and while he still had his hands on them, the door was shoved open violently, hitting his chest and head. He flew backward several steps, finally losing his balance and tripping over his feet. He went down on his back and bumped his head on the carpet. When he regained his senses and looked up, Crusher was inside the door.

From the odor and his unkempt appearance, it was obvious he had been living in his car without washing or shaving. Steve had to say it. "You look like shit."

"Where's the bitch?" Crusher was yelling. "I'll kill her. Where is she?" He kicked Steve's foot and was about to stomp on his ankle, but Steve did a backwards somersault, landing crouched on his feet at the bathroom door. He rose to full height and got ready to defend himself.

While thinking, *wow! I didn't know I could do that,* he got his hands up like a boxer—but Crusher didn't follow up on the attack. This didn't seem like a lovestruck stalker. More like a crazed killer. Steve knew he wasn't Crusher's focus and wanted to get rid of the character without any damage to himself. "Aden? She bailed on me in Las Cruces after you attacked us that night. She's probably back in California or Washington state by now. I can't believe you're still chasing her. You can't possibly think you two are getting back together. How did you find me anyway?"

Crusher blew out a breath and pulled out a pistol. "You're gonna make me do this the hard way. You said you were coming to Mayport to deliver that crappy motorbike to someone at the naval station. I picked the nearest motel and waited for you to show up. Took you long enough to get here. I been here two days." The gun was pointed in Steve's general direction. "Now tell me where the hell she is. I'll shoot!"

His hand seemed pretty shaky to Steve... it looked like an even chance he could drop the pistol or accidently pull the trigger. He was too far away for Steve to try to grab it. "I told you, after you attacked us in Las Cruces, she decided to go back to California. Why don't you point that gun somewhere else? If it goes off, I won't be able to talk to you."

"I don't believe you. Where is she?"

"Do you see her here? I don't know where she is. There are lots of girls in Florida. Find one of those to bother." Steve mentally apologized to the girls of Florida.

"I don't care about the bitch. She's got my money. I need that money!"

"Your money? What money? All she had with her was her tip money. Probably gone by now. Look, I don't know what to tell you about your money. What I will do, if you go away right now, is I'll forget I saw you."

Crusher hesitated. After checking out the area, he had decided to stake out this motel and had parked his car in a back corner, living in the parking lot while waiting for Aden and the asshole to show up. Crusher was watching when Steve first appeared at the motel and knew Aden wasn't riding with him. Maybe she was in a nearby motel. He needed the two to be together, and he didn't know anyplace else to look for her. "She's not here? Did you drop her in Jacksonville?"

"No. She's never been here. She's not gonna be here. She said she wanted to try some of the smaller towns in California. Anyplace you aren't. Try Bakersfield."

Crusher glared at him. "I need that money. Why did you let her go?" He let his arm drop, no longer pointing the pistol at Steve.

"Why? What was I supposed to do? She wanted to go. I couldn't talk her out of it." He marveled privately to himself—he was really getting into the story. "She left you, she left me. That's how it goes."

Crusher finally blew out a long breath. If she had actually left Steve, there was nothing the asshole could do to help Crusher find her. The only good thing, from Crusher's point of view, was that he was in Florida where the drug dealers didn't know to look for him. He still felt he could salvage the situation. "Thanks for nothing, you sumbitch. I gotta think." He turned and walked out.

Steve let his breath out and went to the door, watching the meth-head get in his car and drive off. A huge sense of relief came over him and he sat down, heavily, in a chair. He was shaking as he thought of the pistol pointed at his navel. If Crusher had been a little more careless with his trigger finger, he would be lying on the floor in a pool of blood.

He had regained his composure by the time Frank Kruzick showed up. Kruzick was wearing nice slacks and loafers with a polo shirt, not exactly a motorcycle riding outfit. Steve could see the family resemblance in his face, but he was taller and thinner than his younger brother. Steve could tell he wasn't excited about the transaction. "Hi, Steve? I'm Frank Kruzick. I take it that's the motorcycle outside?"

"Yeah, you want to check it out first or go over the paperwork?" Steve noticed Frank had arrived by himself in a car. He wondered how Kruzick planned to get the bike home.

"Let's talk about this. You are obviously an enthusiastic motorcyclist. I'm not. I told Larry I would buy the damn machine to help him out, but I'm not a motorcycle rider and I don't have the money to spare. My plan is to sell the machine for as much as I can and send the money to Larry. We've been exchanging emails since he got to Japan; he knows I'm going to sell the bike and is okay with the idea. He does expect me to pay him a hundred dollars a month as long as I keep it, but he knows that won't be long. At this point, I don't have any money in it, and I'd like to keep it that way. I have no idea what the bike is worth, but if you want to send Larry a hundred a month, I'll sign a bill of sale and the title over to you. The two of you can negotiate a final deal by email. You can probably get more money for the bike than I could."

"Wow, I wasn't expecting this. The bike is mine for a hundred a month and no down payment?"

"Yeah, I'll take possession as Larry set it up and then transfer everything over to you, if you're willing. I don't want to get involved with the thing if I don't have to."

"You realize you're leaving a lot of money on the table, right? You want to think about this?"

"No, I've thought about it ever since Larry called me. I don't want the bike, my wife doesn't want me to get involved, and I'd rather my kids didn't see the machine. It would just get them excited."

It sounded like Steve could have a Beemer for at least the next three years. He hadn't thought about it, but he realized he loved the motorcycle. The deal wasn't fair to Larry; a more realistic offer would have to be made for the bike. Steve did a fast calculation in his head and worked out that three-hundred and fifty a month would be needed to pay the machine off in five years, more money than he had. Maybe Kruzick would go for a balloon payment after Steve finished school and found a job. In any case, he got to keep riding the Beemer while he worked out a deal with Larry. He wondered what his Honda would sell for. "You got yourself a deal. How do we do this?"

"We need to go the Motor Vehicle Service Center and complete the deal. It shouldn't be complicated, just transferring a California motorcycle through a Florida MVC to a New Mexico owner."

"Are you available in the morning?"

"I think my chief will let me off after muster. I'll call you and give you a time to meet me at the MVC. We have one on base. Do you have your reserve ID card?"

"Yeah, not a problem. I even have it with me."

"Okay, I'll call you in the morning and we'll set up a time to meet."

They said their goodbyes and Frank headed home while Steve went looking for dinner. It was interesting, Steve thought after talking to Frank — he was such good buddies with Larry, but it was obvious he and Frank had nothing in common.

Thirty-one

At seven, Aden walked back to the lounge where a small, raucous crowd was yelling comments at the four band members who were setting up the equipment on the little stage. The band was smiling and yelling back... clearly, they had gone through this before. The instruments consisted of a mandolin, a fiddle, a guitar and a Dobro. The mandolin player doubled up on the banjo. "Hi," Aden offered. It wasn't clear who the leader was, so she addressed the group. "I was wondering if I could sit in for a couple of songs tonight."

They looked her over. "Where you from?" was the first question from the fiddle player.

"California, most recently. I was heading for Florida but now I'm not sure. Thought I'd try to find a job around here."

"What kind of music do you play?" She noticed they hadn't welcomed her in any way.

"Mainly Country and Western. I'll try just about anything. I understand you play mainly bluegrass?"

"Not mainly. Only. I don't know that you'd help us any and we'd just have to split the pot one more way." He seemed to be thinking things over, then he got a gleam in his eye. "Tell you what. You can try one song if'n you want to. We'll see how well it goes over. Be back at eight ready to sing 'Traveling Soldier.'"

They went back to tuning all the instruments.

Aden had a bad feeling about this. They weren't very friendly, and she didn't know the song. She almost told them no, but she decided to go back to her motel and see if she could learn it by eight that night, telling herself, *If I'm going to be a professional, I have to handle all types of situations. If I'm not satisfied with my performance, I won't go back.* She found the lyrics online and memorized them while watching the song being performed on her phone. After playing along with the video several times, she felt like she was ready.

Aden decided this wasn't the crowd for her usual costume. She wore jeans with no rips and her long-sleeved shirt was snapped up instead of tied up. Her boots completed the costume. About eight o'clock she walked to the lounge.

The band had settled in and was playing a song called "Tennessee 1949." They were using a wide-angle mike and the four were doing a dance to let each individual get close to it for their solo. After each had a turn, they all gathered around it to finish singing the lyrics. To Aden they sounded good.

They saw Aden sit at a table. The leader stared at her but made no attempt to welcome her. They just continued through their regular set. The crowd was evidently familiar with the band and their songs. They started applauding after the first couple of notes of each song. Everyone was clearly enjoying themselves and the band picked up on the good vibes. They plainly had lots of experience with the music and the patter between songs. Nearly an hour into the set, the leader said, "We got a girl here who wants to sing a song." Aden didn't like it when he sneered, "A Californian. Let's see what happens." It sounded like she was being set up for something. He beckoned her up to the stage. The crowd chuckled.

It was a disaster from the start. They insisted Aden change the key from the one she had practiced. They started with three different rhythms, none the way she had learned it. The guitar player and the mandolin player seemed to make a game of deliberate mistakes in the chording. It was pitched too low for her voice and, being nervous, she forgot some of the words. When she came to a place for a musical break she said, "take it." but the band just stopped playing. There was no applause, just a few snickers. The leader grinned and said, "Sorry, folks. The least said the better. Maybe that's the way they do songs in Californy." The crowd laughed. As she unplugged her guitar, he bent down and snarled in her ear, "Get lost, bitch."

Aden reddened and turned to her microphone. "I apologize for the... amateurs. They assured me they were musicians." The crowd chuckled nervously as she spun back to the leader. "Thanks for the experience. I don't often get to meet such complete assholes." She wanted to leave before her anger turned to tears. Aden packed up her guitar and started walking out as the band went back to their usual songs.

A man at the bar said, "Sorry, not your day or your crowd. They pull that stunt about once a month."

"I don't know why they even let me sing. They clearly wanted me to fail. It worked." She looked him over—about her age, and he gave her a friendly smile.

"They don't know anything about women. I don't think any of them have girlfriends. They look at you as an accomplished performer who can play something besides bluegrass who doesn't sing through their nose. This small-time band can't play anything else; they had to put you down. I know they never played that song before. I'm shocked they had heard of it, since it's sung by women."

She grimaced. "Thanks for the lesson. Where were you before I started?"

He gave her a grin. "Sorry I didn't say something sooner. Let me buy you a drink to make up for it. Not here. There's lots of bars along here where they didn't see the hatchet job."

She thought it over. "Thanks, but no thanks. I'm leaving town in the morning, and I might as well get a good night's sleep."

He grabbed a napkin and wrote down a name and phone number. "Well, if you change your mind, give me a call. Sorry we had to meet this way."

Aden looked at the name, 'Joe' and said, "Thanks, don't hold your breath. I'm really not in the mood for socializing right now."

"That's what the drink is for. It might have been fun. Have a great life."

She walked back to the motel. She knew the customer was right—it was not her crowd, her music or her situation. Suddenly it hit her. Singing was fun for a hobby. She might even make a few dollars doing it. But she was finding that the audience played a big part of whether or not it was enjoyable and there were lots of situations she couldn't control. Tonight wasn't fun. The episodes with Crusher weren't fun. Her previous office jobs hadn't prepared her for situations like this.

Her first thought was calling her mother for some sympathy, but then she thought about their argument and what she had said to her when she stormed out of the house. Now her humiliation kind of made her mother's point. She needed to talk to Steve. Did this mean she wanted to get back together? She wasn't sure. All she knew was that she wanted to hear his voice. When she got back in the motel room she called him.

"Hey, how are you? Where are you," he asked."

"Hi Steve, did you get to Jacksonville?"

"Yes. It's good to hear your voice. I was afraid you wouldn't call. Where are you?"

"I'm in Meridian. Got here this morning. What would you say if I told you I tried a singing job this evening?"

"From your tone and the fact that it's only eight-thirty in Meridian, I'd say it didn't go well. What happened? It's good you gave it a try, though. I'm hoping I'm wrong about how it went. I'm babbling, aren't I?

"You're not wrong. Worst night ever. I really wish you were here to console me."

"Sorry I wasn't available." It felt pleasant knowing she missed him. "Not counting your first professional show, this is the only one of your performances that I've missed. What went wrong?" Then he remembered his afternoon. "We have a problem. Sort of. Guess who found me here? And what he wants."

"Not Crusher? In Florida? Are you joking?"

"No joke. Crusher. He sounded crazy. He said you have his money. Any idea what he's talking about?"

"I have his money? I have no idea. He must have dreamed something and now thinks it's real. It does explain why he hasn't given up. Where is he now?"

"I hope I convinced him you turned around after Las Cruces and headed back to California. Anyway, he left, and I watched him drive out of sight. So, what was the problem with your session? Most people love your performance."

"It wasn't most people. The band and the audience seemed like they were friends and allies of that redneck pickup driver. It wasn't a session. They only let me play one song that they picked out and they deliberately screwed it up. That's just mean. If there are many people in the business like that, I don't want to be part of it. I haven't met anyone like that since high school."

"Bummer. So, what now?"

"Uh, I was thinking about coming to Mayport. How will that affect your plans?"

"Uh... I don't know if you will find this a deal killer. I contacted Frank Kruzick to unload the bike today and wound up buying it. Long story. We can talk about it and make some plans if you come here. Or I could pick you up there."

"You bought it? And you're riding it back to New Mexico? Well, I'm not sure I'm ready to ride on a motorcycle. Beyond that, I'm kind of wondering about your plans in the near and not-so-near future."

"My plans? As I told you, I'm planning on starting college in September. That's going to last at least four years. My thought is if you want to stay together, you should check out New Mexico. I think you'll like it. You could find plenty of singing jobs or office-type work if you decide not to pursue a singing career. Did you ever tell me what kind of a degree you have?"

"Oh, it's a BS degree. What about us?"

"I hope there is an us. I know we've only known each other less than a week, but we spent lots of time together and you've seen me at my worst. I feel, hope, there's a future for us. And there are lots of tech jobs and singing jobs in Albuquerque."

Aden was silent for a moment. "I hadn't thought about that. You're right, we've only known each other since last Tuesday. I really don't know you that well, do I? I'll call you tomorrow. We'll talk more then."

"Okay. I'm glad you called.

She broke the connection and thought about what he had said. Then she thought about her situation and what she wanted to do. She remembered a Kate Wolf song, "Here in California." The verse said something about going from strangers to friends. Friends, not lovers. A week wasn't long enough to get to know anyone, even if they were together twenty-four hours every day. She lay awake most of the night thinking about her options.

Tuesday

Aden gave up trying to sleep about six am. She got dressed and headed to the Burger King for coffee and a breakfast croissant—whatever they called it—getting there just as they opened. It was a gray morning with heavy clouds overhead; it would soon rain. One of the neon lights in the dining room was flickering, adding to the gloomy ambiance. She spent a moment thinking to herself and wondering if she could write a song with *gloom in the dingy dining room* as the title or in the lyrics. As she sat in the grimy dining room, she came to two conclusions: She really wanted to get out of Meridian, and she wanted to see Steve. Motorcycle be damned. Her phone was right there. She made the call. "Hullo?" a sleepy Steve answered.

"Did I wake you up?"

"Yeah, that's okay. I had to answer the phone anyway."

"I'm thinking I want to go back to work. I could start looking for a job in Albuquerque."

"I don't know what type of work you're looking for, but I'm sure we can find it in town. You won't have a problem finding a job." Steve hoped that was true.

Aden took a deep breath. "I've decided to come to Mayport. I haven't checked the bus schedules, and I don't know how long it will take to get there. You'll meet me?"

"Sure. I'll wait for you as long as I have to."

"I'm leaving now for the bus station. I'll call you when I have some definite information."

"Fine. I'll be waiting for your call. I'll meet the bus. It's really good to hear your voice."

The bus station was a little over a mile from Aden's motel. It looked like rain as she checked out and started walking to the bus station. Fortunately, she still had the plastic sheet that had wrapped the guitar case before. She waterproofed the guitar case but now she didn't have the rain suit, just her jeans and T-shirt. The rain held off until she was halfway to the depot, a real downpour. The guitar stayed dry, but she was dripping wet with a soaked clothes bag by the time she reached the depot, about nine am. The bus didn't leave until three-thirty-five that afternoon. The wait didn't shock Aden, but she was astonished to learn she couldn't get to Jacksonville from Meridian. She would make a big arc north to Atlanta, getting there about eleven that night. Then she had to wait an hour to catch a bus to Jacksonville, putting her at her destination Wednesday morning.

She called Steve to give him the schedule. He sounded happy. "I'm looking forward to seeing you. The trip wasn't the same without you. But I was thinking, if you don't want to ride anymore, you can take the bus to Albuquerque, or we might be able to spring for an airline ticket. You don't have to get on the Beemer."

"Well, we'll discuss it when I get there." They said their goodbyes and Aden went into the restroom to switch from her sodden pants and shirt to a T-shirt and a pair of jeans from the middle of her cloth clothes bag. They were only damp. She waited for the rain to stop before wandering out of the bus station to find a cheap food joint. After paying the Uber driver for her trips and buying her bus ticket, she was just about out of money. It was a good thing Steve had given her the extra fifty dollars. A chicken sandwich without drink or fries would hold her for the rest of the day.

Thirty-two

Frank called Steve at 8:30 that morning. He couldn't get away until fourteen hundred. He apologized and told Steve how to find the MVC on base. He would meet Steve there at fourteen-thirty. He said it would probably take several hours to complete the transaction.

Since he already had his phone out, Steve called his mother and brought her up to date on where he was and that he might bring a new girlfriend home with him. He hadn't thought about the time difference and since it was only six-thirty in New Mexico, his parents were just up and getting ready for breakfast. All his mother said was, "Well, I'm glad you're making friends. We'd love to meet her." There was a pause, and she added, "Sandy had her baby, a girl. I don't know many details. I heard the news at the coffee shop yesterday. Mother and daughter are doing well."

Steve subtracted nine months from the date and realized Sandy and Joe got together about a month after Joe got released from the Air Force, three months before Steve's original enlistment date was up. "Well, I hope Joe does the right thing for both of them and they're happy."

"Apparently, Joe is not to be found. Margaret at the coffee shop was talking to Sandy's mother and learned that Joe quit his job and seems to have left the state."

"I'm sorry to hear that. Sandy didn't deserve a kick like that." They said their goodbyes with Steve feeling like he had just dodged a bullet. If Joe hadn't come along, would Sandy have clung tighter to Steve? It could be him having a child and hurting his chances to continue his education.

Steve had his new, next generation reserve ID card to show at the gate and had no trouble getting on the base. He got to the MVC office ten minutes before Frank. Frank was right about the time needed to handle all the paperwork. After a half-hour wait to talk to a clerk who was upset at the extra work of something out of the ordinary, it was five-thirty when they walked out of the MVC office. Steve turned in the California license plate and left with a registration slip in his name and a temporary tag that he could use to ride back to Albuquerque. After a stop for a meal, he spent the evening at a laundromat washing clothes.

Thirty-three

With nothing else to do, Aden got back to the bus station about one-thirty. The rain had come and gone, and she had worked up quite a sweat walking around out in the high humidity. She admired the pleasant-looking station as she walked up to the front door. It almost looked more like a house with a grass front yard and shade trees around the building. She was glad to get inside the air-conditioned waiting room where she gratefully fell into a chair to cool off and survey her fellow passengers. She was a people watcher and enjoyed observing the fellow travelers. The room was scattered with folks waiting to go somewhere or picking up those who had been somewhere. She chuckled to herself watching all the people staring at their cell phones.

When her bus was called, she found it only half full, giving her plenty of room to store her guitar and bag overhead and settle into an empty seat. Her clothes had dried out and she was feeling much more comfortable. By the time they were out of town, she had drifted off to sleep, making up for staying awake most of the previous night. Aden dozed off and on between stops. She chuckled to herself at the people she watched on the bus. Many had tried to stay on past the destination they had paid for or tried to hitch a ride "just down the road," for free. The driver plainly had experience dealing with both types of situations.

She woke up as the bus was pulling into the Atlanta bus station about eleven-fifteen that night. The station was crowded with travelers, all with some degree of impatience, waiting for their specific bus to carry them on to their destinations. Some were trying to sleep and guard their luggage at the same time. Atlanta was clearly a major hub. Aden hadn't ridden on a bus before and was amazed at the differences between bus passengers—some clearly traveling with all their worldly possessions and glad to have transportation—and airline passengers who usually seemed annoyed, either at their traveling companions or at something the airline had done. At least there was no TSA line.

She settled into a seat in the waiting room and thought about her own situation. Was this the life she wanted? Playing for money in a tip jar? It had been exciting, but how long would that last? Should she quit while she was ahead? Was she ahead? And what was she doing meeting up with Steve again? Was there a future for the two of them? Was she going to go back to New Mexico with him on the motorcycle? She had to admit it was exciting traveling with nothing around you to hide the elements and the scenery, pressed up against the body of a good man who cared enough about you to put your needs ahead of his.

She was still thinking about those things when she started drifting off. She pulled herself up with a jerk, afraid if she really went to sleep she would miss her bus. The PA system did a good job of keeping her awake with announcements every time a bus came in or left, but she found herself drifting off between announcements. She had her guitar in front of her chair, standing upright with her legs over the body. Her bag was on her lap with her arms through the carrying straps, so anyone trying to grab her belongings would have to untangle the pile for success.

Wednesday

About midnight, she decided she needed to stay awake. It was time to check out the vending machines. The candy didn't tempt her, but she had a cup of coffee out of a contraption claiming to make lattes, espressos, cappuccinos and regular coffee. She settled for a coffee with cream. It tasted like it had been brewed last week but it woke her up. A trip to the ladies' room and she was ready for them to call her bus. She was lightly dozing when they made the announcement. At twelve-forty, she was off to Jacksonville, Florida, hoping for right answers and that she was asking the right questions.

It wasn't long until she had an admirer. He came back to her seat and squatted in the aisle, "How's it going?" he asked.

"It's a long trip and I want to get some sleep."

"Scoot over and I'll set here. You can put your head on my shoulder."

"Or you could go away, and I'd sleep better knowing you aren't bothering me."

"Don't be that way. Once you get to know me, you'll find what a fine fellow I am."

"You don't give up easily, do you? Here's as plain as I can make it—go away."

He put his hand on her knee. "You don't really want me to do that."

Aden grabbed his index finger and pulled on it as she bent it up and twisted. The fellow gave a howl of pain. Several passengers looked at the two as he cradled his hand with the other one. The man in the next seat forward pulled the hand up where he had a better view. "You've dislocated your finger, buddy. Better get that looked at the first chance you get."

The character gave Aden a scowl as he moved up to a seat near the front of the bus. The man in the seat in front of Aden grinned at her. "I heard your conversation. I don't think he'll bother you anymore. You clearly don't need any help, but if that should change, let me know."

"Thank you. I hated to cause a scene, but he wouldn't stop."

He pointed to the woman seated next to him. "My wife thinks you're a hero."

"Thank you. No, I'm just going to meet my boyfriend. I don't need any complications."

"Well, anyway, nice job."

Thirty-four

Steve got to the Jacksonville bus terminal about 7 am. He parked the bike and wondered what Aden would think when she saw it. He walked inside and settled down to wait but he didn't have to wait long. The bus pulled in a few minutes early. Steve watched the passengers unload... one fellow seemed to have some problem with his hand. When he spotted Aden in her jeans, leather jacket and sneakers carrying her guitar and duffle bag, Steve walked over and wrapped her in his arms. It seemed to Steve appropriate to give her a slow kiss. Evidently it seemed appropriate to Aden as well. It was a good kiss. A couple just off the bus beamed at them.

They walked outside and she saw the motorcycle. The two of them stood side by side and stared at it. "So, what happened to delivering that to your buddy's brother?"

"He didn't want it. He made me an offer I couldn't refuse. I kind of bought it."

"So that's our ride back to New Mexico?"

"I'm afraid it is. As I said, you can take the bus to Albuquerque. Or we can spend the last of the travel funds for an airline ticket. You don't have to ride with me."

She thought it over. "I guess it should be safe enough to ride as far as the motel."

"Great!" Steve got out the extra helmet and they rode back to Mayport. After Aden put her guitar and travel bag in the room, Steve asked, "What now? We can take as long as you want for whatever comes next."

"I need a shower and food. First, I want some food. I haven't eaten since lunch yesterday. Then we can walk on the beach to stretch our legs. Then the shower."

"There's a diner next door and then it's less than a mile to the beach." They headed out to the diner. Steve hadn't eaten before picking up Aden so they both went for coffee and a big breakfast. Steve struggled for something to say while he watched Aden eat. She was obviously hungry, devouring everything on her plate. "I'm glad you're here. I really missed having you behind me on the ride."

"Well, I can't say I enjoyed going clear to Atlanta in order to get down here, so I guess that's one thing in the Beemer's favor."

After breakfast Aden asked, "Can we walk from here?"

"Yeah, down this street." They followed Wonderwood Drive through a heavily wooded area breaking out on a street leading to the beach. They could see the Atlantic—beyond the surf the breeze stirred up the waves enough for an occasional whitecap until they blended in with the blue leading to the horizon. They were early enough that the sun was still climbing, creating a glitter path over the water. As they stepped off the pavement and out in the deep sand, Aden chuckled. "It looks smaller than the Pacific." "It's weird looking at the sun rising out of the ocean instead of sinking into it."

Steve pointed out the breakwaters forming the channel into the mouth of the St. Johns River. They stopped to watch a destroyer slowing down and entering the channel. It might have been the one he had seen leaving two days before.

"Do you miss it?" Aden asked.

"Well, it's all I've known for the last four years, about three years aboard the ship. It was comfortable because I was used to it. I enjoyed the life, but I'm looking forward to what comes next. Especially if it includes you."

She realized she was glad to be with him and squeezed his hand. Near the water it was easier walking in the damp sand, although they had to dodge the occasional wave breaking farther up the beach than the others. Aden stopped to remove her sneakers and made Steve take his off as well.

"So, tell me about New Mexico," Aden said.

"We've got more beach than this, but no water. For the most part, New Mexicans are nice, friendly people. As far as country goes, we've got mountains to deserts and everything in between. You said you have a BS degree... there are good paying technical jobs and lots of places that have live music, from bars to churches. There's lots of things to see and do, but you have to work for some of them. I had a shipmate from New York City. He got out before I did and stopped in Albuquerque for a couple of days, but he continued on to New York. He wrote that he had trouble adjusting to the lifestyle. He expected someone to entertain him all the time. Our culture is more that we entertain ourselves."

"Do you have real food?"

"You mean other than New Mexican? Sure, French, Italian, American. Anything you want."

"How 'bout you and me. What happens to us?"

"As I told you, I start school in the fall. Clearly you have already gone through that, but if you want a graduate degree, UNM is a good school. I'll have the G.I. Bill and some savings. I'm hoping to pick up a part-time job. I won't be rich, but I'll have enough money to cover living expenses. You could afford an apartment on your own, or if we wanted to get a place together, we could find something in Albuquerque or Cedar Crest, where my parents live. I'd like to make it work. That's me. What about you? What do you want?"

"That's just it, I'm not sure. I think I want to go back to work. I'm thinking singing is a hobby. I can have just as much fun singing at an open mic as trying to do it for a living. Being in the spotlight is fun, until something goes wrong. Those characters in Meridian really put me off my game. I think part of it was because you weren't there. Damn you! Now I feel you're a part of my life I don't want to give up, and yet how well do I know you after just the week we've been together?"

"You haven't told me what your degree is in. Are you keeping it a secret?"

Aden laughed. "I want to surprise you. I'll tell you one of these days."

"I think I know you well enough that I wouldn't be amazed by anything." He thought for a moment. "I think I've shown you the basic me. I don't think I have any bad habits you haven't seen. But maybe I don't see my worst side. What's your worst side?"

"I guess you'd have to tell me. I don't know your taste in movies, books or music. You don't know my tastes except for music."

"I have a good idea about your taste in food and wine. I suspect you have a flair for fashion. I know you are a quick thinker."

They continued down the beach holding hands and talking about things in common and uncommon until hunger drove them to head back to find some lunch. "I'm enjoying eating," Aden said. "I've been on something of a forced hunger strike while we were apart." As they walked up to the motel, they were still thinking about the commitment they were making to each other. But once in the room, words went away as they exchanged a kiss. Finally breaking apart, Aden started a shower which turned into a communal thing, and a hotter excess of gentle caresses that escalated quickly. Finally, they went out to climb on the Beemer.

Thirty-five

Aden was standing next to the motorcycle when the memory of her last ride flashed into her mind. She recalled the terror she felt when the rednecks were chasing them. She hesitated swinging onto the seat as Steve waited for her to settle behind him. Suddenly she felt herself being grabbed by the neck and a familiar voice said, "You don't have to ride on a motorcycle. You can ride with me. In fact, why don't both of you walk over to my car." At the sound, Steve looked over his shoulder to see Crusher's arm around Aden's neck, his pistol jammed in her side.

"Crusher! I thought you were going back to California?"

"You thought wrong... get off that machine." Steve took off his helmet and climbed off the bike. "I thought it over and decided I didn't believe a word you told me about her going back west. I been watching this place ever since you told me she ain't here. I figured as long as you were still here, she'd be coming. Where the hell you been?" He laughed at Steve. "I knew you would lead me to her."

Aden struggled but couldn't break his grip. "You bastard! What do you want?"

"I want my money that I hid in your guitar case. Get in my car, both of you. Bike boy, you drive."

"The case is in the motel room. Why don't we get the money, and you go on your way?"

"I'll get it after I've had some fun with you two. Get in the car!"

Steve got behind the wheel while Crusher and Aden climbed into the back seat. Steve looked for something he could ram while he fastened his seat belt. Maybe he could put Crusher through the windshield.

The car smelled with Crusher's body odor and the faint whiff of urine. Crusher had thrown all the candy and hamburger wrappers to the back on his way to Florida. Aden had to clear the back seat, pushing everything to the floor before climbing in. Crusher looked at Aden. "Leave your seat belt off. You too, bike boy. Take off your seat belt. If you try to crash the car, you two are the ones that will get hurt. If you try to attract a cop, I'll smash your skull, bike boy. What the hell is your name anyway?" He fastened his own seat belt as Steve drove off. "If you think you can outrun me because you're not hooked in and I am, ask yourself if you can outrun a bullet. I don't care how many people are watching, I'll shoot."

"My name is Steve. I won't run as long as you have Aden back there. Where are we going?"

"Steve! How could I forget? Well Stevie, head south down Mayport Road. While I was waiting for you to show up, I found a nice spot where we can relax in private."

"What's this money you're talking about?" Aden asked.

"It's forty grand. I hid it in your guitar case for you to carry to Mexico. I was gonna buy cocaine for you to carry across the border. It would have worked if biker boy, that is Stevie, hadn't shown up. Well, I can get it back now with interest."

"I wasn't ever going to go to Mexico with you. I decided I didn't trust you and clearly, I was right. Where are you taking us?"

"You'll see. It's a place where we can have a little privacy for what I have in mind."

Steve drove south through Atlantic Beach until Crusher yelled, "Turn here, turn here! Right, turn right!"

Steve had to stand on the brakes to slow up for the turn into a residential neighborhood. They were driving past wooded lots and big houses. The farther they drove, the houses got smaller, and the trees got more dominant until the trees took over completely. Crusher told Steve to keep going until they crossed a bridge over standing water. It looked like it might be a tongue off the Intercoastal Waterway. The road ended at a small parking lot just past the bridge; theirs was the only car there. The lot was unpaved, just the sandy soil of the Florida peninsula. Thick brush and pine trees mixed with tall grasses and palms surrounded them on three sides with the bridge and water behind the car on the fourth side. The undergrowth seemed to form a solid wall around the parking lot. "Out of the car, both of you," Crusher ordered.

Steve tried to reason with him. "Whatever you are going to try, you know it won't work. Every time you interact with us, you come out the loser. If Aden has your money, let her give it to you and we can each go our own way."

"Nice try, biker boy. I'll get my money, don't you worry. This pistol says we do things my way and I want a little fun first. Start walking down that path."

Steve looked where Crusher pointed and for the first time noticed a path cut into the jungle-like brush. The pines and tall grasses rose on each side of the sandy path along with palm trees and massive bushes. It felt like a true jungle to Steve. The three started walking down the path as it curved to the right and soon, they were out of sight of the parking lot. The trees soared overhead, forming a green canopy. Steve felt a minor sense of claustrophobia in the green tunnel. They had walked about a hundred yards when Crusher ordered them to stop. "This is the place. Push through there." He pointed to the foliage. "Make a hole there!" indicating they were to push into the brush back toward the waterway. Steve saw several places where Crusher must have broken the branches off a tree to mark the location. He muscled a branch aside and forced his way off the path. He had to hold it so Aden could get through. He thought about letting Crusher start in and letting the branch snap back at him, but Crusher motioned for him to walk on. The thick brush seemed like a solid wall for the first five feet, but Steve could see a faint path indicating someone had been there. Finally, things thinned out, allowing them to push through to a fairly open area. Crusher must have worked like hell to find this place.

He could see the tree line back toward the parking lot stopped about a hundred feet from the water. The area between the open water and the trees was covered with grasses and bushes about three feet high. At the spot where they were, a line of trees ran along the shoreline. Steve recognized them as mangroves. They were in an area of shallow, muddy water with the trees growing out of the mud and into the water. From where they stood to the mangroves some sort of short grass grew throughout the clearing.

The insects were like a solid cloud. They were continuously swatting at the mosquitos and other flying insects buzzing and biting around them. Steve had had it. "What in the world are we doing here? This is hell for all three of us." But at Crusher's insistence, they walked further into the open, grassy area with a couple of palm trees growing in the clearing before getting to the mangroves. Low weeds ended at the shoreline. The mangroves blocked most of the shore, but Steve looked through a break in the trees at a good-sized expanse of water about a hundred feet across, stretching off in both directions before curving out of sight. The far shore had more grasses, trees and bushes. Steve stopped in the middle of the field, about twenty feet from the water. Crusher was just behind him.

Crusher kept waving his free arm to keep the insects off while keeping the pistol aimed in their direction. "Yeah, I'm gonna change my plans. Weren't so many bugs last time I was here. I was gonna tie you to a tree so you could watch me while I rape the bitch, but that ain't gonna work. I think I'll shoot you in both knees and just smash up the tramp's looks." He leered at her. "She won't have so many boyfriends with her face all scarred up. I'll let ya go after that. Maybe you'll live." He continued laughing as he hit Steve over the head with the butt of the pistol. He was trying to knock Steve out, but the edge of his hand cushioned the blow. Steve dropped to his hands and knees in the soggy sand as Crusher whipped around him, shoving the pistol in his pants pocket and grabbing Aden by her hair. She screamed as he slapped her and pushed her down on her hands and knees. He was laughing hysterically. She tried to swing a fist at him, but his arms were longer than hers and she couldn't reach him. His yanking on her hair forced her off balance and when he let go, she fell on her side. He kicked her in the stomach, yelling, "You been spending my money?"

"I don't know what you're talking about!" she screamed. "And why would you hide money in my guitar case?"

"Get up, slut!" He grabbed her arm and pulled her back up on her hands and knees. "I was gonna take you to Mexico, whether or not you wanted to go. It was arranged I'd buy the cocaine that you would smuggle back to the States. Now they think I stole the money, and they will kill me if they catch me. So now I might as well keep the money and disappear. Forty thou ain't gonna last very long. You really screwed up my life. All your fault!" He kicked her again. "How much of my money have you spent?"

"I don't have your money! I don't know anything about your money!"

Crusher pushed her back down and turned to Steve. Steve was still on his hands and knees, shaking his head to clear the cobwebs from his brain. He looked up as Crusher pulled the pistol out of his pocket… it fired as the barrel cleared his pants, the bullet hitting the ground just in front of his feet. Crusher looked shocked as the three of them froze at the sound. Crusher quickly pointed the gun at Steve, who was in the process of standing up.

When Crusher saw Steve on his feet, he backed up a few steps and kept the pistol pointed in Steve's general direction. They were some fifteen feet apart.

"Come on, biker boy, stand up so I get a shot at your knees. Maybe it's you who found my money and has been spending it."

"No one's been spending your money. We haven't seen your money. If you put it in Aden's guitar case, it's still there. Why don't you go and look? Why are we here when the guitar case is back in the motel?"

"You'd like that, wouldn't you? Give you a chance to find a weapon or call the po-lice. I'll look for the money after I finish with you two. If it's not all there, I'll come back and finish what I started." He was waving the pistol back and forth. "Let's see, what knee to shoot first? Maybe I split the difference and shoot your balls." He was still laughing uncontrollably as he started to aim.

Steve, with nothing to lose, feinted left and lunged forward as he got his feet under him, Crusher swung the pistol back and forth, trying to aim as he took another step back. His foot hit a tree root, and he lost his balance, going over backward. The pistol flew out of his hand as he put both hands down to cushion his fall. He fell down hard, landing on his back. Steve and Aden watched the pistol fly over Crusher's head and land at the water's edge behind him. Steve started to run for it as Crusher twisted around to grab Steve's leg. All three missed seeing the large form that lunged out of the pond, grabbing Crusher by the thigh. There was no ignoring the scream, however, when the long, sharp teeth sank into his muscles. Steve spun around to see Crusher being pulled into the water by an alligator. The reptile looked more than ten feet long. An odd fact popped into Steve's mind, remembered from a high school biology class, that the reptiles weighed about forty pounds per foot. Crusher was clawing at the ground as the reptile backed into the pond, pulling the screaming victim along with him. The gap in the mangroves looked like a game trail used by the beasts.

Steve found the pistol in the mud a little farther along the shore. He picked it up and hoped it would still work. He stepped into the water and shook the pistol back and forth to get the mud off. The muzzle was clean, so he aimed at the 'gator's back and pulled the trigger. He saw the bullet hit the water a couple of feet beyond the 'gator. He took a deep breath and tried to concentrate on the sights as he aimed for another shot. By then, the beast had Crusher in about three feet of water. It started to spin along its length, turning Crusher over and over and tearing at the thigh still in its mouth. Steve was afraid he would hit Crusher, but they had to do something. He took careful aim again and pulled the trigger. With all the commotion and splashing, Steve couldn't tell where the bullet went, but after a moment the 'gator let go of Crusher and retreated into the pond.

Steve dropped the pistol and waded out to pull Crusher to dry land. The thigh looked like raw hamburger. A bloody bone end was sticking out of the wound, which was bleeding profusely. Judging from the blood flow, several arteries had been cut. Steve pulled off his belt and tried to make a tourniquet at the groin. It was his uniform web belt with a slide adjustment to tighten and he wrapped it around the leg. "Call nine-one-one! He's going to bleed to death!" he yelled. He got the belt around the upper thigh and slid the buckle as tight as he could get it. Blood was still flowing so Steve found a branch to work under the belt and twisted it to make it tighter.

Aden was back on her feet and asked, "Where are we?"

"We came down Sutter Island Road west from Mayport Road. The nature trail at the west end of it."

Aden pulled out her phone and made the call as Steve tried to stop Crusher's bleeding. Crusher asked, "What the hell happened? Where are we?"

"A 'gator tried to take your leg off. Did a pretty good number on it. I've got a half-assed tourniquet on your leg to stop the blood loss. Aden's calling nine-one-one to try to get you some help."

"Oh God, it hurts like hell. Can't you do something about the pain?"

"As much blood as you've lost, I'm surprised you can feel it. In fact, I'm really shocked you're awake. Lie back and we'll do what we can. We're trying to get you some help."

Aden yelled, "I think the alligator is coming back!"

Steve stood up to look. He could see the nose and eyes of an alligator about ten feet out in the pond. As he watched, the 'gator turned and seemed to be cruising parallel to the shoreline, not getting any closer to the three of them. Steve turned back to Crusher, who had managed to loosen the tourniquet and the wound was squirting blood. "Hey! What the hell are you doing? Do you want to die?"

"That belt hurts, dude. It's too tight."

"It is also saving your life. Man, that animal did a number on your leg. A Band Aid isn't gonna work." He tightened the belt again and tried to take Crusher's pulse. He hadn't paid that much attention to the first aid classes and couldn't find a pulse. Crusher was still breathing, though, so that didn't mean much.

Steve had to fight Crusher to keep him from loosening the belt. Aden finally said, "I got through to the Atlantic Beach police. They said they would get an ambulance started this way right away. I'll go back to the parking lot and lead them here."

"Better mark the path some way so you can find your way back in here."

Aden shoved her way back to the path, forcing her way past the large bush blocking the grassy area from the trail. She scratched an arrow in the sandy path with her foot and ran back to the parking lot, arriving just before an ambulance and the police. Leading a female cop and an EMT with a handful of equipment, Aden ran back up the path. The other EMT was pushing a gurney loaded with the rest of their gear. He followed as best he could. Aden found the spot where they turned off the path and pushed her way into the overgrowth, holding the branch out of the way for the EMT and the cop, who complained about the insects. "What the hell were you guys thinking when you came in here?" the cop asked. With no time to answer, Aden pressed on. When they got back to Steve, he was trying to give Crusher mouth to mouth and chest compressions while keeping the tourniquet tight. "Quick, I think he's dead!' The EMT hurried to take over the chest compressions and had Steve supply air with a manual resuscitation bag. The cop helped the other EMT to force his way through the brush with all the equipment.

When the second EMT arrived, he checked Crusher's vital signs, then sat back on the ground. "Don't bother, he's gone." He looked at the blood trail up from the shore line. "Looks like he bled out."

The cop stepped up at that point; she was holding Crusher's pistol. "So, wanna tell me what was going on here?" She pointed to Steve's scalp "...and why your head is bleeding?"

Steve mustered his thoughts and answered, "Crusher," pointing at the body, "and Aden knew each other slightly in San Diego where she was performing at the bar where he worked. She's a singer. He tried to convince her to go to Mexicali, Mexico, with him for a better job. She wasn't sure she wanted to do it. When she finally told him no, he got abusive and she wanted to get away from him. About that time, I came along and offered her a ride to Jacksonville on my motorcycle and she accepted. Crusher, I think, is—was—a meth user and a stalker and was pissed at Aden for going with me. He knew where I was heading and started following us. He caused problems in several towns where Aden was looking for a job, so I lost him by getting off the freeways and riding back roads. After an incident in Mississippi, Aden decided to stay there and look for work while I went on to Jacksonville. Aden didn't find work she liked in Mississippi, so she called me and told me she would meet me in Jacksonville. She rode the bus overnight and arrived this morning. I picked her up at the bus terminal and we went back to my motel where, it turned out, Crusher was watching the place. He knew I was headed for Naval Station Mayport. He must have made his way here and spotted me near the Navy base. He said he had been watching my motel. He had that pistol you are holding, forced us into his car and had me drive out here. His original idea was to tie me to a tree to watch while he raped Aden. The insects changed his plans. Once he got us off the path, he said he was going to shoot me in both knees and scar up Aden's face. He hit me on the head with the butt of his pistol and I went down. As I started to get back up, he was aiming to shoot me in the knees. I figured I had nothing to lose so I lunged at him. He took a step back and tripped and fell, dropping the pistol. He was down near the shore. That's when the alligator came out and grabbed him, pulling him into the water. I picked up the pistol and fired a couple of shots at the 'gator. Don't know if I hit it, but it let go of Crusher and I pulled him to shore and put a tourniquet on his leg while Aden called the police. That's about it." He looked out at the pond. "Yeah, there it is." He pointed at the dark shape, still watching them from about twenty feet out.

"I ought to interview you separately, but is that about the way you remember it as well?" the cop asked Aden.

"Yeah, that's it." She seemed still in shock. "He's dead?"

The EMT said, "That tourniquet was a good idea, but he must have pretty well bled out by the time you got him back on dry land. The gator cut the femoral artery; he didn't have a chance."

The cop contacted her headquarters to make arrangements for a nuisance alligator contractor to be contacted to collect the 'gator and destroy it.

"You're going to kill the alligator?" Aden asked.

"Yeah, it's killed a human so that's a big strike against it and there's no place to relocate it. There are so many alligators in Florida that moving it to another location would just result in it getting in a fight with the established 'gators in that location. It would kill one of them or they would kill this one. Unfortunately, we have lots of experience with this situation. Putting this one down is the best solution for everybody, except of course, this 'gator."

"Well, I hate to see an animal killed just for acting on its instincts."

"We don't kill all of them. If they are under four feet long, we relocate them. Under four feet, they aren't big enough to be dangerous to people. Still, we removed about seven thousand 'gators last year. Out of a population of over a million."

"And by remove you mean kill?"

"Yes."

The five of them got Crusher's body onto the gurney and they forced their way back to the path. Everyone was covered in insect bites. Steve itched like crazy and wanted a shower. Aden felt the same. While the EMTs took the body to the morgue, the cop insisted on Steve and Aden following her back to the police station. "You will follow me, right? I don't want to turn this into a car chase through city streets."

"Yeah, no problem." They got in Crusher's car and trailed her to the station.

There the police separated them and went over the story several times, filling in missing pieces. They questioned Steve on the car ownership but dropped it after finding Crusher's registration. Steve wasn't sure what that was all about. Finally, the police couldn't think of anything else to ask. Their stories agreed without being exactly the same; clearly, they hadn't rehearsed a story. "Well," the female cop told them, "I'm sure the medical examiner will confirm the cause and manner of death to be consistent with an alligator attack. We have your home addresses in case there are any more questions, so you're free to go."

They met in the lobby but didn't say anything to each other. "Can we get a ride back to the motel?" Steve asked the policewoman.

The woman looked put out. "Yeah, I'll run you back to the motel. Let me check with my sergeant."

On the drive Aden asked, "What happens to Crusher and his possessions?"

"We'll try to locate next of kin. I don't suppose you know where he is from or if he has any next of kin?"

"No. That never came up in our conversations. He has an apartment in San Ysidro, California. I don't know the address, but it's on Tennie Street. He was working at a bar called The Happy Hideaway. They might have some more information about him."

"We'll check it out, but probably everything will be sold as scrap. When we searched the car, it was obvious the guy had nasty habits... we cleaned out enough meth to start a business. That's why we were questioning you about the car ownership," she said to Steve. "We wanted to be sure you aren't a dealer."

At the motel, they thanked the policewoman for the drive and went into the room. Aden looked at her guitar case and asked, "You didn't say anything about the money Crusher was talking about, so I didn't either. If there is any, what do we do with it?"

"That's up to you. I don't think there's any way it could be traced to you, but why take a chance? You could try to give it back, but I don't think I'd want to have any dealings with those people. You could donate it anonymously to a charity. Or charities. But you know your needs. You can do anything you want with it. With all Crusher put you through, I'd say you earned it."

"Don't you deserve half of it?"

"Why?"

"You worked hard to get me away from Crusher. If I earned it, so did you."

"Neither of us knew about it. It's supposed to be in your guitar case. You know where it came from. It's your opportunity to cut a demo and further your career, or you could buy an airplane ticket and fly to Albuquerque, or any other place you want to go. Shall we look for the money?"

Aden opened up the guitar case and started rummaging through the pockets, this time taking everything out and piling it on the bed. As she removed the string packages, they saw the money.

They were both silent as Aden stood looking at the hundred-dollar bills. "Well, it's real."

"We can eat well on our way home. How about a loan? I can pay off Kruzick for the motorcycle. No, it's your money, do what you want with it."

Aden was looking out the window at the Beemer. Finally, she broke the silence. "Well, we've got a long road trip to discuss that. Oh. About that career thing. I find I enjoy playing in small bars and having crowds applaud, but I don't think that's going to be a career for me. I'm going to find a job. I can play music as a sideline."

"Well, that sounds like a plan. Are you going to tell me what kind of a degree you have?"

"I have a degree in electrical engineering and a minor in computer science."

"Wow! I knew we had a lot in common."

"Do you think there will be many opportunities around Albuquerque?"

"Oh, many. Did you know that's where Microsoft started?

"Microsoft? You're putting me on."

"No. They opened the company in Albuquerque in 1975. They didn't move to Washington until 1979. I think Gates wanted to go home. Meanwhile, there are many more places in ABQ that do engineering. I know where I'd like to work after I get my degree. I'll tell you about it as we head home. If it suits you, maybe we can work at the same place. It's big enough that we wouldn't have to work together." He changed the subject. "And now the big question. As you noticed, I still have the bike. Do you think you want to take another road trip?"

"There's a lot of ways to die, aren't there?"

"Uh, yeah. So..."

"I need a shower. So do you. Are you packed?" she asked.

"I can be in about five minutes."

"What the hell? Nobody lives forever. I've seen all I want of Florida and the south. Let's shower and then cheat death again and get this trip on the road."

Steve thought about riding back west on I-10 and the *USS Alabama*. "Let's plan on a stop in Mobile. There's something there I want to check out."

Meet Dick Shead

Dick Shead is a retired computer programmer and private pilot. He has sailed the California coast, the Bahamas, the Dry Tortugas and the Lesser Antilles. His interests include flying, sailing, guitar, and history. His motorcycle is a '56 BSA Goldstar.

Other Works From The Pen Of
Dick Shead

Before a Fall - Remember, pride goes...

June '41 - The beginning of a long, hot summer.

South of San Juan - Tricks of the Trade in the Tropics.

After the Ark - It was a two-week vacation sailing in the Gulf of Mexico. Steve and his friend Tom hadn't planned on stopping an attack on the US.

Dear reader,

I hope you've enjoyed reading this tale of perfect plans that
don't always work out.

Your opinion is valuable to other
readers like you,
who may be looking for books like mine.

Please consider taking a few minutes to post a review,
however brief,
on the site where you purchased this book
or on the Wings ePress web page.

You may also want to visit my author page
at the Wings' website where you can find the

Thank you!

Dick Shead

Visit Our Website

For The Full Inventory
Of Quality Books:

Wings ePress, Inc

Quality trade paperbacks and downloads
in multiple formats,
in genres ranging from light romantic comedy to general
fiction and horror.
Wings has something for every reader's taste.
Visit the website, then bookmark it.
We add new titles each month!

Wings ePress, Inc.
3000 N. Rock Road
Newton, KS 67114